The Last of the African Kin

CARAF Books
Caribbean and African Literature Translated from French

RENÉE LARRIER AND MILDRED MORTIMER, EDITORS

The Last of the African Kings

Maryse Condé

Translated
by Richard Philcox

University of Virginia Press
Charlottesville and London

The University of Virginia Press is situated on the traditional lands of the Monacan Nation, and the Commonwealth of Virginia was and is home to many other Indigenous people. We pay our respect to all of them, past and present. We also honor the enslaved African and African American people who built the University of Virginia, and we recognize their descendants. We commit to fostering voices from these communities through our publications and to deepening our collective understanding of their histories and contributions.

This translation has been supported by a grant from the National Endowment for the Humanities, an independent Federal Agency.

This is a work of pure fiction. The king in question had no Caribbean desendants.

Originally published in French as *Les derniers rois mages*
© Éditions Mercure de France, 1992

University of Virginia Press
Translation and preface © 1997 by Richard Philcox
Printed in the United States of America on acid-free paper

First University of Virginia Press edition published 2024

ISBN 978-0-8139-5180-5 (hardcover)
ISBN 978-0-8139-5181-2 (paper)
ISBN 978-0-8139-5182-9 (ebook)]

9 8 7 6 5 4 3 2 1

Library of Congress Cataloging-in-Publication Data is available for this title.

Cover art: From *Procession,* William Adjété Wilson, 2014. Collage, 67 × 89 cm. (© William Adjété Wilson)

Cover design: Cecilia Sorochin

Contents

Preface

Translation is a form of cannibalism. And to translate the Caribbean text is doubly cannibalistic since the Caribbean work of fiction is, in the words of its own writers such as Aimé Césaire, Edouard Glissant, and René Depestre, already a cannibalization of the Western canon. When Maryse Condé writes a novel I read what she reads, I see what movies she sees, and I listen to the music she listens to. I try to gauge what is influencing her at the moment of creation so that I can formulate a strategy for translating her novels. In the case of *Les derniers rois mages*, or *The Last of the African Kings*, I know that she would listen over and over again to African American music, and especially the blues — be it Lena Horne or Billie Holiday. Lena Horne's rendition of "Stormy Weather" inspired the book's epigraph, reflecting the troubled relationship and disintegration of the two main characters. The rain and their hostile environment play an important part in the book. African American music influences not only the atmosphere of the novel but also its structure. The isolated chapters called The Notebooks of Djéré, rewritings of African myths of origin, should strike the reader as solo improvisations in a jazz concert. They are lyrical impromptus that clash with the haunting, bluesy mood of the rest of the book as Spero, the main character from Guadeloupe, reviews his life over a twenty-four-hour period on an island off the coast of Charleston, South Carolina. Just as jazz is a reworking of African rhythms so the structure of the book reworks the links between Africa, the place of origin, and its Diaspora of Guadeloupe and South Carolina.

In addition to the music I know that there was one book that was an important source of intertextuality for *The Last of the African Kings*, a little like *To the Lighthouse* (New York: Harcourt, 1927) by Virginia Woolf was for my translation of

Condé's *Crossing the Mangrove* (New York: Doubleday, 1995). And that is Bruce Chatwin's *The Viceroy of Ouidah* (London: Picador, 1982). Not only is there a similarity of structure, starting with the present and moving further and further back in time, but there is a similarity of tone — that terrible irony. The Western writer can get away with irony because his works are not required to be true representations of society. As Tzvetan Todorov says in *Poetique* (Paris: Ed. du Seuil, 1968), "To ask whether the discourse of literature is true or false is meaningless. The discourse of literature is fiction."

Writers from the South, on the contrary, have inherited the legacy of commitment. They are expected to give a positive or at least sympathetic image of their people and their society. They are seen as teachers. V. S. Naipaul from Trinidad has been attacked by every Caribbean writer from George Lamming to Derek Walcott for his uncompromising portrayal of Caribbean society. In his essay entitled "Hopes and Impediments," Chinua Achebe calls him "a modern Conrad, although partly native himself." The sense of derision that pervades Condé's novels could be matched with *The Viceroy of Ouidah* since Bruce Chatwin's novel deals with a similar subject, that is, the fortunes of the dynasty of an African kingdom.

Both novels are delightfully iconoclastic, unorthodox, and nomadic, favorite themes of Condé and Chatwin. Let's listen briefly first to Chatwin:

Each year with the dry season he would slough off the habits of civilization and go to war.

His first task had been to reform the Dahomean army. He and the king got rid of the paunchy, the panicky and the proven drunks. And since Dahomean women were far fiercer fighters than the men — and could recharge a muzzle-loader in half the time — they sent recruiting officers round the villages to enlist the most muscular virgins.

The recruits were known as the "King's Leopard Wives."

They ate raw meat, shaved their heads and filed their teeth to sharp points. They learned to fire from the shoulder not the hip, and never to fire at rustling leaves. On exercises they were made to scale palisades of prickly pear, and they would come back clamoring "Hou!

Maryse Condé

Hou! We are men!" — and since they were obliged to be celibate, were allowed to slake their lusts on a troop of female prostitutes.

And now Maryse Condé in *The Last of the African Kings*:

Agnes Jackson was a childless ninety year old who had been living alone in the eyes of God for over forty years, ever since her husband left her in Hollywood for a male tap dancer. In her youth she had been a real beauty. A photo conspicuously pinned to her living-room wall showed her sitting behind a piano, her long, light brown hair touching her shoulders. She had been close friends with Langston Hughes, Paul Robeson, and Richard Wright and had maintained a lengthy correspondence with Zora Neale Hurston. Debbie had therefore requested a large grant from a foundation, which was awarded without any hemming or hawing, and for almost four years she had been collecting Agnes's memoirs with the idea of publishing them in a collection of "oral history."
Unfortunately everything got muddled in the old woman's head. She could no longer recollect with whom she had gone to bed and with whom she hadn't, nor with whom she had gone round the world. Was it really Diego Rivera who fell in love with her in Mexico? So the two women got nowhere, a bit like that famous tapestry that was started afresh each morning only to be undone each night.

Unlike *Crossing the Mangrove*, *The Last of the African Kings* is not what the critics would call a Guadeloupean novel. In fact there are very few Creole expressions and the place of action is not solely Guadeloupe. Most of the descriptions are limited to a tightly knit urban community and there is very little reference to the fauna or flora of the island. Which leads us to the question, what constitutes the Caribbeanness of a text?
In his remarkable book *The Repeating Island* (Durham: Duke University Press, 1992), Antonio Benitez Rojo says, talking about the Caribbean novel,

it is a double performance, a representation containing another representation. The first, or rather the most visible, is directed toward seducing the Western reader; the second is a monologue that returns towards the I, toward the Caribbean self, intending to mythify and at the same time transcend symbolically its unnatural-natural genesis, that is to assume its own marginality vis-a-vis the West and to speak of its Calibanesque Otherness, an Otherness deriving from the violence of conquest, colonization, slavery, piracy, war, plunder, occupation, dependence, misery, prostitution, and even tourism.

He illustrates the element of cannibalism, which is at the core of Caribbean creativity. The Caribbeanness of a text cannot solely be defined by its language — French or Creole for a writer from Guadeloupe, Martinique, or Haiti. Among the writers of the Francophone Diaspora living in the United States and Canada a number are writing in English and expressing their subjectivity in another colonial tongue. It cannot be defined by what Fanon would call "the visible coating": landscape, forms of entertainment, magical and religious practices. It is very much the inner relationship of the individual to his or her environment, culture, or self.

We should not forget either that the original text of *The Last of the African Kings* is already a translation into French, a European language, of a non-European perspective. The English translation is therefore the translation of a translation. It is thus through a European linguistic system, a European literary tradition, that we communicate with a Caribbean society. The English translation, consequently, could follow the same process and convey the Caribbeanness of the text.

The American reader should be able to hear Maryse Condé and understand her characters and her culture that are fundamentally different. So it was with Bruce Chatwin's voice in the back of my head that I set about translating *The Last of the African Kings* in the hope of communicating the palimpsests of Caribbean discourse.

RICHARD PHILCOX

The Last of the African Kings

For

Arthé

Debbie

Janis

Nebbie

Rita

Rosalind

Vévé

Sue

and the others . . .

I

The crabs emerged from every hole in the gray volcanic sand that was papered with dead leaves and closed ranks. Jostling each other's purplish shells, waving their powerful, pincerlike claws, they careened and clawed their way to Spero's body. They plodded on unrelenting up his thighs and encircled the massive hump of his manhood before tangling their claws in his pubic hair and scampering up the calabash of his belly. Their claws drew droplets of blood. Just as they were about to reach his throat, Spero woke up in broad daylight. He had been having the same dream for two years, three or four times a week. He did not know what caused it. What sadness was hidden at the bottom of his heart. His eyes opened on the portrait of his great-grandfather that he himself had painted at the age of fourteen from the photograph that for three generations had adorned the dining-room wall of the family home. His great-grandfather had brought with him into exile five of the Leopard wives, his daughter the princess Kpotasse, his son Ouanilo, and his *honton*, his alter ego, the prince Adandejan. The ancestor's eyes were hidden by thick sunglasses. His cheeks were eaten up by a beard that had not yet turned gray. In fact, all that could be seen of his face was a big triangular nose and a large forehead receding under his headdress, a miter decorated with the traditional pearls. Djéré, Spero's grandfather, was cradled on the far left in the arms of the oldest queen; this blissful, apparently beloved illegitimate son, however, would be left behind by the family together with other relics when they returned to Africa. This abandonment would drastically affect Djéré's entire existence and that of his descendants.

Spero was now wide awake. Although strongly built the frame of the house was being shaken by the wind and was creaking in every corner. September had long gone. Yet people were still frightened, wondering whether another Hugo would come to sow death and destruction as it did the year before. Downstairs Debbie was rummaging around in the kitchen. The smell of coffee wafted up the stairs and mingled with the powerful, nauseating stench of the swamps. The entire region was swampland, and the water mixed with the mud to form blackish pools that lapped against the feet of the tall trees. There were few houses on the island because of this insalubrious air, the closest being nearly ten miles away. So the days flowed by without a sound. Only at dusk was the air filled with the cries of seabirds flocking amidst the foliage. When the noise became too deafening Debbie would go out into the dark and set down bowls of milk and slices of fresh fruit under the pines and live oaks festooned with moss, in keeping with a tradition dating back to the time of Eulaliah, who had been the first to live in this house and fill it with children. The spirits of the ancestors were grieving. Spero had had trouble getting used to these surroundings and he still shivered sometimes when he looked outside. He sat on the edge of the bed and then stood up without too much difficulty, without feeling the pain that sometimes seared him from knee to groin. He went down into the kitchen. The television had already been switched on and a red-cheeked, dark-suited preacher with the blond hair of a choirboy, carefully parted on one side, was promising hell to the infidels and the halfhearted. That's how he knew it was Sunday. He gave Debbie the usual peck on the cheek and sat down on the other side of the table. She looked at him strangely. Then after a while, with her mouth full of grits, she said, "Don't you remember today's December Tenth?"

He was taken aback. He had somehow managed to forget this anniversary that had marked his childhood. On 10 December 1906 Djéré, his grandfather, had performed a ritual from which Justin, his father, had never shirked. Justin, who never paid attention to anything except the curves and contours of a woman's body, had a requiem mass celebrated regularly in memory of the ancestor who had treated his Caribbean lineage so badly and reminded his sons that if it hadn't been for those wicked French they would all be rich and powerful and living in Africa. On that date the house was as dark as a catafalque. The windows remained closed. The radio was switched off. The mirrors were veiled in mauve crepe while incense burnt in front of the photograph whose frame had been polished the day before with a mixture of lemon and ashes. Marisia, Justin's wedded wife, wrung the neck of a chicken, cooked it without salt, and served it up with okra, dasheen leaves, crabs, and mashed yam from a recipe by Hosannah, Djéré's mother. Marisia obeyed orders, but in her heart she was furious. She had no patience with this nonsense of a royal ancestor that was merely an excuse for Justin's idleness, as it had been for his father's. Neither Djéré nor Justin had ever done a day's work in his life. It wasn't money that attracted women to them, that's for sure, but something in their aspect that you couldn't help noticing. Marisia had thrown into an iron trunk under the bed the pipe, the metal nose shield, the pair of sandals, the snuffbox, the fringed parasol, the spitoon, and the headdress of discolored pearls that had belonged to the ancestor. But she had been unable to unhook the photograph taken one morning in 1896 in Bellevue, Martinique — Djéré had just turned one — that hung imposingly over the Henri II sideboard, ruelle 4, Morne Verdol, La Pointe, Guadeloupe. It was the first thing Hosannah had hung on the wall after she left Martinique to follow a worthy Guadeloupean home to his island to bring up her illegitimate son.

As for the boys, they never looked at the photograph and ignored their father's ramblings. All sorts of meaningless and senseless words flew out of Justin's mouth like silk-cotton tree flowers drifting here and there. Of the three boys only Spero paid scant attention to what Justin said, probably because his father spoiled him so much, calling him his "ray of sunshine" and going so far as to feed him morsels from his own mouth. This alliance had been cemented one Tuesday when the history teacher at the lycée during a class on the colonial conquest had mentioned the same name and told the same story Justin had been filling people's heads with for years. That day Spero dashed home where Marisia, her mouth full of pins and her hands white with chalk, was fitting a wedding dress on a customer. He slowed down in front of the photograph, then shot into the bedroom, where Justin was nursing a slight chill with doses of rum and lemon, sprawled out in his locust-wood bed.

"Papa, Papa," he stammered. "The teacher mentioned your grandfather!"

Justin found strength to sit up.

"What did he say?"

Spero dragged him in front of the picture in the dining room and, lowering his head, recited, "He said the French took his kingdom and gave it to his brother. They made him cross the sea that otherwise he would never have set eyes upon. In February 1894 they exiled him to Martinique where he stayed six years. Then he was allowed to leave. He returned to Africa and died in Algiers, like you said, on December tenth."

Ever since then father and son had spent their evenings whispering with their heads together, much to the irritation of Marisia. Spero was already a bad example to his two brothers, a good-for-nothing interested only in drawing and painting, without putting all sorts of other nonsense into his head.

African king or not, Djéré's papa had behaved like all the other black papas on this earth. He neglected his child. He left him behind in the care of his poor single mother. He never answered the cards he received from his son every New Year, nor the letters from Hosannah who, encouraged by Romulus, the man she lived with, demanded money to cover expenses.

The child, it must be said, was never in want. He had sandals. He had shorts. He had shirts. He always had enough to eat. But was this life among the poor children of the Morne Verdol befitting a child of his blood?

Men are not fashioned the same way as women. In the bottomless calabash of their heads they cultivate ambitious nonsense that makes their existence even more difficult for them to bear.

Instead of forgetting all this past and quite simply looking the present straight in the eyes, Djéré and Justin alike had clung to the remnants of a bygone age. As soon as he was old enough to understand what he was reading, Djéré laid hands on everything he could concerning the history of Africa, especially Dahomey, which today they call Benin. He was not content with reading the worm-eaten books that lay dormant on the shelves of the Lambrianne library. No! He cut out coupons in catalogs and mailed orders to France. All with the money from his mother and the worthy Romulus, a nurse, who to make ends meet climbed up and down the Morne Verdol four times a day before climbing up and down the Morne Vert on which the hospital was perched.

Djéré thus built up a magnificent collection of leatherbound books and illustrated magazines. Unfortunately the hurricane of 1928 carried everything off, scattering them over the coolie plum trees, and on his death just before the Second World War, his legacy was nothing but a series of notebooks numbered one to ten that were found at the bottom of a wardrobe. "The Notebooks of Djéré." In them he had attempted to recount who his father was and who his mother was as well.

As regular as clockwork, the ancestor would amble down the steep path that folks in Martinique have since named the "royal way," clasping his son's hand. He would step out onto the road to Schoelcher and stride along under a parasol that one of his queens held open over his head. The inhabitants of Bellevue would come out on their doorsteps and with a total disregard for his dignified appearance double up with laughter and mimic his gestures as they watched him go by.

An African king? Whatever next? Whoever heard of kings in Africa? Those people boil each other in cauldrons.

It was a December Tenth, 10 December 1954 to be exact, on returning home from the requiem mass at Saint-Jules, that Spero had given Justin the picture he had secretly painted from the old photograph in the dining room. He had taken particular care in depicting his grandfather Djéré's chubby baby face. Wearing a black tie and an armband on his left sleeve, Justin took the picture in both hands. Then the salty tears of pride and emotion flowed down his cheeks to his chin.

Although he never got angry like Marisia when he saw Spero idly daubing large sheets of drawing paper instead of studying to become an elementary-school teacher, he had never taken his son's taste for painting very seriously up till then. But he thought this picture extraordinary. Stunning. Frederic Devaux, the Frenchman who had painted the frescoes in the market and the subprefecture, could not have done better. He started filling in forms and applications for Spero and within a year managed to get him a grant to a school of fine arts in Lille.

That's how Spero came to spend five years in that cold, windy, often snowed-in town where the people are not very talkative. Once he had settled down in a hostel he could be seen more often in the library than at his drawing classes. Shutting himself away from morning to night he would devour every document imaginable written by historians on the defunct kingdom of Abomey. That's how he began a correspondence with Monsieur Bodriol, a former colonial administrator who had spent twenty years putting together the chapters of a work—which the critics agreed was monumental— on the god-kings of Benin, and how he came to visit him in Paris. For reasons he kept secret, this visit was not a success. Nevertheless, like a *kpanlingan*, a herald, he now knew by heart the kings' genealogy from Huegbaja to that day of mourning in 1894 when the egg of the world had been smashed to a thousand smithereens. Spero liked to think he resembled his ancestor, whom even the most colonial of historians depicted as being a man full of fervor and charm. One thing bothered him: his color. Justin had apparently given in to that very Guadeloupean liking for light-skinned women and married Marisia, born from dealings with a *béké*, a white creole planter, which meant Spero turned out decidedly red of skin and hair. This troubled him. Couldn't this be taken as one of the deformities the dynasty detested? Hadn't King Agonglo rejected his firstborn because three toes were missing from his left foot? Hadn't Adandejan banished his son beyond the Zou

River because there were gaps between his upper incisors big enough to insert the tip of his tongue?

During these four years of living and studying in Lille, Spero had told nobody his secret, not even the few women — linen and chamber maids at the hostel, peasant women from the north, sympathetic to immigrants — he was bold enough to seduce and make love to.

In fact, either because he feared ridicule or quite simply because he did not like talking about himself, he had never told anyone about the secret of his royal blood. Except Debbie.

Debbie!

He looked at her across the table, her eyes full of malice, her graying hair shaped into a ship's prow over a smooth forehead, her body, approaching fifty, hunched in her housecoat, and he felt bitter. Distressed at heart, he saw her again as she was some twenty-five years earlier when she had walked into his life.

After two years back home in Guadeloupe he had still not found a job. By his own choosing. He had turned down a teaching job at the technical college in Saint-Claude because he couldn't face crossing the bridge over the Gabarre and being away from Justin, who, despite his ramblings and what Marisia called his laziness, had always preferred him to his other two boys. He refused a job in Le Moule because it was too hot and the reflection of the sun off the sea hurt his eyes, which, as weak as the ancestor's, were always carefully shaded behind sunglasses. He got into the habit of selling his watercolors — a genre he came to prefer over all others while working with Jean Lapouille, the well-known painter from Lille — to the passengers from the cruise ships that docked in the port twice a month. All he had to do was set up his paintings under the almond trees and wait. The silver-haired Americans would limp to a halt, utter cries of admiration, and end up digging out dollars from wallets as roomy as suitcases. Spero could speak a few words of English. "You like it? Not expensive, you know. You give how much?" And at the end of the afternoon, under the contemptuous gaze of Marisia, who had never been very fond of this eldest son who was too much like his father, he would pull out of his pockets as much money as his younger brother Maxo earned after a month pushing paper in the local office of an insurance company from Le Mans. One fine day a young black girl stopped in front of him. Tall. Very tall in fact. Her head positively soared into the air, with a huge mouth and black eyes full of the same sadness he himself felt at the bottom of his heart when the sun ends its day and the earth is left to the terror of dreams. Suddenly he felt ashamed sitting there holding out his hand to white folks (for what else was he doing? Marisia asked) and he jumped up. But she was captivated like the others and asked in a fairly respectable French, "How much is this one?"

At the school of fine arts Spero had been one of the last in his class. The teachers had never paid much attention to this Guadeloupean who swallowed his *r*s and often missed classes.

He didn't mind. He had no ambition whatsoever. He painted because he hated everything else and did not want to become an elementary-school teacher to help out his parents. When he stood in front of his easel, wings grew out of his shoulders. He thought of nothing. Nothing that would make him think about how to spend the time we have to spend on this earth.

Debbie's admiration had the effect of a shot of rum on an empty stomach. Somewhere inside him he found the courage to invite her for sugarcane juice at the Palmeraie and was staggered when she accepted. So they left the curve of the docks, walked down the main street that ran straight between balconied colonial facades protected by wooden canopies, and plunged into the chaos of the rue de Nozieres. He very soon realized that Debbie had an awful lot to say. Words gushed out. This Caribbean cruise organized by the Black Caucus, an association of black teachers from South Carolina, had been a present from her mother as a reward for getting through college, and it was not a great success. Far from it. They visited a different island every day, and every one was the same as the next with its facade of palm trees and paradisical beaches. On board everyone seemed to be forgetting the convulsions

Maryse Condé

shaking America at the time. It was all games, entertainment, and laughter fit for children. Three years earlier she had lost her father to political violence and her heart would not heal. She had buried herself in her studies and emerged at the age of twenty-two with a history degree. Her only regret was that her studies had taken her away from more burning issues. She had never taken part in any major demonstration and the only militant act she could boast of was a sit-in in Woolworth's cafeteria.

Spero knew nothing at all about girls. After the glass of cane juice he shyly proposed a meal in a restaurant at Bas-du-Fort and got it accepted as well. This time they climbed into a bus parked in the market square, and never had the town they traversed seemed to Spero so congested, so small, so poor in architectural monuments and unworthy of the attention of such a beautiful foreigner. As they crossed the Carenage district the sky darkened and there was a violent cloudburst. In seconds the streets were swollen rivers, and picking up their petticoats, the women ran to take shelter under the balconies of the storied houses. Debbie didn't see a thing. She went on talking as if she hadn't found a sympathetic ear for years! Her family, the Middletons, came from Barbados, which partly explained her mother's good intentions. All that, however, had been lost in the mists of time and they were now considered to be one of Charleston's oldest families. She lived in a hundred-year-old house on Crocker Island, a swampy, half-deserted place that was linked to the mainland by a dilapidated ferry. It rained all the time and on some days you couldn't tell the sky from the sea.

When the little church nearby rang three in the afternoon she was thinking of returning to the docks when Spero, spurred on by despair, managed to invite her to look at his paintings.

The bus stopped at the foot of the Morne Verdol, which had to be climbed head-down under the hot sun. Spero felt ashamed. Although the top of the hill was covered with a wonderful crown of tamarind trees and ylang-ylangs, the perfume trees, halfway up it was an ugly mess of corrugated iron shacks connected to the street by two or three planks laid over a ditch filled with blackish water. The place stank of filth and sewage. Thank goodness Debbie was still talking and paid no more attention to this than she did to the blue sea at Bas-du-Fort or the madras headties of the women who came out on their doorsteps to look suspiciously at this new face. She stopped talking only to inspect with authority the paintings piled up just about everywhere in the house, lingering over the few compositions in oil and mentioning names that Spero had never heard of but was suddenly convinced he could match, even outdo. Beauford Delaney. Jacob Lawrence. Romare Bearden. When she thought about getting back to the docks he did not know what came over him. He started telling her where, despite unfortunate appearances, his family came from. He had to have this woman in his life. At the end of the day, sitting side by side on a wicker trunk, they watched the SS *Mariposa* slip majestically out of Pointe-à-Pitre harbor. A tangled pile of pink and white clouds veiled the shipwreck of the sun, and Spero reveled in this first so very extraordinary victory of his life, which had been so arid until then.

You can imagine how pleased Marisia was to see this intruder turn up at her house!

Until then her three sons had not caused her any trouble and the neighbors on the Morne Verdol had had no need to lock up their chicks. Suddenly, one of them was bringing home a woman. And what a woman! A woman who didn't speak Creole. A woman who felt the cold and asked for hot bath water twice a day. A woman who suspiciously inspected everything she was given to eat and drink. What annoyed her even more was that Maxo and Lionel had fallen under the spell of the American, too. On weekends, Maxo, an ardent sportsman, accompanied Debbie up to the top of La Soufrière to compare the colors of the volcanic peaks. Some Saturdays he would even drag her along the Victor Hugues forest path to contemplate the massive outlines of Mount Carmichael and the Grande-Decouverte. Lionel, more bucolic by nature, was content to have her admire the *Bauhinia variegata*, the orchid tree, at the Tambour nurseries. Every afternoon she would be enthroned in the dining room beside Spero, getting in the way of customers and their fittings, deciphering Djéré's notebooks with the aid of a dictionary.

In his exile in Martinique, it was not so much the extreme solitude of his existence that saddened the ancestor's spirit. Nor his downfall, pronounced by white men who meant nothing in his eyes. Nor the dethronement of his brother, which he had learned about from press clippings read to him by Ouanilo. It was the thought that he had been too busy fighting for his throne, which in the end he had lost, to think about performing the first funeral rites for his father. Only forty-one young boys and forty-one young girls had been sacrificed. Wouldn't the *daadaa*, the ancestors, hold it against him? How would he be welcomed when his turn came to enter Kutome, the City of the Dead? As a result, he had one nightmare after another. His wives, left untouched, heard him cry like an infant in the middle of the night.

Debbie still found time to give the boys a lesson in politics. What? They knew nothing about America and its problems? They had never heard the names of W. E. B. Du Bois? Malcolm X? Martin Luther King Jr.? They had never heard of the concept of nonviolence?

Ashamed, Spero stammered out a dubious answer. As for Maxo and Lionel, they couldn't find any excuses.

Justin, too, cast a disapproving eye on this love affair between Spero and his American girl. Up till then his boy had been only his. His and the ancestor's. Now a woman had come between them. He had already found him changed — for the worse — on his return from Lille. On his first December Tenth back home on the Morne Verdol, Spero had had to be persuaded to attend the requiem mass, and as soon as he swallowed the yam mash he had washed his mouth out with a glass of rum as if the insipid taste disgusted him. At present there was no time left for chatting with his papa or for reading him pages out of Djéré's notebooks. As soon as the news was over on the radio he locked himself away with Debbie in his bedroom. There was no need to press your ear against the wooden door to hear them laugh and make indecent noises. When oh when would Debbie take herself back home?

One September evening — the rainy season had been particularly rainy, swelling the ditches with torrents of water and pounding the mud — Spero and Debbie pulled out a bottle of Moët et Chandon that had been chilling in an ice bucket, and looking into each other's eyes they announced to the bewildered family their plans to get married and leave for Charleston.

"Did you really forget today's December Tenth?"

Debbie couldn't believe it, suspecting a ruse she didn't understand. He nodded.

Hadn't he in fact started to forget this date twenty-five years earlier, as soon as he had set foot in Charleston? When he realized he was not much different from those around him who changed their first names, draped themselves in African wrappers, and wore a triple necklace of cowries? Their fantasy matched his truth. Gradually he had left the ancestor where he belonged and only Debbie remained the princess, till she became the queen mother.

As soon as their child was old enough, every December Tenth Debbie made her join hands in front of the framed portrait of the ancestor that she had hung on a wall. On a kind of altar she kept candles burning and placed a bunch of fresh flowers. The child adapted perfectly to this atmosphere, to these litanies her mother had her recite, and was delighted with the story her mother told her.

Spero remembered his joy when his daughter was born. Neither of them had wanted a child, for they sensed that as a couple they were not destined to last a lifetime. Their love resembled a tropical storm: sudden and violent, then evaporating into space. Why had Debbie interrupted her cruise so easily? That's anybody's guess. And why did he go into exile and follow her to Charleston? Had either of them ever believed in a glorious future in his painting? Had she perhaps merely made him dream of another place, of another land less irksome and mean than his own?

When he hugged his daughter warm up against his chest Spero had nurtured the illusion that his real life was finally beginning. In his breast his heart had melted with love and hope. A daughter! A daughter!

On the Morne Verdol, people said the family had no luck with daughters. And it's true that first Cyprienne and then Marisia had produced only boys. During her third pregnancy Marisia was convinced from her shape that she would give birth to the long-hoped-for daughter. So disappointed was she that she refused to kiss baby Lionel for three days. Justin, however, adapted very well to his paternity, saying that the descendants of such an ancestor could only be male.

As for Debbie she wanted a boy, and without consulting Spero went through some highly symbolic first names. Malcolm. Sekou. Jomo. Kwame. Modibo. Patrice. When their baby finally arrived the names looked silly, and Spero quickly came up with the name of a blues singer he liked.

A daughter! A token of fertility and a promising future. From now on he would paint for her and make a name for himself.

Very quickly, however, he had become disillusioned. Claiming the infant was sickly, Debbie monopolized her entirely. She took her into her own bed and banished Spero to one of the guest rooms facing north on the third floor. Alone under his sheets he could hear the long talks between mother and child, and once again he felt a foreigner, an exile.

It's true that when she was little Anita was whimpering and wan! Nobody could have foreseen the young beauty she was to grow into once her puberty was over. She did pick up a little the year Debbie took her to Balsa Muir, a small town in South Carolina where a certain Victoria, who had received the gift of God, practised the laying on of hands and advised her to dress the child in red on Fridays and white the other days of the week. Perhaps Spero had begun to forget the ancestor the day his daughter was born: her birth had broken the tradition of boys, and this transgression rooted him firmly in the present, demonstrating that yesterday was well and truly yesterday and today was the only thing that mattered.

He could do nothing about Debbie filling the child's head with these old stories that were better left forgotten. She embroidered on them as she pleased. Djéré was no longer the illegitimate son abandoned with his servant mother like a bundle of dirty linen in a villa on the outskirts of Fort-de-France, but the son of a young lady, a proud example of Martinique's upper class who had not had the heart to leave Papa, Maman, and her island. During his exile in Algeria that followed his exile in Martinique, the ancestor had not let a single day go by without mentioning the names of Djéré and Hosannah. After his death, the Caribbean lineage had been constantly urged to return to the motherland and take its rightful place.

How could Spero have contradicted such fantasies when the colors of reality were so somber? In Charleston the blood of martyrs had not made the ground fertile. Schools and housing still remained de facto segregated. The black schools were in a terrible state! At the college where Debbie taught history, revolver-holstered vigilantes made the students empty their bulging pockets of jagged-edged knives, six-blade pocket knives, razors, and other arms. Right in the middle of East Bay a man had killed two blacks who thought the South had gone with the wind, and he was still on the run. At Sunday services worshippers swayed and clapped, wondering when the famous dream that had got so much media attention would finally come true. It's been so long coming, O Lord, we've lost faith. Was he too just another false prophet?

Debbie wanted Anita to know Africa. So year after year she inked in for her the lengthy forms from Operations Crossroads Africa whereby the children of America are initiated into the realities of the Third World. Alas, year after year, they were returned marked "Refused for health reasons." Africa had therefore remained a blank until Anita flew off to Benin after four years of development studies at Liman College. She left without asking anyone's permission and her departure seemed very much like a final farewell. During an entire year Spero and Debbie received only two postcards from her, each with a flag printed in the left-hand corner. The first pictured rows of women with identical headpieces, dressed in wrappers of the same color and design. The second portrayed children, also in rows, giving a vaguely martial salute. Worried, Spero tried to make enquiries and was given to believe that the military leader who had been in power for ten years had been driven out by a palace revolt. Apparently this did not reassure Debbie, for he continued to hear her sob her heart out night after night. What's more, all Debbie's letters went unanswered. So it was all he could do to prevent her from joining a package tour to the old forts of Ghana. Elmina. Dixcove. Cape Coast. Anomabu. Prampram. Once she had set foot on the soil of Africa, she hoped to take leave of her traveling companions and set off in search of her daughter. If their daughter did not want to see them, wouldn't it be better to respect her decision, for love's sake?

Debbie got up awkwardly to plug in the toaster and asked with a touch of pity in her voice, "What are you thinking of doing today?"

He hesitated. Her own schedule was rigorously organized. Black Baptist Church of Samaria until around 2 P.M. For she was not content with attending services, singing the psalms louder than anyone else, and if need be, whenever the nurses were overworked, rubbing the hands or sponging the forehead of a believer gripped by the Holy Spirit. In a back room whose only decoration was a crucifix she gave inspired readings or dealt out forceful sermons to the few stubborn, sulky teenagers whose parents had managed to drag them into the house of the Lord.

Then she walked to Agnes Jackson's house, a quarter of an hour away.

Agnes Jackson was a childless ninety year old who had been living alone in the eyes of God for over forty years, ever since her husband left her in Hollywood for a male tap dancer. In her youth she had been a real beauty. A photo conspicuously pinned to her living-room wall showed her sitting behind a piano, her long, light brown hair touching her shoulders. She had been close friends with Langston Hughes, Paul Robeson, and Richard Wright and had maintained a lengthy correspondence with Zora Neale Hurston. Debbie had therefore requested a large grant from a foundation, which was awarded without any hemming and hawing, and for almost four years she had been collecting Agnes's memoirs with the idea of publishing them in a collection of "oral history."

Unfortunately everything got muddled in the old woman's head. She could no longer recollect with whom she had gone to bed and with whom she hadn't, nor with whom she had gone round the world. Was it really Diego Rivera who fell in love with her in Mexico? So the two women got nowhere, a bit like that famous tapestry that was started afresh each morning only to be undone each night.

After her tête-à-tête with Agnes, which kept her to around 6 P.M., Debbie found the energy to dash to the other end of Charleston to the African Ballet Theater, whose director, Jim Marshall, had studied traditional dance in Ashanti country. Debbie gave her stamp of approval to the choreography and advised on the costumes. Up till very recently she had bravely attended the meetings of the Support Nelson Mandela Committee that went on until it was time to catch the last ferry, but now that our hero had fortunately been liberated the meetings had lost their point.

As for Spero, he spent his Sundays alone on Crocker Island.

Sometimes he found a thousand and one things to do. After hurricane Hugo, for instance, he rebuilt with his own two hands the third floor, which had been carried off by the great wind as far as the ocean's edge, hanging blankets, clothing, tattered books, and old family photos on the trees as it went. He learned to his great surprise through letters from Maxo and Lionel that Hugo had also struck Guadeloupe and that the island was nothing but a desolate wasteland. Most of the houses on the Morne Verdol had been flattened or had slid down its side, ending up at the bottom inside out. Their house was still standing, and it was the second great hurricane it had come through, counting the one of 1928.

More often than not, though, Spero did not do much with his Sundays. Sometimes he obeyed Debbie and set off on long walks, even under heavy winter rains. A sunken path filled with joggers ferried over from terra firma circled the island. In summer, when the days took on their glowing colors, he would set up his easel and paint the landscape he had never gotten used to. The sea thick and viscous receding to the back of the horizon; the black boys fishing for crabs with their long nets, sinking the soles of their feet into the soft, black mud that covered the shore like a carpet of volcanic ash; bunches of black seaweed here and there tangled up like the hair of the drowned. Sometimes he didn't move from the house. He would sleep and always have the same dreams. Of crabs. Of seaweed. Of creatures of the deep.

Sometimes his dreams took him back home. Marisia, her hair turned white but finally wearing a smile on her face, would be waiting for him at the airport beside Justin, as proud as a peacock with his son. In actual fact, Marisia had died the year after he left from a cancer she never mentioned to anyone. Justin was still living, but senile at seventy-two, taking himself for the ancestor and telling stories of widows buried alive with provisions of brandy, tobacco, clay pipes, and three-cornered hats.

Debbie closed the door of her room behind her. A place where Spero never set foot, her room resembled a museum dedicated to the goddess "Black Americana": photos of Paul Robeson as Othello, Mahalia Jackson in curls and concert dress, Martin Luther King Jr. in front of the Lincoln Memorial, Andrew Young at the UN, Jessie Jackson with finger raised against a rainbow backdrop, and her numbered reproduction of the *Legend of Amistad* by Romare Bearden. She was very proud of her library, which contained not only the novels of Toni Morrison, Alice Walker, and other up-and-coming writers, but conversation pieces such as a first edition of writings by

Jupiter Hammon, the first black American poet, a slave who lived at the end of the eighteenth century, and first editions of Frederick Douglass's *Autobiography* and *Uncle Tom's Cabin* by Harriet Beecher Stowe, with illustrations by Jonathan Daimon. When she came out of her room, she would be transformed. Thanks to the creams, makeup, and perfumes from her bathroom she fabricated that solemn, haughty, slightly intimidating mask with the nonetheless benevolent smile she put on for others. As for Spero — he was getting ready to spend the entire day in his dark blue sweatsuit that he had slipped on over his not very clean pyjamas — she rightly remarked that he was letting himself go. It's true in the past he had been a real *bodze*, a real dandy. Justin had handed down to him the liking for white starched underwear, shirts with pleated fronts, and trousers with creases as straight as plumblines falling on impeccably polished shoes. Sometimes he was even bold enough to wear a fedora tilted over his left ear. Now, without even taking the trouble to look at himself in the mirror, he was pulling on a pair of jeans, a sweater and jacket, and with his feet ensconced in a pair of Nikes, voilà!

Ever since Anita had abandoned them Debbie and Spero had nothing left with which to weld together the pieces of their life. They had nothing much to say to each other. They seldom shared a meal, since Debbie sat down to eat with a book. They had not made love for two years, since Debbie took his affair with Tamara Barnes as an excuse to banish him from her bed.

So shy and unsure of himself, when had he started looking at other women? When had Debbie found nothing more to say to him, turning their hours into days of silence? When had they started to live side by side without communicating or reciprocating? You can diagnose the first symptoms of a disease but not the beginning of the end of love. When they first arrived in Charleston, they were so inseparable they were nicknamed "Him and Her." He had forced himself to accompany her on visits to her circle of friends as if he were impervious to these people who didn't trust a nigger speaking English with a French accent and who made fun of Debbie's stories about a royal ancestor behind her back. He accompanied her to her lectures at the neighboring black campuses — and once even to North Carolina. For she was considered to be one of the leading specialists on the Reconstruction. It's true she had had access to some exceptional research material, since Moses, one of her great-great-great-uncles, had been one of the ten black state senators in the first chamber of representatives elected after the Civil War. The white politicians at the time ridiculed him, claiming that he hardly knew how to sign his name, and doubled up laughing every time he opened his mouth.

Spero had also accompanied Debbie to concerts by black musicians, for she had taught him to like jazz. On this point he was more flexible than she. He had tried in vain to get her to vibrate to the rhythms of the *lewoz*, *toumblacks*, quadrilles and especially the *kaladjas*, the Guadeloupean love dances he was so fond of. Whenever the moon was full, the men would mount their drums — their *kas* — Justin as well — and there would be dancing on the Morne Verdol. She had remained as cold as ice, merely comparing this bacchanal to the Kongo dances of the slaves in Louisiana. (It had been their first little quarrel.) A nonbeliever, who while he lived in Pointe-à-Pitre only set foot inside Saint-Jules on December Tenth for the ancestor's requiem mass, he had also accompanied her to Sunday services. That was a strange community, the black Baptist Church of Samaria. During slavery its preachers had hidden in the barns to teach the slaves how to revolt. Now women had the right to preach, and Debbie standing at the foot of the altar would often improvise with that resounding voice he once compared to a *boula*, a Guadeloupean drum.

"Generations come and generations go, while the earth endures for ever. The sun rises and the sun goes down; back it returns to its place and rises there again. The wind blows south, the wind blows north, round and round it goes and returns full circle. All streams run into the sea, yet the sea never overflows; back to the place from which the streams ran they return to run again."

For several months now the black Baptist Church of Samaria included a feisty woman preacher by the name of Paule from Washington DC, who had made a name for herself electrifying the congregations in storefront churches there. She was Spero's latest conquest; he had courted her without any real conviction simply because she was his wife's best friend.

Thanks to women, Spero had made his discovery of America. The good souls of Charleston — and there were a good many of them — informed Debbie of each of his infidelities, and she treated them with the utmost contempt. It's a common fact — isn't it? — that African, American, or Caribbean, the black man is not hewn from the wood of monogamy. In private she likened herself to a *bara muso*, a first wife sharing her husband's bed with co-wives yet managing the household finances. She was caught off her guard only once. And that was because of Tamara.

Before his affair with Tamara Barnes, Spero was recovering from a stormy liaison with Ruby, whose life could have been the basis of a short story — hardly original, it's true — on the Old South.

Ruby came from Clarksdale, in the Mississippi delta, and had been given her first bottle to suck in the cotton fields where Julia, her fifteen-year-old mother, was working herself to the bone for four dollars a day. That was in 1943 on the Hammond plantation. All you needed to do was stand at six in the morning on the corner of Fourth Street and Issaqueena, the main thoroughfares of the black district, and wait for the trucks from the plantation. Ruth, her mother's twin sister, had taken Route 49, made famous by the blues; a drop in the human tide moving north, she emigrated to Chicago, where she hired herself out for seventy-five cents an hour. She urged Julia to come and join her in paradise. But Julia could not take the plunge because of a cotton picker she had fallen in love with who had a wife and family of his own and would father her two children after Ruby.

In 1958 — Ruby was then fifteen — the wretched sharecropper her mother was living with tried to rape her. She sunk a pickaxe into his back, and without a glance at the color of his blood took off and ended up in Memphis. How she managed to survive nobody knew. Some say she spent her time in some institution. Anyway, a few years later she turned up in a relatively smart club, I must say, wearing camellias in her hair and singing songs by Billie Holiday, who had just died in New York. That was how her career — which never really sparkled — had begun. Spero had unearthed her in a seedy, half-empty club in Charleston. But Ruby had already put up with too much from men and was not going to be a loser any more. She used to search Spero's pockets and sniff his underwear; she would stand watch a few steps from his studio, and when he wasn't in her bed she would call him in the middle of the night disguising her voice. He had had to break it off.

With Tamara Barnes, Spero found himself at the other end of the Old South. A statue of her forebear, W. G. Barnes, a staunch advocate of slavery, stood on Citadel Green. Tamara had converted the twelve-room mansion, unfortunately the only piece of property her parents had left her, into a hotel. Camellia House. Four lines in the visitors' brochure recalled that the house was built in 1778 and that the rates were reasonable. One morning while Spero was having breakfast with one of his numerous one- or two-night stands, he had encountered Tamara's white waxen face, her mauve eyes, and that ginger head of hair, carefully brushed back with jasmine-scented water into a chignon, that she had inherited from a White Russian émigré who was well beneath the station of the great-grandfather who married her. Almost forty, Tamara's heart still mourned a cousin who had plucked her virginity before going to study at Harvard and becoming the leading historian of the Civil War and Reconstruction. (A racist, the black historians have decided). An only daughter, she had laid her father to rest at the age of fifteen. For seventeen years, she looked after her mother, whose heart and body had been broken by the death of her husband, then in tears drove her to her last resting place. And finally she remained alone to defend the honor of the family name.

However furtively her neighbors in East Battery, where Camellia House stood, kept watch day and night they had never seen a man say a word to her, except for a tradesman or a customer. The trip from Ruby's bed to Tamara's had captured

Spero's imagination — although he was not particularly attracted to white women, contrary to common assumption about black men. Admittedly he was fascinated by this side of America. Fatally wounded by history since the end of the nineteenth century, Camellia House stubbornly clung on with grace and dignity. Crowds of obese people trampled its lawns and admired its azaleas while munching on hamburgers. Adulterous couples slept between its sheets. So what!

On the screen of Tamara's body Spero projected a miniseries. The landing of the *Caroline*. The unsteady steps of a handful of Englishmen from Barbados with their slaves (including Senior Middleton, Debbie's ancestor). The arrival of other Englishmen and the slightly belated appearance of the Africans, the thriving plantations of cotton, indigo, and rice, the burning of Columbia, the surrender of the Confederates at Appomattox, the end of an era . . .

He liked the fact too that she was so infatuated with making love. It seemed that in one fell swoop she wanted to make up for all those years of lost pleasure. She melted into water and burnt with passion under his hands and mouth. Together they talked the night away. At first light, when he managed to drag himself from her bed, he stumbled like a man leaving a rum shop and could only find words in Creole to express the infinite satisfaction of his body: "Mi mal-fanm, mi!" (My, what a woman!)

One day while they were lying side by side, worn out by their lovemaking, he found himself sharing his secret. Oh, no, he wasn't just a painter without talent, a foreigner who massacred the English language, a womanizer who disrespected his wife while living off her. He was something else. In short, he told her about the ancestor. But Tamara had already read *Roots*. And when you are a descendant of the Pilgrim Fathers on your mother's side and one of General Lee's barrack buddies on your father's, all those stories about black royalty don't amount to very much! She scarcely bothered to listen, yawned, and turned her back on him in bed. Mortified, Spero spent a good week without seeing her, and for weeks there was a certain chill in his words.

Although he had lived in Charleston for many years, Spero had never sized up the town's mentality, and the fury that his affair with Tamara unleashed caught him by surprise. Debbie made him understand that it was a slap in the face not only for the black community of Charleston, but for the black race in America, constantly being put to shame in its fight for dignity. And also that he was a traitor. For months he rejected such an amalgamation of charges. He even tried to laugh about it. Then in the end it spoilt his pleasure and he yielded to the general outcry. And yet when he thought about it it seemed to him that Tamara had got him out of the jail where he had been imprisoned, where he had gradually forgotten the sweet taste of freedom.

He really was suffocating in Charleston! He had had his fill of black churches, black universities, and black stories by black friends! Sometimes he was taken with the urge to go home. Take a plane. Land at le Raizet. The pods of the flame trees would have burst into flower and the tarmac would lie bleeding at their feet.

But can you return home empty handed with holes in your pockets? Can you go back with nothing to show but mossy white hair and osteoarthritis? He hadn't exactly made a fortune in America. He hadn't earned a piaster, neither in gold nor in copper! He was one of those immigrants whose stories are best left untold so as not to frighten candidates about to leave. But in actual fact do you ever make your fortune in America? A pack of lies! Rubbish! *Pawol an bouch pa chaj!* — You can't rely on words! Unfair advertising! For every person who saves his body, ninety-nine lose their soul. The mind loses count of those who came knocking on the door of dreams and now sleep with nightmares.

All set for the day, Debbie came out of her room and once again held her cheek out for Spero. He accompanied her to the porch, the piazza as they say in Charleston. While she carefully set her feet down on the large flat paving stones leading to the former stables on the left side of the house, now converted into a garage, he looked around. A wall of trees soaked by last night's rain blocked the view and nobody could see what lay beyond. In the distance you could hear the sea howl with anger. The sun was up, however, and remained seated like a convalescent on a cushion of clouds. In a while he would go out for a walk.

Justin, Spero's father, had been one of those children who seem to be in mourning for the mother they buried at childbirth. Moreover, Djéré, Justin's papa, was so taken up with writing his notebooks that he paid him no more attention than he did the paint peeling off the walls of the house on the Morne Verdol or the ever darker spots on the ceiling made by the water dripping from the roof nobody repaired rainy season after rainy season. Fortunately there was Hosannah, his grandmother, who treated him like the apple of her eye. She dressed him in velvet and silk poplin with wide sailor collars tripleedged in blue. She fed him chicken fillets and creamed mashed potatoes. Never breadfruit or dasheen, none of those basic foodstuffs the poor have to make do with as an accompaniment to their codfish and salt pork. The neighbors jeered at all the trouble she went to, for the child made no progress at school. It was obvious he'd end up like his father, who was bone idle, his mind muddled by constant swilling of rum and that nonsense about a royal ancestor and exile in Martinique. Some people were only too quick to blame Hosannah, who after having spoilt and mollycoddled her own son was now doing the same with her grandson.

Constantly hearing Djéré churn out his nonsense at the Cerf-Volant, a rum shop at the bottom of the hill where he was one of the regulars, some smart alecks had nicknamed him "Wise Man" Djéré, a name that was later passed on to his son. At Epiphany on 6 January, a golden paper crown was placed on his head and he was obliged to buy a general round of rum or absinthe. He complied with the money that Hosannah stuffed into his pockets and recited pages out of his notebooks, which nobody listened to.

Maryse Condé

Justin could not bear his father. Throughout his childhood he had wondered why he didn't have a papa who on weekdays went off to work with his lunch tin at the d'Arboussier factory like everyone else and on Sundays dressed up in a white starched drill suit. Why did Djéré just sit at the dining room table, dipping his pen into a glass inkwell, scribbling and scratching from morning to late afternoon on pieces of paper, and in the evening when he was drunk telling stories that nobody could make head or tail of? He could not bear his grandmother either. Hosannah was a sad-looking black woman, a genuine beast of burden who worked and worked and worked. Insensitive to the treats she dealt out in silence, he blamed her for a surely unwarranted devotion to Djéré. For worshipping him as God In Person. Instead of treating him as an egoist, a swiller of rum and an incredible bore who ignored everyone around him.

It was only when a bad bout of pleurisy blew her out, in two days, like a candle that he missed her, for then he had to set about looking for work.

Justin had no time for Djéré's stories. They only came to life when he left for Martinique with some other Guadeloupeans to do his military service. Unlike his fellow islanders who, without knowing exactly why, nurtured little fondness in their hearts for Martinique and Martinicans, he was happy to be boarding the ship. Because of his grandmother's poverty he had never left La Pointe. Even during the long vacation he stayed behind and roasted on the Morne Verdol. His only distraction was to set off for the port and watch the great liners that crossed the Atlantic, without even taking the trouble to dream that one day he would "stride over" the water. Sometimes he made a bit of money carrying the passengers' iron or wicker trunks, for he was very tall and very strong since Hosannah kept him well fed. And then his family on his mother's side came from Martinique. On one of the rare occasions when she had opened her mouth, Hosannah told him that people called Jules-Juliette were two a penny in Rivière Prêcheur, the village in Martinique his mother left to look for work in town.

The barracks where they kept him locked up were situated in the district of Bellevue. Now it so happened that the pride of this neighborhood was a pink-stoned house hidden at the bottom of a garden filled with hibiscus, Joseph's coats, and multicolored crotons. It was encircled by a huge veranda supported by six white columns, vaguely and somewhat surprisingly Doric in form. If you stuck your nose through the gate that was always locked with a heavy iron chain you could catch a glimpse of an old round pond made of stone and a flute-playing cherub whose plaster was peeling. They called it the King's House.

For six months Justin passed by the house without stopping or bothering to cast a sideways glance. Then one day he remembered the nonsense his father used to tell him. Who had lived here?

Oblivion scrubs the memory clean, they say. The Martinicans had forgotten their jeering of times gone by. Grandparents had passed on to their children who had passed on to their children a magnificently edifying story. Everybody was sure they had seen with their own two eyes the old man amble along beside his *honton* under a parasol held over his head by one of his wives. Sometimes he took his son walking with him and the child who answered to the name of Ouanilo passed by, his head held high as was befitting a prince. With a wealth of details people described the sabre with the wide engraved blade he wore on one side and especially the fringe of blue pearls that veiled his face. They had never seen anything like it: it reminded them of blue flakes chipped from the moon. People also recounted how a carpenter from Terres-Sainvilles had carved out a throne in mahogany from a drawing the *honton* had carefully made in a school exercise book and how the old man sat on it as stiff as a poker. Almost a century later people were offended by the story of a French teacher, one of those French French who came to idle away their time under the Caribbean sun, who had given Ouanilo a kick and then crowed all over town, "I booted the butt of a prince!"

For the first time these stories made Justin think that Djéré had not been just talking through the top of his head. He began to interrogate the inhabitants of Bellevue, but they could not remember very much. Someone suggested he look in at the Schoelcher Library, so he shut himself away there on his day off. It was here he found some dusty newspapers of the day that did in fact mention this African king and his suite exiled by the French: five wives, two children, plus his alter ego the prince Adandejan. In the 13 December 1894 issue a long article described the arrival of the king's son Ouanilo at the lycée in Saint-Pierre. "The young prince appears fairly intelligent," wrote the journalist. "He reads quite well and is quite skillful at forming his letters." However there was no mention anywhere of a local family lineage. Yet Justin was as delighted as a detective who has the proof in his hands. And greatly encouraged, he returned to La Pointe a different young man from when he left.

Since Hosannah had left this earth three rainy seasons earlier he tried to draw closer to Djéré. But rum had finally disposed of Djéré's mind and Justin could get nothing out of him. He wanted to read his notebooks, but never managed to get his hands on them, since Djéré had double-locked them in his wardrobe now that his hands trembled too much to hold a pen. So Justin began to haunt the municipal libraries of La Pointe, and even the history shelves in the bookstores. When he came back from Martinique everyone agreed he was just as boring as his father.

What's more, he was arrogant. The Morne Verdol was too small for him. He assured everyone he would not end his days there — another land was awaiting him. One day he quarrelled with his boss, Hassan el-Nouty, owner of the Garden of Allah, where he sold bales of printed calico, and called him "filthy Arab." Hassan el-Nouty did not stand for it and straightway sent him packing.

It was at that time he married Marisia Boyer d'Etterville, and what an extraordinary marriage it was. Marisia Boyer d'Etterville had first been a Boisripeaux, like her mother, Lacpatia, and her grandmother before her. Then a fit of anger had put at death's door the *béké* who eighteen years earlier got Lacpatia pregnant — Lacpatia the daughter of a penniless mulatto from the Hauts-Fonds. In his terror of the flames of hell the *béké* legitimized his sixty-one illegitimate children scattered throughout the savannas of Grande-Terre, then passed on to the other life.

The year Marisia changed names was the year she fell sick, so sick that Lacpatia set about sewing her funeral dress.

Why did Marisia fall sick?

Those who know something about these things claim that a name passes the essence of life from one generation to the next and is moored fast in the unfathomed depths of the soul. From the very first day Marisia was born, or perhaps even as far back as when she had started to swim in Lacpatia's womb, generations of Boisripeaux women, born and died long ago, had passed onto Marisia their valor, their hopes, their stifled ambitions, and even their malice, which makes people human in the infinite forgiveness of the Lord. Brutally snatched from this lineage and transposed into an unknown line of descendants, Marisia's spirit had been unable to resist. It had collapsed and her body had followed.

Yet Marisia came through. So pale she looked as though a monster of the night had sucked all her blood and so thin the ends of her bones were sticking through her skin. On the evening she left the hospital, while Lacpatia was tenderly settling her into a rocking chair, she announced her decision to marry and the name of the man she intended to wed.

Her poor mother wept.

The doctors are still intrigued by Marisia's recovery. They say it was a miracle, a word that doesn't mean very much. What we do know is that she had met Justin. Marisia and Justin met at the hospital, where ever since he had been kicked out of the Garden of Allah, Justin had been sliding basins under patients' behinds, so thankful to have found a job even if it was foul smelling. After forty-five days of illness with her spirit floating out of reach of her body — between heaven and earth — Marisia's blurry eyes had seen a tall man enter her room and approach her bed. While he lifted her up and placed the cold enamel object beneath her he whispered:

"You think I'm a good for nothing, a common nigger, isn't

that right? A collector of excrement. The shit man. Mr Caca. Well, I'm going to tell you something, tell you who I am. Listen to me carefully because I'm not going to start my tale with a *Once upon a time* or *Tim-Tim* or *Is the court asleep?*"

Marisia never repeated to anyone what Justin whispered in her ear. Perhaps she kept it locked up in her memory to brighten the dark days of her marriage, and, Good Lord, there were enough of those. The fact is that when Justin had finished, her mouth, which for forty-five days had barred every sound, opened and let fly a shrill laugh that quickly changed into a gasp of pleasure under his onslaught. The next morning she was able to sit up in bed and swallow a little chicken broth. Ten days later the doctors signed her release. The neighbors on the Morne Verdol learned with stupefaction of Justin's marriage to a deserving young girl from a respectable family. They were lost in conjectures.

What was going on here, for goodness sake?

Justin had nothing to his name. Apart from the shack on the Morne Verdol, he had no property, no land under the sun, no house in the hills. No diplomas. No light skin. His father was the joke of La Pointe, with his bouts of drunkenness and stories of a royal ancestor. All he possessed was the fond memory his devoted grandmother Hosannah had left in people's minds.

But people could go on being surprised as much as they liked: the date fixed for the wedding drew closer. One Saturday, the last before Christmas, two green rented Oldsmobiles draped with narrow garlands of jasmine flowers drew up in front of the church of Saint-Jules. Justin, Marisia, her young brother Florimond, and Lacpatia got out followed by Djéré, for once in his right senses, wearing a bow tie over his Adam's apple and the three claws of the Leopard sparkling on his temples. People noticed with surprise that despite the blackness of his skin he had a regal air about him. The wedding was no crowd-stopper. People felt there would be no happiness here and the bride would soon have nothing but her two eyes to cry with. No reception followed the ceremony at the church. There was no wedding cake. Lacpatia heated up the black pudding and the curried goat she had brought, and the wedding party ate in gloom.

No sooner had he married Marisia than Justin quit his job at the hospital and bade farewell to work forever. From that time on he divided his time between music and the bar at the Cerf-Volant. He had always liked music. But how could he study it when Hosannah earned scarcely enough to feed the family? Then he heard of a group with a teacher who had learned the art in Haiti, and he joined them in a house in the outlying Nassau district. Justin could have become a famous musician, another Siobud or some other legend of his time. Alas! He was not persevering. After an hour practicing on his clarinet he would drop everything and run to the rum shop, where he would soon be spouting off his usual nonsense and forget about those who were waiting for him. Poor Marisia had her hands full with both Djéré and Justin, two good-for-nothings, two rum guzzlers who sometimes turned violent. Until God in His goodness recalled Djéré to Him; Marisia was then eight months pregnant with her first child.

Nobody knows what finished Djéré off. Probably an existence of sorrow and disillusion lived in the memory of his failed ancestry.

Justin did not cry. This shocked the neighbors on the Morne Verdol.

You only have one papa. You don't have two or three. The next morning after they had taken away the coffin, Justin splintered the door of the locustwood wardrobe at the head of Djéré's bed under Marisia's consenting gaze. All he found were some old things belonging to the ancestor, some newspaper clippings, the *Histoire Illustrée de l'Afrique* by Henri Veyrier with a large yellow mark on page 216, and the famous notebooks numbered from one to ten. They were nicely written in straight characters with blue India ink. On the first page Djéré had drawn a family tree that ended with that arrogant word ME. Then he had jotted down sentences that seemed completely meaningless. For instance:

"The lightning struck the coconut palm but the dum-dum palm is untouchable."

"The cardinal does not set the bush on fire."

"The world holds the egg that the earth desires."

There then followed some fairly crude colored drawings. A tree. A pineapple. A fish. A cutlass. An elephant raising his trunk. A lion.

Finally a list of dates aligned in a column:

January 15, 1894.

February 14, 1900.

December 10, 1906.

Intrigued, Justin buried himself in the notebooks themselves. To the surprise of Marisia, who had never seen him read as much as a newspaper, he buried himself for three whole days and nights. When he emerged he had a strange air about him, as if he had discovered the secret soul of his father after his death. Justin was in fact filled with belated remorse. Instead of despising Djéré and taking him for a wretched swiller of rum he should have tried to understand him, to talk things over with him. How could he repair his indifferent behavior?

After having racked his brains he got an idea: how about having the notebooks published?

Not knowing how to go about it he went to see Monsieur Timoléon, his former elementary school teacher, who at that time had a soft spot for Justin because he had a green thumb and raised pumpkins in the school garden. Mr Timoléon appeared knowledgable because he liked to quote expressions in Latin. Yet when Justin consulted him he didn't think himself scholarly enough and advised him to send the notebooks to a certain address in Paris. You never know what might come out of it.

Paris? France?

The two words frightened Justin. And then there was the war with the Germans. The French must have other things to think about! So he put the notebooks back where he had found them and turned the key twice in the lock. Besides, the birth of Spero was soon to become his number one preoccupation.

Spero was born on the stroke of midnight a few days before Christmas, several weeks later than scheduled as if he could not make up his mind to come and see what was happening in this world of ours. In every church mass was being said for the young Guadeloupeans who had gone off to fight. In front of the church of Saint-Jules a board gave the list of casualties. Yet the Morne Verdol was in a festive mood. Madame Mondesir was inviting neighbors for her Christmas carol sessions as she did every year and families were fattening their hogs. Light-skinned like his mother with somewhat yellow hair, Spero was covered with dark freckles down his back from his shoulder blades to the small of his back. However much Marisia repeated that it was a mere craving for black olives she had had during her seventh month of pregnancy, Justin could not get it out of his head that it meant something quite different. He was convinced it was the Leopard!

When his son was a few months old he circumcised him himself. Then on the boy's temples he engraved the ritual scars his father had worn, something his own father had neglected to do. As soon as Spero knew how to read, Justin placed Djéré's notebooks in his hands, and the child recited the first sentences in his thin little voice until he grew to love the stories more than his lessons at school. He was particularly fond of the chapter recounting the origins of the ancestor.

Despite Marisia's fits of anger Justin took Spero with him everywhere he went. To the bar at the Cerf-Volant where he had him drink aniseed-flavored lemonade. To the *lewoz* evenings at Chauvel and Besson. To the concerts at "La Minerve" and "La Semeuse." People even said he took him to his mistresses, where he sat in a rocking chair sucking a barley sugar and waited till his father had finished with his carnal pleasures.

At the age of thirteen he had his first suit made of raw silk, and Justin took him on Saturday and Sunday afternoons to dance at the *bal titane* to the sounds of the El Calderon band.

But the boy was scared to ask the girls to dance and stood rooted to the spot. What did Justin expect from Spero? That he'd take him back to Africa? To Dahomey? Nothing was less likely. All that business about the ancestor bordered on the mythical and it was highly unlikely he could have lived far from his world on the Morne Verdol. More likely he expected Spero to make a reputation for himself from one end of the island to the other, to polish the family name and gratify his father, who had always been treated with derision.

He was shattered when Spero left for America. It was as if he had watched him take the road to the cemetery in the undertaker's four-horse carriage. His sense of things was offended as well. Since when did a man walk behind a woman? It was up to Debbie to settle down where her husband wanted! In public he claimed his boy would be unable to live without him and would return to the Morne Verdol. When the years came and went and Spero never returned, he became a bag of bones. His royal palm of a figure bent in two. His nimble steps turned to a shuffle. He was so locked in his gloomy thoughts he no longer recognized anyone, passing by acquaintances without as much as a "Good morning" or a "Good night." He even lost interest in rum and no longer headed for the Cerf-Volant, where his former drinking companions waited for him in vain. All that remained was his music. He sat on the veranda, put the clarinet to his mouth, and would play you an old beguine from the time he was a young fan of Siobud's. The neighbors on the Morne gathered for these free concerts and applauded loudly before moving off while shaking their heads. It was a real shame to see what this poor devil had become since his son had left. Nobody knows exactly when he began taking himself for the ancestor. He started mumbling incomprehensible speeches about burial grounds, ritual offertories, taboos, and cult worship. With an air of conviction he would cut chickens' necks and let the blood spurt out. He stubbornly refused to eat wrasse, a spotted fish, on the days when Alexia, the servant Maxo had had to hire to take Marisia's place in the kitchen, seasoned it in a *blaf*, a traditional fish stew. Every evening at dusk he walked down the Morne Verdol, head forward, elbows in, hands behind his back, gripping between his teeth a long, black, silver inlaid pipe that had belonged to the ancestor, removing it from time to time to spit into a silver spitoon he pulled out of one of his pockets. People came out on their doorsteps to watch him go by. The kids followed on his heels. Because of his pipe they nicknamed him "Metal Mug."

After Debbie's four-wheel-drive vanished through the trees, Spero remained a good while standing on the piazza with the fog-laden air smothering his face. Crocker Island had little in common with the Morne Verdol! How come he was ending his life in this lonely spot after having grown up amid chaos, heat, and promiscuity? There was something in this setting that he positively hated, something that corresponded exactly to who he was. Something that corresponded to the real Spero.

Childhood for him had been a never-ending corridor, a path that snaked across a desolate savanna. He had emerged in pitiful shape, not at all equipped to pursue a career, meet women, make love to them, and have children, and even less teach them the meaning of life.

On the outside Spero was a strapping young man, the spitting image of Justin only lighter in color (in fact it was he, more than the other two, who had inherited Marisia's white blood), and he was wild and reckless. His school friends had learned better than to call him "Wise Man," for his fists knew how to hit hard.

On the inside, deep down, he was the insecure little boy who dreamed of becoming a virtuoso on the violin without even having played it and who suffered agonies over his mother's hardness of heart. For him there was never a kind word or an embrace, yet she showered Maxo and Lionel with kisses. Every mother prefers her first son. Why didn't Marisia?

Because of her attitude he would remain behind after school

and play *mabs*, marbles, in the storm channels. Often he did not return home for lunch and reappeared only when the daily obituaries were being read after the evening news at 7 P.M. Because of this, he was inseparable from his father, laughed like him, was uncouth, and consoled himself with being his favorite.

Marisia nevertheless remained the great love of Spero's heart. No woman ever had the same effect on him. He couldn't help comparing Debbie's heavy, sturdy, somewhat hefty figure with his mother's slight, frail build, weakened even further by her terrible illness. When he lived on the Morne Verdol he would glue his eyes to the gaps in the walls of the outhouse shower and watch the contents of a *kwi*, a calabash, stream down his mother's pale body. He would have liked to be that water. Above all he loved the undulation of her breasts and the dense forest of her pubic hair. Because of this picture deeply engraved in his mind he remained a virgin up to the age of seventeen, when during a church wedding of a neighbor's daughter, a pretty little bitch by the name of Delices did the job for him. In fact when he met Debbie he had had very few mistresses and his passion compensated for his lack of experience.

He decided to go indoors, carefully bolting the complicated locks he had had installed on the front door. Debbie had laughed at such precautions and reminded him that nobody had ever been attacked or burglarized on the island. But he was scared of what he read in the newspapers. What on earth had given Thomas Middleton Senior the idea of purchasing this land on Crocker Island and building a house on it? The island swamps had never attracted anyone. Even when rice was king, the source of wealth for the plantations around Charleston, the only inhabitants of this island eaten away by oyster beds were the crabs. It's a fact that Thomas had bought these acres for next to nothing at a time when General Sherman was allotting land to the newly freed slaves.

Spero went back into the kitchen, sat down, and filled his cup with hot coffee from the coffee pot.

He followed Debbie in his thoughts. Soon she would be driving her four-wheel-drive down the ferry ramp and then turning into the heart of the black district where the Baptist Church of Samaria stood. When she arrived Paule would have already donned the turban and floating white alb in which she officiated. Sitting under a cross she would reread the words of the Holy Bible that would illustrate her sermon.

If we do not mend our ways, God sharpens his sword,
He bends his bow and keeps it ready,
Against the evil-doer he prepares his formidable weapons.

Paule! Spero could not get over how easily he had seduced this servant of God. One day he returned home unexpectedly and found Debbie deep in conversation with this *capresse*, this light-skinned woman with a full head of hair, who was vivacious enough to set a font on fire and who for years had claimed as her sole companion the Good Lord. Between them stood a child of ten or twelve with that overwhelmed look common to boys raised by a single mother. Debbie and Paule were discussing how to make the empty Sunday schools more attractive, to lure the youth away from drugs and easy money. All it had required from Spero were a few intent looks, a few skilfully placed words, a slight pressure of the hand, and he had her telephone number, a rendezvous and, to cap it all, a place in her bed. They met twice a week in the early afternoons in her tiny apartment cluttered with indoor plants, religious pictures, and, like Debbie, the Romare Bearden reproductions and photos of Martin Luther King Jr., Malcolm X, and Jessie Jackson. Despite everything, she continued to be inseparable from Debbie, who helped her prepare her sermons, fetched her son Chaka from school, or drove him to his violin lessons. She continued seeing her and talking to her on the phone every day for hours on end.

Even so, Spero had the intelligence not to despise her, understanding full well that she was a victim of this great solitude of black women, the constant subject of articles in *Ebony* or more serious magazines. This solitude had thrown dozens of women into his arms! Some of them wore mourning for a

Maryse Condé

lover who had met a violent death in an urban wasteland or was locked up for life behind prison bars. For others, horror of horrors, their lover had left to share the bed of another man. Others had met an even crueller fate when their lover betrayed the race and went off to join the enemy camp on the arms of a blonde. They had all remained behind with a heart and a body for the taking and their two eyes to cry with.

Sipping his coffee Spero imagined Debbie and Paule in the neon-lit church hall, each keeping her smutty secret to herself, sitting among the congregation possessed by the Spirit, singing, clapping, swaying from left to right, raising to the altar their faces soaked in sweat and tears. Although Paule was often carried away in the heat of a sermon and lost control of herself, moaning and shouting with passion, Debbie never gave in to such emotions. In the midst of the utmost chaos, she would remain seated or stand stiffly, back straight, singing with the beat. And Spero would blame her for it as if it were a disability. He had always dreamed of joining in this collective frenzy and saw himself standing, sweating, stumbling, possessed by the fury of God. For he had never seen anything like the services at the Baptist Church of Samaria, not even in the excitement of a *lewoz* at Chauvel and Besson. So it was the anniversary of the ancestor's death and he had forgotten the date!

The first December Tenth they spent in Charleston had also been the date of their first major quarrel. Without asking for his opinion, she had invited to spend the evening on Crocker Island a professor emeritus of African history; a novelist, who, after the publication of her first book thirty years earlier with a modicum of success, was constantly rewriting a second one on the Civil War; a former Alvin Ailey dancer, now obese; two reverend ministers and their wives; as well as her best friend, the sociologist Jim Marshall. After having solemnly paid their respects to the portrait of the ancestor that had been brought down into the living room for the occasion and placed above a vase of flowers, all these people, as sober as employees at a funeral home, gulped down the gumbo soup, the stuffed oysters, the fried chicken, the rice pilaf, the candied sweet potatoes, and the pumpkin pie she had spent the day preparing. The conversation focused on W. E. B. DuBois, whom the professor emeritus had known very well before he had left for Africa. Then the novelist read large extracts from her future novel amid a religious silence, and Jim Marshall followed up with a description of his stay in Kumasi during the 1960s and his relations with the Osagyefo Kwame Nkrumah and the Asantehene Agyeman Prempeh II — the former representing modern political power and the latter, the seat of traditional power. After the guests left Spero reminded Debbie that the anniversary of December Tenth was strictly a family ceremony inaugurated by Hosannah when she had learned of the death of her child's father. He therefore requested her to mind her own business in future.

From that moment on he made it his responsibility to have a mass said at the Catholic church on Hill Street and decorated the house with white roses for remembrance and burned incense in small earthenware pots. As for the tradition of the meal without salt, for a host of reasons, it was lost.

Spero washed his cup in the sink, put it away, and went and sat down in the living room in his favorite armchair with its faded blue velvet and its golden fringes.

Through the wide-open window he watched the sun climb up and up to the top of the sycamores.

Djéré was only five when his father left Martinique, and yet he thought he could recall every detail of his appearance and every word he had spoken. His head was solidly set on his shoulders, one of which was rubbed with oil and always bared so that it shone like a lighthouse, while the other was covered with a richly embroidered toga. He was so tall that when he walked, the yellow flowers of the ylang-ylang and the red blossom of the flamboyant caught in his miter. His temples were scarred with the three claws of the Leopard, whose vigor and grace characterized his entire person despite his great age.

When he set foot on the ground wearing brocaded slippers or buffalo-hide sandals, the earth sank under his weight. He loved to talk about his father, the greatest of the Huegbaje-hennu, he too a victim of French treachery. His voice grew hoarse when he recalled how certain members of his court had betrayed him: his high priest, his soothsayer, so many members of his own family, perhaps even his brother whom the French had placed on the throne after him. Hadn't he accepted defeat merely to save the kingdom? Had he been afraid to see it pass into the hands of an *anato*, a stranger to the royal blood? When he learned that the French had deposed the *anato* in turn, he remained locked up in his bedchamber for three days and three nights without eating or drinking, and the royal Leopard wives could hear him sob and call out to the *daadaa* for help. Sometimes in the evening when Djéré refused to suck Hosannah's breast and go to sleep, he would rock him in his arms and sing in Fon with his warm, melodious voice:

The Danhome of Huegbaja is a dazzling sun,
No eye can bear to look.
The Danhome of Huegbaja is a rock,
Where no foot can tread without bleeding.

He also liked to talk about his wars and his battles, especially the last one, the one he had lost. His eyes flashed when he described the treachery of Dodds, the massacre of his Amazons, and the slaughter committed by the French. Sometimes he asked Ouanilo, perched on a stool, to read aloud passages from *La gloire du sabre* by Vigne d'Octon that he never tired of listening to:

There is not a single road or path that is not marked by many similar staging posts, sites of death and crimes, the remaining traces of the only commerce that flourishes in these lands under the protection of our flag.

After these readings he fell into a deep despondency. Every morning his wives would throw the water he had used for his bath under the tulip tree in the garden. To eat and drink he would lock himself up with Hosannah in one of the rooms of the house where nobody ever went, and Djéré knew that it was on one of these occasions that he had been conceived.

One morning Hosannah, red and puffy-eyed, slipped him into his best suit: a pair of dark blue velvet short trousers, a white shirt with a large sailor's collar, and patent leather shoes with a buckle. Then she soaked his hair with Jean-Marie Farina eau de cologne and gave it a good brushing. A great commotion had been under way in the house since first light. Heavy iron trunks, wicker baskets, and bundles were piled up in the yard. Draped in brocade wrappers, the royal Leopard wives, who now spoke perfect Creole, stopped chewing on their toothpicks to give orders to a myriad of porters with sweaty chests and spindly legs. Wearing an organdy dress the princess Kpotasse was attempting to entice the birds from her aviary into a cage: hummingbirds, ring doves, black woodpeckers, and yellow-headed thrushes. Everyone was running in all directions. Only the old man remained silent, seated stiffly against the back of his armchair, his miter set somewhat askew, his hands gripping the knob of his cane. At 9 A.M. on the dot they all set off for the docks.

His father's departure was the first trauma in Djéré's life. Up till then he had been the son of a king in exile, cherished, coddled, and cradled from arm to arm. He grew up in a colonial villa that could rival any belonging to the *békés* up on the *route de Didier*, a villa that had two guards idling outside in the wind with guns slung over their shoulders. The royal Leopard wives would carry him around on their backs and the little cherub would gurgle with delight as he watched the clouds drift across the sky above his head. From one day to the next he became nothing but a papa-less illegitimate son of a maid in a hovel at Terres-Sainvilles that belonged to his grandmother, who was as black as the coal she once shoveled into the bellies of the ships of the Compagnie Generale Transatlantique sailing for Saint Nazaire, Santiago de Cuba, or Veracruz.

Why hadn't his father taken him with him? He seemed to love him so much. The only word he screamed out furiously from dawn to dusk to convey his pain and his outrage was "Daadaa!"

At night he would wake up shouting the name of his older brother, whom he worshipped: "Ouanilo! Ouanilo!"

He hated the *lakou*, the tenement yard where he lived. He hated Terres-Sainvilles, derisively nicknamed the neighborhood of "les Miserables," a dank, evil-smelling place where carts regularly spilled their loads of excrement. He hated Mayotte, his grandmother. He hated Hosannah. When she came home, sweating and worn to a shadow from scrubbing the floors of a *béké*, he would bite and scratch her and spit in her face. He dreamed of drawing blood and knifing her to death. Hosannah did not beat him or flinch at the horrid things he said and did.

"I ké vini! I ké vini chèchè'w!" (He'll come! He'll come and get you!) she would repeat as if she herself didn't believe a word she was saying.

One midnight a series of rumblings rattled the silence and a series of tremors shook those who were fast asleep in their beds. Frightened out of their wits, the inhabitants of Terres-Sainvilles gathered on their doorsteps, their eyes still heavy with sleep, looked up at the inky sky streaked with orange, and wondered what new piece of misfortune fate had in store for them. Mount Pelée had started to erupt. The next morning the Savane, the plaza in the center of Fort-de-France, had been transformed into an open-air hospital that had difficulty accommodating the injured from the northern districts of the island, whose mouths, lips, and stomachs had been seared and burned. The soldiers were unable to contain the crowd of idlers pushing for a look. It was rumored that the town of Saint-Pierre itself had been destroyed to the very last stone. There was talk of forty thousand dead! Not a single *béké* had survived in Martinique, it was said.

Hosannah's marriage to Romulus somewhat improved Djéré's existence. She had at last quit wearing her knees out scrubbing the *béké*'s floors and found a job as a hospital orderly at the municipal home for the needy at Pointe Simon. There she made the acquaintance of a male nurse from Guadeloupe who, after a bitter fight with his father over some land and a house, had resolved to put the island of Dominica between himself and his native island. The nurse was so taken with her big, languishing eyes and the dimple in her chin that despite the child she had been saddled with he didn't take long to propose — not to move in with her, but to marry her at the city hall and at church. At this point he was an attractive proposition, for his father had passed away and the property he had been so unjustly denied became his. Nevertheless Hosannah hesitated a long time before saying yes: as an only daughter, she didn't have the heart to leave her poor mother behind. So Romulus, after almost a year of waiting and hoping, had to accept the inevitable and offered to take care of the old woman as well as the illegitimate son. Finally, in March 1906 — Djéré had just turned eleven — the new family piled its meager belongings — three beds, two rocking chairs, a chest of drawers, and a lovely locustwood pedestal table — aboard the steamer *Jesus Marie Joseph* and set sail for La Pointe. Djéré was clutching his school satchel with his only possession: the photo taken when he was one year old, laughing like a chubby cherub in the arms of the oldest of the queens. Standing a few steps away, arm in arm with Romulus, Hosannah was wearing a yellow and violet checkered madras dress that the wind was puffing up like a bell over her petticoat; to his amazement he noticed that she was young and beautiful, not the mother he thought he hated.

Like most of the passengers, Djéré was as sick as a dog during the thirteen-hour crossing and did not open his eyes until they were entering the harbor of La Pointe. He was captivated. A multitude of little green islands floated on the water like confetti, decked here and there with a rickety cabin, a slanting coconut palm, or a seagrape tree whose leaves were painted in red and green. La Pointe spread out in the curve of a bay bounded on the right by the chimneys of the d'Arboussier factory that constantly vomited flaky ashes. On the wharfs, customs officers looking like martinets were watching over the harrassed dockers amid the smell of fresh fish. Djéré's heart was won over. Immediately he preferred La Pointe to Fort-de-France. The town was bravely and gracefully recovering from an earthquake, a hurricane, and two major fires.

They walked up the rue de la Loi, where old-fashioned til-
burys passed six-cylinder Chandlers and Clevelands, and
headed straight for the foot of the Morne Verdol. What a
contrast with the *lakou* at Terres-Sainvilles! The four-room
wooden cabin with a wide, wrap-around veranda that death
had forced Romulus's father to bequeath him was an enchant-
ment. A guava tree, a lime tree, and some congo pea bushes
loaded with pods were growing in a plot of land close by. That
was already a sign of happiness!

Yet the first few months were not easy. Although Mayotte
had no trouble finding a job heaving coal, Hosannah wasted
hours at the market where they hired *das*, nursemaids. She was
frowned upon for being Martinican, for speaking a Creole that
nobody understood, and for hitching up her dress over her
petticoat in a strange way. It was eight months before Romulus managed to find her a job as an orderly at the general hospital. In the meantime she took in washing at home, inhaling
the smell of the upper classes' dirty linen. Djéré was also called
"Martinican" at the private school in the Faubourg Vatable
where Romulus had enrolled him, for the Brothers of Ploer-
mel had refused to accept him because of the incontinence that
he never quite got over. People found him a bit too black, and
in particular laughed at the beautiful scars Prince Adandejan
had chiseled on his temples. He learned very quickly to keep
his mouth shut about his father being an African king, for
teachers and pupils alike would laugh till their sides ached.

"An African king! Ka sa yé sa?" (What on earth's that?)

He had no friends and played hooky all alone, idling days
on end among the tough customers and ladies of easy virtue
of the Dino district.

In June 1907 Mayotte collapsed on the heap of coal she
was attacking with a shovel, and the doctor could do little but
confirm a cardiac arrest. Hosannah, who despite Romulus's
considerateness had always felt a stranger on the Morne Verdol, now fell into a deep affliction.

Romulus Agenor, whom she had just married, was a man
with a warm and sensitive heart. His father had given him so
many beatings on the slightest pretext that he hated the way

adults exerted violence on children. He understood his step-son, his fury, his revolt, his fits of tears and brutality. So he never attempted to take the place of the old man whose portrait shone at the bottom of the child's heart like the Blessed Sacrament. That was why — and many people could not understand this — he did not legitimize him at the time he got married, wanting to leave the door open for the future. Who knew if one day the real father might not change his mind and send for his child? The years that went by did not discourage him. New Year after New Year he had Djéré send his good wishes to his father on greetings cards he chose and also addressed himself:

M. Gb — —
African king in exile,
Blida, Algeria.

Since Hosannah could not — or would not — give him any information on the ancestor, he plunged into his own research. At that time, I'm talking about before the First World War, nothing was coming out of Africa. The entire continent was under the boot of the French and the British, who had dismembered it like a piece of game. All the history books showed you were slaves chained together or held by the neck in a forked brace called *mayombe*, Senegalese infantrymen, and so-called plate-lipped Negresses. Romulus would spend hours and hours in the municipal libraries but never found very much. One day, however, at the Lambrianne Library, rue Peynier, he came across a complete set of the journal *L'Echo des colonies*. That's how he learned that the old man had died in exile in Blida almost four years previously. It said that for security reasons the French government had refused to have the body sent back to Dahomey.

Romulus was stunned. How could he break the news to Djéré? Although Hosannah never wanted to hear the name of her child's father again, considering she'd been cheated and abused, Romulus knew the feelings Djéré carried for his father in the secret of his heart. For three days he hesitated. Finally, in front of a picture of the Sacred Heart of Jesus on one of the wooden walls, he revealed what he had just learned.

The ancestor's death was the second major trauma in Djéré's life. Secretly, he had always hoped he would once again become the child of one of the great men of our times and go and live somewhere else. Anywhere but this *krazur*, this speck of land tossed on the ocean! Anywhere but in this promiscuity and sweltering heat of the Morne Verdol!

When he learned the sad truth he began by throwing himself into the harbor, heading out to the open sea, then letting himself drift with the waves. Some fishermen hauled him up in their nets just as he was about to drown and brought him back to the docks at La Pointe. Hardly had he dried out on the Morne Verdol than he swallowed some paraffin oil, and as if that was not enough tried to slash his wrists with a razor blade. The hemorrhage laid him up in the general hospital for four days. It was only after these unsuccessful attempts on his person that he resigned himself to putting up with life.

Hosannah, for her part, showed neither grief nor emotion. You would have thought it did not even concern her. And yet on the following 10 December she had a requiem said at the church of Saint-Jules, which she attended dressed all in black. Then she served Djéré and Romulus the first meal of remembrance that started the tradition.

Whereupon life resumed its normal routine in the house on the Morne Verdol. But misfortune never gives up. It strikes and strikes again, and breaks the human spirit.

Romulus was as good a husband as he was a stepfather. He belonged to that rare species of men who never missed a meal at his wife's table and never missed a night in her bed. Only one passion drew him outside the home: the passion of cock fighting. Since Hosannah would not tolerate such horrors in her house, he kept his fighting cocks at the home of his childhood friend, Saturnin Rosebois, who lived in the Canal Vatable district. He owned six, to be exact, six that came from Cuba, fierce birds with scarlet, shaven necks that answered to the preposterous names of Kou Pliché, Gwo Modan, Zyé Koklech, Ti Bonda, Lévé Fésé, and Ayin pou Ayin.

Every Saturday, come rain or shine, Romulus set off for the Canal Vatable where Saturnin was waiting for him. Carrying the iron cages containing the birds fed for three days on egg yolk pellets seasoned with cayenne pepper, the two men took their seats on board the steamer that conveyed them to the wharf at Petit Bourg across the bay. They paid no attention to the landscape that unfurled in front of them. The steamer hugged the coastal mangrove that covers the low, muddy banks of the Riviere-Salée, then sailed along the forest of swamp bloodwoods around the mouth of the river Lézarde, where the outlying houses of the town start to rise in tiers. Their thoughts were on the cockpit where they were going to spend a good part of the day and on the rum shop called the Rendez-Vous des Amis where they would celebrate their winnings. Now it so happened that one Saturday when Kou Pliché had won for the eighth consecutive time and filled Romulus's pockets with a small heap of dirty bills, the owner of the last cock to lose, an awkward customer and drunk into the bargain, accused Romulus of casting a *kimbwa*, a spell. A quarrel followed and amid the confusion somebody dealt Romulus a fatal blow with a cutlass. He lost his life within the hour.

Not only did Hosannah almost die but this third terrible blow dealt by fate marked the beginning of the end for Djéré. He left school, where, as the last in his class, he was a bitter trial to his teachers, and refusing to look for work locked himself up in his room. It was at this point he began to write in his notebooks, based on his real and imagined memories and on what Romulus had told him. One October morning, the neighbors on the Morne Verdol saw him leave home looking like death warmed over and head for the Fessoneau bookstore and stationery shop and return with some ink, some paper, and some Sergeant-Major pens. From that day onwards, locked up from morning to night, he scribbled in his school exercise books. He was driven by no particular ambition, no exact desire. But when he delved back into the short period he had lived with his father and put it in writing, he simply felt better, free from those impulses that one day, if he wasn't careful, would make him do somebody in, man or woman, who

Maryse Condé

knows, and land him in jail. By writing he gradually attained a great serenity and a perfect detachment. At the same time he made daily visits to the Lambrianne library. Here he read books whose pages still remained uncut and browsed carefully through rare journals and magazines wherever Africa was mentioned. But he saw nothing concerning his father.

At that time Djéré did not touch a drop of alcohol. Yet, on leaving the library, he would spend hours at the Ancre Rouge, a bar of somewhat ill repute in the harbor district, a bit of a bordello. He liked the chaos and the commotion: the rattle of iron-wheeled carts over the paving stones, the neighing of horses, the cries of the coconut, soursop, and orange sellers coming from the Saint-Antoine market, and the hollering of the drunks. The Ancre Rouge was squeezed in between two stores belonging to the *békés* piled high with barrels of codfish from Saint-Pierre-et-Miquelon and boxes of soap from Marseilles. The oxen from Puerto Rico were being whipped off the ships with excruciating bellows. With a sad, vacant look, *koulis*, indentured East Indians who had requested their repatriation, all skin and bones, were climbing on board the steamers.

One afternoon while he was sitting at his usual place someone wiped the counter in front of him and asked in a shrill voice, "What will Monsieur have?"

Djéré looked up. Up till then he had been too preoccupied with his father to cast his eyes on a person of the opposite sex or be tormented by what hung between his legs. Yet he was over twenty years old. The girl he was now looking at could not have been more than thirteen or fourteen. Jet black with pearly white teeth and eyes to give a priest a turn, Cyprienne helped her mother with the cleaning at the Ancre Rouge, and when there was a crowd she served the customers, although she was not supposed to. Nobody called her by her first name. Anticipating what she would turn out to be when she came of age, a choice morsel for unscrupulous men, they had nicknamed her "Suzie Soon"!

For Djéré it was not soon enough. That same evening he followed the mother and daughter home. Chance had it that they lived a few steps away from him with five squealing brothers and sisters in a shack that leaked all over.

We know nothing about how Djéré and Cyprienne began their love affair. Nothing about what he said or what he did to court and retain this girl who was still a child. Nothing about what he promised her mother, who despite her poverty was said to respect the church and the Lord's commandments and take the good behavior of her daughters very seriously.

Be that as it may, in the month of March 1917, Cyprienne walked up the Morne Verdol with a determined step carrying a wicker basket on her head. The neighbors were shocked. Hadn't they heard her the previous year at church renouncing Satan, all dressed in white, her hands clasping a candle singing she would live like a good Christian?

To heck with what people thought! Djéré was in seventh heaven. You could hear the sound of his voice. You could see the whiteness of his teeth. He said "Good morning" to his neighbors. On 28 April, the day of his birthday, he even gave Hosannah, who wept all day long, a bouquet of lilies with a fern arrangement. Soon little Cyprienne had grown a belly out front. But the Good Lord does not approve of forcing the body of a young girl, of penetrating her before it is time, of taking pleasure and planting a son. However much Hosannah prepared herb concoctions of worm bush and dog grass, ground cerulean seeds and rolled them in tallow to make poultices, Cyprienne had to take to a bed in the general hospital as soon as she was four months pregnant. Here it was the doctors' turn to keep her calm, have her swallow potions so bitter that her eyes filled with stinging tears, and three times a day crucify her with intravenous injections. To no avail. In a flow of blood her hardly developed body refused the burden imposed on it. Djéré frantically pressed his lips to her flaking mouth and begged her not to leave him.

Nevertheless, on 15 August, the day of the Virgin Mary's Assumption, in a colorless predawn, Cyprienne expelled from her womb a baby boy whom doctor and midwife alike forgot amid the dirty linen, so busy were they trying to save the mother. The death of Cyprienne was the fourth great trauma

Maryse Condé

in Djéré's life. After that he drifted into an existence of rum and cheap absinthe, and soon no longer deserved the name of human being. He was even oblivious to the hurricane of 1928. They say he came home drunk as usual, lay down on his *kabann*, and woke up the next morning amid the rubble of corrugated iron, wooden beams, clothes scattered throughout the garden, and an uprooted lime tree, asking in a stupor, "Siklónla ja pasé?" (Have we had the hurricane yet?)

And yet if he had continued his visits to the Lambrianne library as he had done when Romulus and Cyprienne were alive, he would have come across an issue of *La Dépêche africaine* that would have informed him of the whereabouts of his half-brother Ouanilo. Now a lawyer, he had founded in Paris with two other Dahomeyans the Universal League of Defense for the Black Race.

Unfortunately the pages of this March 1928 issue were not to be read until years later by a young French history teacher at the Lycée Carnot.

As for Hosannah, she was to live for another twenty years and had to provide for the needs of a real child as well as a man who had lapsed into second childhood through rum.

As senile as he was, Djéré sometimes reread his notebooks, always stopping at the same place.

The Notebooks of Djéré *Number One*

The Origins

The forest shakes its foliage and whispers, "I am the oldest of them all."

And it's true the forest has always been there. The old folks say that when man was nothing but a gray fleck bobbing on the hard, gray shore of the ocean it was already there. When all the bits of earth were tied together end to end, it was already there. It was standing firmly on its feet calloused with elephantiasis and cankers, it was hanging barrettes of scarlet flowers in its tangled mop of hair. It was knocking against the sky and barricading the light from the sun and the moon. The forest is a fortress. Behind its walls it cages the red-and-blue-crested macaws, the quetzals that set the branches on fire, the howler monkeys hanging upside down by their lianalike tails, the macaques with their hairy, ancestral look, the gorillas with their faces daubed in black, the pachydermatous pachyderms, and the swishing butterflies as they fly eyes wide open into the dark. Between the toes of its tentacular feet that snake under the leaves and roots to suck up the clinging mud, the tarantula and iguana lie in wait for the toad freshly painted in red and the leaf-cutter ant that never sleeps. The forest is a labyrinth. The green python and the cat-eyed snake lose their sense of direction.

But they are all afraid of Agasu, the Leopard.

The old folks say the forest hauls its trunks up high to inhale the blue oxygen that blows in from the ocean. Lower down, amid the dank smell of sweat from its armpits, the bromeliads germinate where the slime solidifies into tadpoles.

In the forest there is no dry season. Water is everywhere. It falls from the sky, it floats in the air, it laps against the soil where larvae swim. The crabs hang their nests in its branches and the piranhas swim between the feet of its trees preying on the red fruit of the sarawak mistletoe.

One day the forest spread its thighs.

And one by one the round huts with their straw roofs fell out of its belly, and the men brandished their assegais and went off to hunt the elephant and the okapi while the women lit a fire between three stones and gave the children milk from their breasts.

This was the first village of the Aladahonus.

The forest provides for each and every one. Honey from the bees, nectar from the orchids, the hard fruit of the wild avocado, the flesh of the caterpillars, and meat from the agouti.

The night Posu Adewene made up her mind to leave the waters of her mother's womb and join the ranks of other human beings after nine months, one week, and three days, the forest lost its voice. That evening not a whine of mosquitoes nor a whoosh of bats, vampires out for blood, could be heard. Not a *shh shh* of a hummingbird looting the juice of the pollen, not a *croak croak* of a toucan made hoarse by its beak. Not a sound of a royal antelope stealthily treading the forest floor. Agasu the Leopard was prowling in the darkness.

But it was not out of fear of Agasu the Leopard that the villagers were huddling in their huts. It was because the queen had already given birth twice to a dead son who had to be left to rot deep under the earth. This time, however, when the midwife scooped up the bundle of flesh soaking in fresh blood and saw the shell-like vulva under the navel, she said happily, "This one will stay. It's a girl!"

Posu Adewene raised her head towards the sunlight like the tendril of the passion flower or the philodendron. At fourteen she had the complexion of a young wild banana plant. When she smiled her eyes and teeth glistened like the milk of the rubber tree. Her rounded breasts bobbed in front of her and the elders told her father to give her only to the man who drew the first fatal arrow against the elephant. But her blood had not yet flowed between her thighs and her father merely laughed . . .

One day Posu Adewene set off to look for snails and mushrooms for a sauce her father's wife was making. A few yards from the village the hunters were seated around a royal antelope they had just carved up. They were recounting their struggle with the animal and flies were buzzing around their heads. On seeing Posu Adewene they began to sing a song of admiration, but she passed by haughtily without looking at them, for she did not like the smell of entrails and steaming blood.

Agasu the Leopard had his belly full.

For days he had found neither monkey nor capybara, neither deer nor lizard, neither bird nor peccary, but on descending to the riverbed his fierce jaws had feasted on the flesh of fish and tortoises that swim among the mud and silt. He had just laid down on a bed of mongongo leaves when he saw Posu Adewene stepping along between the massive trunks carrying a basket on her head. Immediately he felt his blood rise. His scarlet tongue hung out of his jaws. His eyes filled with stinging water, and rising up on his hind legs he uttered an uncontrollable howl. Posu Adewene heard it too. She stopped, looked left and right, and saw his spotted coat.

Posu Adewene already knew a great deal about the Leopard. Often of an evening the hunters would lower their voices to talk of his ferociousness and cruelty. She had imagined him as ugly as a black, hairy orangoutan, the very caricature of a man. She wasn't expecting so much beauty and stood spellbound, not even thinking of taking to her heels. Even his enormous scarlet erection seemed to her like a savage flower.

Agasu and Posu Adewene stood staring at each other eye to eye and all around them the forest held its breath. Then Agasu bounded forward.

That was how my ancestor Tengisu, the founder of our dynasty, was conceived.

Then nine months later to the very day Posu Adewene gave birth to a monstrous, deformed boy with spotted skin and the cruel claws of his father: they say the midwife who brought him into this world could not help letting out a cry of terror and was beheaded on the spot. After that, people who saw him were careful not to show their feelings out of fear of undergoing the same fate.

Tengisu was always the favorite in his mother's heart and preferred to all the other children.

When my father sat me on his knee and told me this story it didn't seem at all irrational. He spoke calmly, somewhat gravely, and I was captivated by the flame in his staring, glittering eyes. I accepted this cruel tale as God's truth. It didn't seem any more disconcerting than the story of Adam and Eve I was being taught at the same time by the queen Fadjo. I too lost my way in the labyrinth of the forest. I lay down between the roots of its trees and the powdery wings of the giant carnivorous bats brushed against my face. The darkness grew darker and darker and I could hear the commotion of the invisible monkeys from the forest canopy to the spongy soil. When at last I found my way back I snuggled up against my father's shoulder wishing that this moment would never end, as if I felt I was soon going to lose it and that I would no longer be the son of the Leopard to anyone.

Spero realized he had dozed off in a light sleep, permeable to sounds, propitious for insignificant dreams, a splinter of the sun embedded in his left eye. What was he going to do with his day? Since it hadn't started raining yet, why not jog to Indian Swamp?

That was the name they had given to the middle of the island, where the soil, already as flat as your hand, sank into a depression covered with brackish water. Under the trees as dense as a forest, shrubs with foliage as closely knit as *banglins*, thorny scrub, grew with their feet in the mud. History or legend had it that on this very spot in 1675 a handful of renegade British soldiers massacred a tribe of Kiawah Indians to the last man. Then they laid hands on their women. Since even in the afterlife these unfortunate women could not erase from their minds the offense they had been subjected to, you could hear them wailing in the voice of the wind at any hour of the day or night. It was also said they drew into the swamp people who had lost their way, in revenge for the humiliation of the past. And it's a fact that mutilated bodies had been found in the mud. After sunset nobody jogged in the vicinity of Indian Swamp.

Paradoxically, Spero liked this desolate spot that reminded him of the technicolor films he had seen during his childhood when he sneaked into the Renaissance movie theater with Maxo. Indians riding across rivers. Runaway slaves splashing through swamps. That too was America: childhood images. Once he was outside he checked the sky. It wouldn't rain for hours. He walked down the steps of the piazza, strode to the creaking gate that marked the limits of the garden, then started to jog, working his elbows against his body. Other joggers, taking advantage of it being Sunday, were thronging the roads and paths on the island, and lines of men and women, features taut with the same physical strain, were running to God knows where.

At this moment the service would be ending at the Baptist Church of Samaria in a final commotion of cymbals and tambourines before the worshippers filed out glumly at the thought of returning to their daily routines. Ever since Paule had preached there, all those who for a time had shunned the church for more flamboyant and appealing sects had returned. Even Spero, who had not set foot inside the church for ages, sometimes came to listen to her. As a sinner, she could preach about sin. And about remorse, anguish, terror, and punishment. The first time she made love to Spero, she wept, and he had really felt her tears were sincere. He himself felt little remorse, convinced that Debbie knew perfectly well what was going on behind her back and, in a certain way, encouraged it. One Sunday, when he had accompanied her and Paule after the service to Agnes Jackson's, Debbie had looked them straight in the eye and asked whether they had nothing better to do with their afternoon.

Spero was very fond of Agnes Jackson, who, in the disjointed ramblings of her old age, retained a sense of fun and humor that was cruelly lacking in Charleston. He loved to hear her talk about her family. If he had been Debbie, that's what he would have interviewed her about, and not about all those celebrities she claimed to know.

On 24 March 1810 Dr. James Hill laid his right hand on the Bible and swore before the court of St. Paul in the district of Charleston that James Earl Jackson, locksmith by profession, whom he had brought into this world twenty-eight years earlier with his forceps, thereby causing the death of his mother, was in fact white. Consequently, he was entitled to enjoy all the privileges the law granted to this category of individual.

Four years later, after some incident or other, the decision of the court of St. Paul was overturned, and James Earl Jackson was declared a mulatto.

He made an appeal. Over a period of three years witnesses filed onto the stand to protest that a man's race must not be judged solely by the color of his skin, but above all by his reputation and the manner in which he behaves in society. To no avail. Mulatto he was declared to be. Mulatto he remained despite the three slaves in his locksmith shop and the tax per capita he was sentenced to pay. The Jackson family never got over their incursion into the forbidden world of white folks. It left a trace of folly in the minds of all its members, a mental unbalance more or less pronounced according to the individual temperament. In Agnes the folly consisted of a pathological hatred of whites. So light-skinned that the most expert eye was often mistaken, she had nothing but tales of injustice to tell, snubs and police brutalities she had been victim of because of her color, as far back as her schooldays and throughout her career as a pianist.

She would tell with infinite detail how she had been converted to communism after meeting Aragon in Paris where he had written her a poem on the back of a menu.

She also claimed to have discussed ideas with the dark and handsome Jacques Roumain, who had just founded the Haitian Communist Party and, convinced he was being followed everywhere he went, always wore a wide-brimmed fedora to hide his face.

Spero did not believe a word she said and understood full well that the Sunday meetings with Debbie were merely designed to let her relive her past the way she wanted it to be.

But Debbie set a tape recorder in front of the old rambling mouth, overwhelmed her with questions, jotted down notes, and took herself very seriously. Debbie was like that. No cliché ever seemed suspect to her, no stereotype too exaggerated, and when she discovered the truth she couldn't look it in the face. For her the history of blacks in America was like a plant that grew firm and straight, an edifying era written in black and white where there were only tormentors and martyrs. That's why she had started, and abruptly stopped, writing the story of George, her father.

They called him George Middleton, "handsome George," because they had never seen so straight a nose on a Negro. His female admirers would pass by again and again in front of the barber's shop on Meeting Street that had belonged to his great-great-grandfather, and then his great-grandfather, where his father and he himself never set foot except as customers once they had become schoolteachers. Past fifty, he met Martin Luther King Jr. and began to attend every one of his rallies. That's how he met his death in Stokane, another dusty, insignificant little town that was preparing to boycott its buses.

When she saw him laid out and set for eternal life, Debbie, who had worshipped him, made it her mission to perpetuate his memory. But when she started to question people — the very same people who had followed him in tears to his grave in the cemetery at Orange that had just been desegregated so that blacks and whites could spend their time in eternity side by side — she learned some very strange things. Those who had been his students on Sea Gull Island, one of the most destitute among the destitute islands that hug the shore of South Carolina, could still recall the young teacher who kicked them in the butt and in his frequent fits of anger called them good-for-nothing niggers. Some even went so far as to suggest that his great concern for the race did not stem from a meeting with Martin Luther King Jr., whom he had never met in flesh and blood, but from one day in April 1960 when, taken with an urgent need, he relieved himself in the Whites Only restroom of Woolworths on Lime Street. Caught in the act, he was soundly beaten and thrown into the street, even though he was George Middleton. Was that the hero she was about to immortalize? Disheartened, Debbie had put away her typewriter. She had the need to revere. Reverence was her religion.

It had taken Spero time to realize that in actual fact she despised him. He thought he made her happy, dispensing tenderness by day and pleasure by night, and enough to dream for all seasons with this story of a royal ancestor and the notebooks of Djéré she had carefully transcribed and once even planned to translate into English. And then gradually, the truth emerged as a great pain in his heart. His wife despised him.

Why, for God's sake?

He had thought it over so often he had come up with the

answer. The reasons were many and ranged in importance. No, alas! He was not the worthy heir of his royal ancestor. He himself had no ambition. No ideals! No interest in politics. Nor in the future of the black world. And then he spoke broken English. He came from a godforsaken island that nobody could locate on a map. He didn't like pumpkin pie. From 1 January to 31 December his paintings, hanging from the rails in his studio, collected dust. Not a single buyer. Not a single collector.

Yet on this last point perhaps she was the one to blame, for he had obeyed her and silenced his inner inclinations. It was obvious: he was not made for these symbolic and signifying oils she encouraged him to paint. His field was watercolors. The play of light, air, and sun. He kept hidden away in his portfolio like a shameful secret the series of watercolors he had accomplished in which he had celebrated Charleston with his eyes and heart: *Drayton Hall*, *The Battery*, *The Slave Market*, *The East Bay Promenade*. It wasn't his fault if that's what attracted his brush! Colonial houses with their stone facades worn with age. Gardens overflowing with azaleas and rhododendrons. Live oaks festooned with Spanish moss.

When he first arrived, Spero had fallen in love with Charleston. He had never dreamed of a town like this. Although he loved La Pointe as one loved one's mother and the familiar faces of childhood, it was clear to him it was just a former slave-trading post, a place for storing and selling goods with profit as the sole concern. Lille and Paris had been too hostile for him to embellish them with any charm. On the contrary, these two places on the planet were linked in his memory with times of solitude, poverty, and humiliation of all sorts due to his color, for often people took him for an Arab and spared him little in the way of insults.

One evening in a bar in the Tourelle district of Lille a waiter had refused to serve him a beer he had shyly requested. When he went up to the counter to complain, a colossus loomed up who almost smashed him to pieces.

Nothing had prepared him for his encounter with Charleston. Captivated, he discovered the beauty of stone when it is married with flowers and trees, harmoniously arranged by the hand of man. He never tired of strolling the crisscross of streets in the center, tempted at each step to sketch a facade, an architectural detail, or a monument. He walked back and forth along the sea that set off the town like jeweler's velvet. But he soon realized that this liking for Charleston hurt and annoyed Debbie. For her, Charleston was based on the exploitation and servitude of her own people. Charleston could flaunt the aristocracy and grace of a Southern belle because she had never dirtied her hands. She had never done anything but dress up for dances and balls while others attended to her whims. The old slave market was the face of a past that no black should forget. Debbie told him of W. E. B. Du Bois's visit to Charleston, when he had refused to admire the accomplishments of the slave owners and urged his brothers to build their own Charleston.

Spero also liked to paint children's faces. He had painted his daughter's at every age. From the time she was a baby, when Debbie laid her gurgling under the trees in the park, up to her teens.

Hardly had they moved to Crocker Island than she had asked him to stage an exhibition to mark his breakthrough in the American art world. The exhibition was to be held at Chez Marcus, a small gallery-cum-bookshop on Market Street that was the literary and artistic heart of the black Charleston elite. It had played host to Du Bois, James Baldwin, Reverend Ralph Abernathy, who had taken over from Martin Luther King Jr., the historian Nathan Huggins, and other illustrious guests whose signed photos covered the walls. Spero had immediately shaken off the natural indolence he had inherited from Justin (Marisia used to call it quite crudely his laziness) and had worked like a slave. His inspiration came from the masters dear to Debbie and, without ever copying them purely and simply, he had produced thirty-six canvasses in record time. Yes, thirty-six! He was quite proud of a composition entitled *New York*, inspired by a poem by Léopold Sédar Senghor, also one of Debbie's favorites. It represented a narrow street running between the steel-blue legs of the skyscrapers

on which snowflakes were falling in the shape of winged ser-
aphs. Right in the middle of the whitened macadam the body
of a young black man lay in a pool of blood that was soaking
into the depths of the earth and nourishing the roots of a tree
whose branches, overgrown with vines and tendrils, brushed
the tops of the skycrapers.

The guests, most of them friends of the Middletons who
knew Debbie's family tree like the back of their hand, came
in a crowd. They drank to the last drop the white wine from
California and devoured to the last cube the cheese that was
served. They were not sparing either in their words of praise,
since a professor of art history compared *New York* to a painting by Frida Kahlo. And yet they did not buy a thing, and the
Black Sentinel of Charleston, which since 1840 had informed the
black community of events worthy of their attention, did not
devote a single line to the exhibition. Debbie was mortified.
For weeks afterwards, with furrowed brow, even though she
did not breathe a word about it, Spero could hear her telephone the newspaper's artistic correspondent who, as if by
coincidence, was never there.

She did not give up, however, and shortly after this fiasco
leased a studio on Meeting Street for a small fortune. Nobody
ever came in. Spero spent his days there because he did not
know where else to go. When he was tired of putting brush to
canvas or just idly drinking in the wind, he went off to breathe
in the briny smell of the sea and watch the tourists do their
little tour of the historic district, looking for souvenirs of slavery and the Civil War in horse-drawn carriages. At five in the
afternoon he got behind the wheel of his old green Volvo and
went and downed a few glasses at the Montego Bay, a piano
bar on Lime Street.

The Montego Bay was rather an odd place. It was as dark as
a tomb, so dark that the regulars had to grope for their tables,
and it was not unusual for newcomers to take a tumble down
the few treacherous steps. The place was of somewhat ill repute. The regulars consisted of black pimps built like baseball
players, their pockets stuffed with filthy, foul-smelling dollar
bills, and curvy black prostitutes who would down a few

drinks between customers, wearing identical wigs reaching halfway down their backs that made up for the unkempt straw on their heads, as well as a crowd of women out for a one-night stand that would save them from the boredom of their lives and help make ends meet. There were also a few young black hoods openly smoking fat cigars of marijuana while plotting some dark deed, and the jobless, who, finding life too long, were shortening it in alcohol and the racket of rhythm and blues. Over all this humanity, Linton, the boss, would cast his piercing, prying eyes, squinting under his fleshy eyelids through the smoke of a cigarette constantly dangling at the corner of his mouth.

Linton was Spero's only friend, a Jamaican by origin, brought up in Cuba, who emigrated to Montreal and then ended up in Charleston, which meant he spoke three languages fluently. Linton had first made a bit of a name for himself by blowing on a saxophone. Photos on the wall of the Montego Bay showed him dressed in a jacket with silk lapels, his hair plastered down with brilliantine, in the center of an impressive band. Nobody knows why he gave up playing and settled in Charleston in the 1970s. The people of Charleston don't like strangers. In fact they were suspicious. For some, Linton was a drug dealer secretly involved in all those crimes reported in the newspapers. For others, an anti-Castro activist in league with the Cubans in Miami. And for others, an abductor of little girls. On several occasions, Debbie had taken the liberty of remarking to Spero that he was not a reputable person. But Spero, who usually acquiesced, resisted, for Linton was a failure and a foreigner like himself. And not any foreigner — a West Indian! For Cuba, Jamaica, and Guadeloupe were by far and away the same thing, joined together in solidarity like the teeth on a comb.

Spero and Linton drank together, and amid the vapors of Barbancourt rum that Linton had shipped by the case from a Haitian wholesaler in Brooklyn they ruminated over their aversion for America. Sometimes Linton took up his saxophone and the darkness inside the Montego Bay became less dark. Flecks of stars glowed beside the dim light bulbs, and even the most jaded customers stopped drinking, bickering, and talking nonsense to turn toward the spot where the magic was coming from. For a moment even Spero forgot who he was and became the son of the Leopard.

When Linton put down his instrument, however, he became himself again. Alas, no! He had nothing out of the ordinary to report. It was only Spero Debbie had married, Spero, and not the ancestor. So he would set off back to Crocker Island just in time to catch the last ferry. As far as the eye could see the water splashed black, and an old black man, adrift in alcohol as well, was telling him the story of his life, as sad as a song by Lena Horne. Spero recalled that brief time he had lived in Guadeloupe with Debbie and it seemed to him these had been their only moments of happiness. He now understood that the Debbie he had known and loved at the time was not real. In Guadeloupe she had suddenly discovered a kind of freedom. On the Morne Verdol there were no constant reminders of Jim Crow. No incessant outbursts about the wickedness of white folks or arguments about all the wonderful things blacks couldn't do because of them. Yes, they were poor and exploited on the Morne Verdol, but the heart was content even so. While Justin rambled on with his nonsense and Marisia, her mouth full of pins, tried patterns on her clients, Maxo would boast of the exploits of La Gauloise, the soccer team he played in. Lionel, who had just found a job at the botanical gardens in Tanbou, could only talk of orchids and the complex and slightly obscene contours of labella, anthers, bracts, retinacula, and corollas. Every Saturday Spero took Debbie dancing in the racy *koré varé* clubs of the Bas-de-la-Voute district and pressed his burning pelvis against hers. Back in Charleston she returned to the prison of race. Once again she was the daughter of George Middleton, presumed martyr.

Worst of all, she had communicated her contempt for Spero to their child. Anita had never asked Spero if the full moon gives birth to rabbits or if a rainbow in the morning brings sorrow and one in the afternoon brings hope. Whenever he drew her close to him to eat her up with kisses she lent herself to such demonstrations of affection out of charitable politeness. Like her mother, she was only interested in the ancestor in him. The first time she questioned him about his past he was dumbfounded. Here she was at seven already familiar with the name of every battle the ancestor fought against the French, every detail of his long pursuit in the bush protected by the devoted peasants, plus a series of facts he did not know himself that she had learned with her mother from books by American historians at Yale. She could draw from imagination the royal palace, its bas-reliefs, and its ring of orange and palm trees. And finally, more courageous or more naive than any of them, she had not stopped there and had made the long journey in reverse.

Spero decided to turn back. He had run for over an hour and was out of breath. As sinuous as a viper the path snaked all round the island, locking it in its coil. Here it delved among the trees, there it reemerged into the light and hugged the shore.

When he had first arrived on Crocker Island, Spero could not help thinking of the ancestor, who, at the end of his journey by sea, had landed in Martinique. He must have been terrified. What! He was going to finish his life on this *krazur* of land? It was this speck of dust he had exchanged for the green of the still-virgin forests, the realm of Agasu, the dark brown lagoons of brackish water, and the yellow savannas of his kingdom?

In fact, hardly had he set foot off the boat than he began to dictate letters to President Carnot explaining the great injustice he had suffered and requesting his return home. Every month, Prince Adandejan, who served as his secretary, used up twelve reams of Rosseler paper, ten boxes of envelopes by the same manufacturer, and dozens of bottles of China blue ink, a color the ancestor was particularly fond of as it reminded him of the color of the sea he had crossed despite the warnings of the gods and the elders.

Hosannah, Djéré's mother, had long believed she was destined
for a good life. When she was a little girl, no taller or bigger
than a clump of lemon grass, playing in front of the house of
Mama Mayotte, a middle-aged woman stopped to look at her
and began to prattle away. The woman's name was Chechelle
la Folle, a humble "coal woman" by profession, who liked to
sit at people's deathbeds and recite the prayers for the dying
and who claimed to see what the future had in store. Nobody
paid her much attention because of her foul breath, although
she did predict the great fire of June 1890 and the hurricane of
August 1891. She had just left Zephyrine's deathbed, another
coal woman who had passed away in her fortieth year, when
she saw Hosannah and immediately began her chatter. On
hearing the noise Mayotte came out onto the porch and
Chechelle la Folle addressed her sharply.

"Is that your child? And you let her play like that in the gutter? Let me tell you something: that's no ordinary girl you've
got there and it's not any old sort of nigger who'll mount her
one day. Oh no! he'll come from the other side of the ocean.
His papa's the Leopard. No food or drink ever passes his lips."

The neighborhood gossips, who heard her speaking, split
their sides laughing.

There was Chechelle la Folle at it again! And since it was
early January and the time of Epiphany, a ridiculous story
began to circulate around the *lakou*. Hosannah was going to
marry Balthazar, the Wise Man who brought myrrh for the
Infant Jesus. They only stopped their silly jokes when Mayotte,
whose barbed tongue had a fearful reputation, started to hurl
obscenities left right and center. She, however, had faith in
Chechelle la Folle's predictions and brought her child up with
the conviction that her life would not resemble her mother's
and even less her grandmother's, who had been whipped by
white folks. She taught her religion. Every Sunday Hosannah
knelt down beside her on the cold cathedral tiles and looked
intently at the wall lamps, the candelabra, and the crystal lights
while the voice of the organ responded to the verses of the
soloists and the choirboys. After mass mother and daughter

sat down on either side of the kitchen table and the memory of Chechelle la Folle's words shone in their eyes. Too poor to send Hosannah to school and teach her how to read and write, Mayotte nevertheless found her a good job. Hosannah hired herself out to a baker's shop on the rue Isambert that made its own bread, *bordeaux*, *flutes*, and *Marseillais* loaves. She got up before dawn, washed herself with rainwater from the barrel behind Mayotte's shack, ran to take her load of bread, then set off to deliver it. Agile as a goat, she would climb the hills and leap over the gullies, soaked by the rain and dried by the sun, always a smile on her face. It so happened that one morning in June she delivered some bread to some new customers who had recently moved in to a twelve-room villa with a garden up front and a yard round the back in Bellevue. The villa plagued the neighbors' curiosity.

At the beginning of the year it had been leased by the Governor's services from a mulatto lawyer who had left to practice his profession in Saint-Pierre. A whole set of furniture had been moved in: consoles, couches, sofas, a dining-room table, a card table, a pedestal desk, two dressers, all carved out of locustwood, three sleigh beds in walnut, half a dozen canopy beds topped with big wooden knobs for mosquito nets, rocking chairs, and cane chairs. At the last minute, as if all that was not enough, an Erard piano had been added while two guards dressed in khaki took up their positions in front of the freshly painted white gate. Given such preparations the neighborhood assumed they were expecting some important people, probably some high-ranking French government official transferred to the colonies with his family.

Around the middle of March out of three horsedrawn carriages stepped two men, one still young, the other already almost an old bag of bones, five women, and two sullen teenagers, a boy and a girl who looked around themselves arrogantly. What struck everybody with amazement was the color of the new arrivals. They were black, but black! Blacker than black! Blue! They were blue! As far back as they could remember they had never seen such a color in Martinique. The older of the two men was particularly intriguing. His face was virtually

Maryse Condé

hidden by fringes of colored pearls that hung from the lower edge of his headdress like a thick curtain. He was wrapped in a blanket like a tapestry made from rainbow-colored fabric. His feet fitted into wide Moorish sandals with gold embroidery on a scarlet background and pounded the paving stones. His arms were weighed down with silver bracelets. They soon learned he was a very warlike African king who claimed that he had stood up to the French in their undertaking to pacify Africa and that all these women were his wives. It was whispered that over a hundred more back home were lamenting his departure and there was no counting the number of children. At the moment of leaving for his exile he had picked out his favorite two.

Some declared themselves shocked at the proximity of such neighbors who were an offense to a Catholic education. But the idea of sending a petition to the local council was not adopted.

We don't know exactly how the old man came into intimate contact with Hosannah. The latter never gave details of these meetings to anybody, not even to Mayotte. It appears it was an idea of Fadjo's, the Leopard's first wife.

Ever since his arrival in Martinique the old man had been melancholic. Once full of fervor and humor, never refusing to compose a song for the occasion, he now spent his days in silent gloom. He missed his *bokono*, who used to read him his future every day. So Prince Adandejan started to hunt around. A few weeks after their arrival in Fort-de-France he entered the old man's bedroom followed by a frail little man with a reddish skin, barefoot and wearing a *bakoua* hat. The man's name was Zephyr Marboeuf, the most famous *gadé dzafé*, leaf doctor, on the island. Every Day of the Dead he would take on his real shape and spirit people away. It was whispered he had carried off Marguerite, the blue-stocking Negro girl, forty years earlier in Basse-Terre on Guadeloupe, for he could travel at will from one island to the other. Zephyr Marboeuf had to strain his ear to hear the question the old man was asking.

"Will I ever regain my kingdom?"

He peered into the invisible and at first could see nothing

but a bare, white tomb in the desert of Arabia. Then his ears heard the sound of a bugle. He squinted through his eyes and saw a large crowd in tears in mourning under the sun. He understood.

"Yes! But you will already be in *Kutome*!" he said.

On hearing these words, the old man burst into sobs. From that moment on he refused to eat. He pushed away the freshly ground *pakala* yam, as white as cotton; he refused to eat the smooth, creamy sauces made of okra and the *kalalou*, crabs and greens, so like a dish from his own country. He lost his taste for *akras*, fritters made of *titiri* (small fish), and for brains, codfish, crayfish, chou, or Bodi beans. The Leopard's wives prostrated themselves in front of him and sobbed, "Master of the universe! If you go on like this the sun will burn out!"

At night he wanted nobody in his bed and stayed smoking his long pipe until the first glimmer of day whitened the louvered shutters.

Often he would recall the fire of Abomey.

One morning, when Hosannah, then in her sixteenth year, had come to deliver the crusty, fresh bread that Ouanilo cut into fingers and dipped into his soft-boiled egg, Queen Fadjo came face to face with this beauty. Posu Adewene could not have had breasts more pointed nor a rump more rounded when she tempted Agasu! There was no doubt that the most weary, withered male member would harden at the sight of her!

Queen Fadjo enquired about her, was convinced that she was a virgin lovingly protected by her mother, and with the help of Ouanilo, who could already speak Creole, offered her a wage five times higher than the daily franc plus a loaf of bread that she received in the rue Isambert. Hosannah was put in charge of serving the ancestor's meals. The first time she entered the room where he rested during the day her heart was thumping. She was carrying a tray laden with granadillas with a scent like the melons of France, water lemons still with their ring of sepals, white guavas, cashews topped with a nut like a crown, Amélie mangoes with a slight scent of terebinth, and a goblet of chilled pineapple wine. The old man was slumped on his throne. With his shiny black eyes deeply set in their wide-open orbits, he was daydreaming. One year ago he had been sitting on the bank of the river Tago after the ceremonial bath that allowed him once a year to discharge his faults on a young child. How content he was to feel his body and soul regenerated! He did not know at the time that his days as king were numbered. Why is it that misfortune turns up unannounced, without ever beating its drum?

Hosannah set down her tray on the floor, prostrated herself as she had been told to do, and murmured, "Master of the pearls, I am here."

Thereupon she got up, letting the white cotton wrapper she had been given drop to her hips, revealing her virgin breasts. The old man was spellbound in front of this supernatural apparition. A sensation he had not felt for a long time flared up inside him, and that which was nothing but a mass of flabby membranes, withered skin, and flesh swelled up, distending the fabric of his long English underwear.

"Who is your father? What name did he give you?" he stammered in Fon.

Hosannah uttered a giggle of incomprehension, throwing her head back to reveal a shiny set of teeth set like pearls in her black gums.

Regaining his strength as the Leopard the old man jumped up and drew her against him.

When he penetrated her Hosannah uttered a cry that the queen Fadjo heard with satisfaction as she listened at the wooden door. Then, since you can never be too sure, she went and inspected the soiled sheets.

Henceforth she took Hosannah under her wing. She taught her the names of the kings and the prayers in their honor, the rules of succession, the rules of enthronement, the oblations, the sacrifices, and the taboos. When Djéré was born she took full charge of the baby.

Hosannah had a heavy heart. She was far from content with her situation. Was this the extraordinary future Chechelle la Folle had predicted for her? By day the old man took no interest in her. But night after night he had her come to him and possessed her like a wild animal in the forest. His uncut nails dug into the tender flesh of her body, his teeth sunk into her neck, and she had to suffer in silence. His sighs of sexual satisfaction sounded like growls. Sometimes he reared up as if on hind legs. And because of these nights that were torture to her, the wives of the Leopard hated her. For fear of their poisons, Fadjo did not allow Hosannah to touch any food without first tasting it herself. As for Ouanilo and Kpotasse, the children, they treated her like dirt, forcing her to empty their chamber pots full of feces and constantly heave jugs of hot water for the big basins in which they washed themselves. She no longer saw her maman but once a month when she had her day off. And Mayotte spent it complaining and grumbling.

Chechelle la Folle certainly lived up to her crazy name! Was that the brilliant future she had seen for Hosannah? In her mind's eye Mayotte had seen her Hosannah walk up to the altar arm in arm with a handsome Negro, dressed in a long skirt revealing a glimpse of embroidered petticoat, wearing an elaborate short-sleeved blouse, a heavy four-row choker around her neck, bejeweled with *zanno a klou* on her ears and a *tranblant* pinned to her madras head tie. Or else a wealthy mulatto, even a *béké*, would take her in. It happened every day.

Instead of which she was carrying a baby she hadn't asked for by a Negro from Africa!

When she took the newborn Djéré in her arms, blue as Kongo cane, shaven *koko sek*, as smooth as a coconut, and scarred like a tabby cat thanks to Prince Adandejan, she wept all the tears out of her body.

Hosannah refused to listen to Mayotte's cheerless words. She put up with them again and again and turned a deaf ear. But when the ancestor and his family left without as much as a glance behind them she had to admit that her mother was right. The old man left her penniless with an extra mouth to feed and her two eyes to weep with. Her heart learned the meaning of hatred. It seemed her youth had been robbed and nothing given in exchange. A fine African king indeed! King without a crown or legacy! King without gifts of incense or myrrh! She directed her hatred in particular against Queen

Fadjo, who had treated her like a daughter and an equal. Hadn't she repeated every day that the Leopard wives, those who give birth to the kings, must be children of the poor like Hosannah and that her own mother was nothing but a cloth dyer from Abomey? She herself had started out in life as her apprentice, carrying on her head the heavy bundles of wrappers she sold in the markets of the kingdom.

Romulus's love took Hosannah's heart by surprise and made it bloom again like a garden after the dry season. She was overjoyed when on his arm she left Martinique, where she had known nothing but misery, and came to live on the Morne Verdol. Although she never fully took to the Guadeloupeans, whom she found rude and uncouth, it seemed to her that the sun once again was shining over her. Alas! The premature death of Romulus came and destroyed her fragile hopes, and up till her death she was never to know happiness again. She placed her memories in a secret recess of her mind and never entrusted them to anyone. When Justin returned from military service and pressed her with questions she categorically refused to answer. Yesterday was yesterday and what was gone was gone. Hosannah passed away in March 1936, one of the fifteen hundred victims of the great typhoid epidemic that cut down men, women, and children from north to south and east to west across the island of Guadeloupe. The doctors claimed the fever had been introduced by bulls from Puerto Rico that had drunk poisoned pond water back on their home island. The governor decided to have them slaughtered, and it was a real massacre, all those tons of red meat thrown into the sea when so many people were living in poverty. The sick poured in to the Camp Jacob hospital in Basse-Terre and the general hospital in Pointe-à-Pitre in such numbers that the army was requisitioned to erect tents under the tamarind trees.

A lot of people attended Hosannah's wake and burial, for they found her deserving and honest. Even those who had criticized her while she was alive because of her inordinate weakness for Djéré and Justin began to talk about her as if she were a saint.

Justin followed his grandmother's hearse without a tear in

his eye. As for Djéré, he had not even realized that the person who brought him into this world was no more. Drunk as usual, he was snoring like an accordion on a bench in the Place de la Victoire when the police shook him like a plum tree and hauled him off to jail to work off his sleep. When at dawn he managed to find his way back home he was amazed by the smell of flowers and melted candles as well as the violet drapes over the mirrors. He went to bed for another forty-eight hours, mumbling over and over again, "Ka ki pasé isi dan?" (What's going on here?)

Spero turned the key in the lock, entered the house, and automatically headed for the kitchen. When Debbie went off for the day, she always made a point of leaving him a meal: some salad, a single slice of whole-wheat bread, a chicken leg with no artificial coloring or preservatives, and a piece of organic fruit. The chicken was a concession for his hearty appetite, for she herself had become a vegetarian following a dream she had on the anniversary of her mother's death, a dream that cured her of the sin of eating flesh. Contemplating this anemic food, Spero had the feeling he was taking stock of the twist their married life had taken. Little by little, Debbie had eliminated the salt that accentuates the flavor, the sugar that provides the sweetness, the fat, the succulence. She had wasted her time on only one point: she had never managed to get Spero to steer clear of alcohol. And to think that twenty-six years earlier they had met and loved amid the fun of eating, drinking, and other sensual pleasures.

Marisia had not been a bad cook, but not as good as Spero's godmother, Sidoine, who kept a hotel in Grande-Savane at the sign of the Grand Gosier. And then Marisia was not an agreeable person, almost a sourpuss, tormented by her open conflict with Justin and the education of her three sons. So on Saturdays Spero and Debbie would flee the heat of the Morne

Verdol for Grande-Savane and take the *charabanc*, the country bus that served the entire district of Petit Bourg, chugging up and down the hills. Ah, those Saturday feasts washed down with rum punches after which they tumbled into bed! In the morning neither the blackbird noisily clearing its throat on the veranda nor the sun indiscreetly slipping between their sheets managed to wake them. When they first lived on Crocker Island, before the fateful dream, Debbie used to take him sometimes to one of her aunts who could cook you up one of those succulent traditional dishes from the South. Alas! All that was long over with. If only Debbie realized the importance food had acquired because of her. When he went visiting Linton at the Montego Bay he could start to desire a woman from the way she crunched her nachos. Most of his affairs started like that: sharing a dish. Placing his chicken leg in the microwave, his body aroused, Spero recalled one of his recent and juicier love affairs. Last year they had been unable to resist the ritual, and Debbie and he had gone to New York for Anita's graduation ceremony. For eighteen years Debbie had saved every penny to ensure her daughter the best education money could buy at one of the best universities in the country. She herself had studied at Spellman, a prestigious black college in Atlanta where duty towards one's race was taught as devoutly as science and literature. Without ever admitting it publicly, nevertheless, she realized that those times were over, now that the yuppies had made a place for themselves in the sun, and it was the end of the eighties, when the concept of race was no longer a winning ticket. Far from it! So she had dreamed of Yale, Harvard, and Princeton . . . like so many other mothers. But there was Anita, categorically rejecting these shrines of learning and setting her heart, goodness knows why, on a small college in the Bronx that was far from anywhere.

There she lived in the basement apartment of a house belonging to Paquita Pereira, a Mexican immigrant. As soon as she got out of the cab Debbie put on the airs of an outraged princess. She didn't like this narrow alley, this seedy apartment, those untidy dreadlocks on her daughter's head she had so often beribboned and oiled, and as for that shapeless dress that shrouded her body! As soon as his eye glimpsed the flaking stone facade Spero, on the contrary, knew where he was and had no desire to be anywhere else. Nobody here in this neighborhood, painted with the colors of mediocrity, would blame him for being something he wasn't or remind him he was living off his wife. At the corner of the street a handful of ragged men signalled a bar, the Black Dove, to which he promised to pay a visit. Paquita, the landlady, who seemed to be accustomed to Anita's ways, invited them for dinner that very same evening. She too was a painter. Her paintings filled every space on the living-room walls, the two stairwells, and the landings on the second and third floors. They also decorated the bathrooms, including one called *Mariposa* over the washbasin that served as a mirror. Since she dreamed of becoming the new Frida Kahlo, Paquita left her mustache unshaved, tied ribbons all over herself, and wore a cabalistic sign tattooed on her forehead. Over dinner she explained in very poor English how the artists of the Third World had their hands tied because their societies were intent on controlling their vision of things. No room here for the wandering artist enamored of love, flowers, and birdsong. If she had been born in other climes her name would now have been written in letters of glory. While Debbie listened to all this with a little pout of contempt, Spero was captivated.

Not by her chatter, but by the way Paquita wolfed down her lamb with eggplant braised in peppers, tomatoes, and ginger, the very smell of which made your mouth water. When they made love a few days later, her overripe flesh was as succulent as a wedding banquet.

Following Paquita from restaurant to night club to art show, Spero, who had hated New York, completely changed his mind about the city and almost began to like America. He realized he did not need to join the stream of immigrants who, years earlier, had mistaken Ellis Island for a gateway to hope and crowded through it to grab the best out of life.

Amid this fraternity of fellow creatures whom Paquita introduced him to — musicians without any music, guitarists without a guitar, boxers without a right or left hook, businessmen without a business, poets without rhyme or reason, novelists without a novel, and stars without a star — he felt at home. Something he had not felt in a long time, for those around him had nothing left to hope for but death. Like himself.

And yet it was during this stay in New York that Anita broke his heart by announcing she was leaving for Benin. For some years now Anita had not been Anita. She had been transformed. Her skin was velvety, her cheeks dimpled, her eyes blazed while the contours of her body rounded in readiness. People, in amazement, could no longer believe this was the rough and ready beanpole they used to know and told Debbie that some man would soon whisk her away. Alas! This transformation of the body coincided with a transformation of the mind. The new Anita burnt what she had once idolized. Not only did she refuse to sing in church, she refused even to go inside and sit next to her mother who had been so proud of her for so many years. She sat at the table with such an expression that neither Debbie nor Spero nor Mamie Garvin, the servant who had been with them since Anita was born, dared say a word to her. At night she locked herself away in her room. She gave up her piano and karate lessons, keeping only her African dance lessons taught by Jim Marshall. Plus her grades were terrible and her teachers could not understand what was happening to the student who used to be the pride of the school. Although Spero, secretly content that she was growing apart from her mother, put it down to a mere teenage crisis, Debbie seemed shattered and even aged. Anita broke the silence she had been keeping for years. She sat her parents down in the tiny dining room of her apartment and served up the news. She was going to put her theoretical knowledge into practice in a village of Benin called Paogo. Hadn't she been studying development for four years?

While Debbie burst into tears — and Spero realized with a bitter heart that he had never seen her cry, even in the worst cases when he had cheated on her — Anita brazenly remarked unfeelingly that her mother was being illogical. Hadn't she, Anita, been brought up to worship Africa? Was she forgetting that their family, more than most, had intimate links with that continent? Wasn't it high time to renew them? And her eyes, which usually passed over Spero without stopping, thereby signifying he was a negligable quantity, amounting to zilch, suddenly pleaded with him, clinging to him as if she was counting on his agreement and support.

It had been a long time since Spero had flown into such a rage. His blood burned. His body shook. Usually so sparing with words he was unable to control all those that were now jumbling out of his mouth. Can't we ever live our lives in the present? And, if need be, bear the ugliness of its wounds? The past must be condemned to death. Otherwise it will become the killer. Wasn't it all that nonsense about an ancestor and Africa that turned Djéré and Justin into what they were? Two Wise Men, two drunkards, the laughingstock of the Morne Verdol? Wasn't this the misfortune of too many blacks they knew who were so busy building imaginary family trees they had lost out on conquering their own America? What was she hoping for? What did she expect from this voyage to the very beginning of times long ago?

Anita turned her head. Her eyes were expressionless. In any case, her mind was made up. She was leaving in two weeks.

After that the days and nights dragged out in pain and suffering. Letting Debbie return home alone, devastated, to Charleston, Spero remained behind in New York. Paquita tried to console him in every way imaginable. She entertained him endlessly with those fables that illustrate the ingratitude of a child's heart that leads so many parents to their graves. Hadn't she herself left Mexico at the age of sixteen, determined to go back only once she made a name for herself? In other words, never. Her father had died without her being able to give him one last kiss. And what about himself, was he irreproachable when it came to his own family?

Spero didn't even hear her. Somewhere inside he was amazed at the extent of his own suffering. He had not realized he loved his daughter to such an extent. It's true he possessed nothing else. Nothing. She was his only treasure. His goose with the golden egg. During this sad period Spero took the remedy that had comforted his father and grandfather before him. He downed gallons of alcohol. Every evening he was a regular customer amid the warm smoke at the Black Dove, a bar that was the spitting image of the Montego Bay except that the customers looked more dangerous, desperate, and cynical.

There he met Abiola, a brother from Nigeria, who had been driven from his country by repeated coups d'etat, and who only reinforced Spero's bitter disillusionment with Africa.

Spero had told nobody what had happened in Paris and during his stay in Lille.

Around the second year of his studies — and the time seemed endless with no women, no heating, penniless, poverty-stricken — he had come across an advertisement in the daily paper for a history, *Les rois-dieux du Benin* (The god-kings of Benin), whose title first intrigued him, then kindled his imagination. He made enquiries and learned that the author, Monsieur Jean Bodriol, was a former colonial civil servant who had served twenty-five years in Africa and administered other territories with an iron rule. Spero pretended therefore he was something he wasn't, a student working on a history thesis, and asked to come and see him in the capital. For a Guadeloupean, nurtured with fantasies of the City of Light, Paris can be full of surprises. Was this the city so extolled? Lackluster stone facades, greasy sidewalks shiny from the rain, foul-smelling metros besieged by shabby, exhausted crowds, and bars filled with drunkards seeking consolation in red wine. Spero dined on skate in brown butter sauce in a noisy brasserie. The next morning, armed with a map, he stepped out of his hotel in the fourth arrondissement, walked down the rue de Rivoli, and managed to find his way to the banks of the Seine and the Library of Overseas Worlds, which was under the direction of Monsieur Bodriol. He waited almost an hour in a hallway covered with huge color photos whose captions he read attentively to kill time. "The Piton des Neiges taken from the Cirque de Salazie." "A road in present-day old Saint-Paul." "A halt beside the Etang Salé." "View of Assinie in 1904 from a postcard." Finally he was shown into a dark, narrow office decorated with tapestries from Abomey and photographic enlargements of relief work on the royal palace in Singboji: horses, mules, roaring lions, trumpeting elephants, and chameleons. A wooden object, whose curved section sheathed in silver represented a fish, was on show in a display case along with a set of tiny metal umbrellas. All these artifacts seemed strangely familiar to Spero, who had seen the exact same drawings pencilled in Djéré's notebooks and was convinced he could name them one after the other. He handed Monsieur Bodriol his most precious possession: the photo depicting the ancestor, Ouanilo, the queen Fadjo with Djéré in her arms, and the other Leopard wives, with "King Gb — — with his family, Fort-de-France, March 1896" written on the back.

Monsieur Bodriol examined it carefully in silence, then looked up.

"Have you got your grandfather's birth certificate?"

Spero hadn't even thought of it. In any case Djéré had been declared at the city hall in Fort-de-France under his mother's very Martinican name of Jules-Juliette, the name borne by all his descendants. Monsieur Bodriol then made a gesture that could have meant anything.

"You have no proof of what you are advancing. If your story were true, we would have had wind of it. Prince Ouanilo kept a very detailed diary of his father's last years. There was never any mention of this birth."

Spero left feeling like an impostor.

Leaning against the stone parapet he stared into the muddy waters of the Seine, and it seemed he had never been so humiliated in his entire life. Whom did they take him for? Someone looking for a job? A good-for-nothing trying to attract attention and clinging to the branch of a dynasty? What good would that do him? Whatever could they be thinking? He was expecting nothing and seeking to gain nothing.

Darkness fell while anger was still boiling inside him. Suddenly the city took on a grace of its own. While the Seine flowed black between the legs of the bridges, the neon displays, the wide-open eyes of the cars, and the brilliance of the terrace cafes composed a symphony of light. And the men and women swept along, a sense of mystery in the somber folds of their clothes. He pushed open the door of a bar, where a woman sitting alone was soon attracted by his solitude and wanted to know who he was and where he came from. He shrugged his shoulders and said mockingly, "I'm the son of one of the last African kings!"

In fact, the old man was not as guilty as Spero believed.

The year prior to his departure he suffered a terrible loss: Prince Adandejan left him. He returned home, leaving only his body in the land of exile.

Nobody knew exactly why the prince died.

He had never got accustomed to the climate in Martinique, which he found cold and damp. He was constantly coughing and blowing his nose. The winds in particular frightened him. Whenever they started to blow he would barricade himself inside his room, and however much rum he drank with lime and cane sugar he could never manage to keep warm. The black, foul-smelling steam that Mount Pelée spit as far south as Fort-de-France scared him, too. What did it mean? Surely it was a sign that the *daadaa* were angry. Like the old man, he repeated that the honors due to the last master of the pearls had not been performed and he predicted his revenge.

The wives of the Leopard expressed surprise. In times past the prince had had a great liking for women. In Abomey, after a campaign, everybody took offence at the number of Mahi captives he kept for himself instead of sending them to be sacrificed. But in Fort-de-France it seemed that his body had lost all its desires. The nights when he was not playing an unending game of whist with the old man he would spend alone in his bed as innocent as a newborn babe.

One morning he woke up with such violent pains in the back of his neck that he had to be admitted to the military hospital as an emergency. That very evening he fell into a coma and died two days later without ever having regained consciousness.

The wives of the Leopard thought the old man would pass away in turn. Prince Adandejan was the son of his father's sister. Together they had suckled the same wet nurse chosen from the hardy matrons from the region of Zogbodomé. They had taken their first steps together in the same private quarters of the palace, behind the walls spiked with human skulls, watched over by slaves. When he had been chosen over his brothers as heir apparent they had celebrated his victory together and got drunk on white wine from France and genever from Holland. In the ancestor's retreat at Atchérigbé, after the rout from Abomey, he had always been beside him, always.

During the twenty-four-hour wake the old man remained seated motionless to the left of the deathbed clutching the hand of the corpse. At the graveyard he stood staring at the soil as it fell onto the coffin. After that he was never the same. However hard Ouanilo, who served as his secretary, recited articles from the papers by French people demanding his return from exile or read out draft letters to be sent to the President of the Republic, his mind was elsewhere. It was as if nothing any longer mattered. Nevertheless, just as he was about to leave Martinique, he remembered his youngest son and asked to take him with him. But the colonial administration would hear nothing of it. The royal family numbered eight people. No more! The old man, however, had no material resources of his own. The French had dispossessed him of all his gold, the income from his lands, and the millions of francs his father had amassed from the palm oil trade. The colony of Dahomey paid him a ridiculous pension, forcing Queen Fadjo to pawn her jewels on the fifteenth of each month at the jeweler's on the rue Perrinon.

What could he do?

He emerged from his torpor to dictate to Ouanilo a letter to the Governor requesting the fare for the passage of his youngest son. But it remained unanswered.

He had no choice then but to leave.

While crossing the Sargasso Sea he took off his sunglasses

and was stunned at the sight of all this blue that never failed to amaze. It was there the sun dealt him a treacherous blow and carried off his senses. Nobody noticed at first what had happened. The voyage had begun peacefully and the *Marechal Bugeaud* rolled gracefully on a sea of oil. The Leopard wives and Princess Kpotasse, who were unable to put up with this swaying motion, locked themselves up in their cabin with cotton handkerchiefs soaked in eau de cologne held to their nostrils. Occasionally they would rush to the portholes and vomit up the little food they had swallowed. The old man strolled on the deck with his rolling gait in the company of Ouanilo. He paid no attention to the odd looks from the other passengers or to their whisperings. He liked to sit in the bow of the ship and watch for hours as the sun painted the sky. At certain times of the day it was pink and yellow. At other times it was white, blue, and green like a huge banner. Schools of shiny flying fish, like fireflies, flew over the crest of the waves. Sometimes happy dolphins jumped out of the water.

It was Queen Abuta, the youngest of the Leopard wives, who first realized something was wrong. The old man was lying on his bunk and she was gently fanning him to sleep with a fan of ostrich feathers when he suddenly sat up and asked in a distraught way, "Where is Ahanhanzo?"

Now Ahanhanzo was his brother who had disappeared under mysterious circumstances years earlier. It was even whispered the ancestor had called in his witch doctors and brought his brother down with smallpox to take his place on the throne.

Terrified, Abuta laid down her fan and ran to fetch Fadjo, who was quietly smoking a little pipe in her cabin.

As the voyage gradually progressed it was obvious that the old man had forgotten he had used up the years of his existence — that he was nothing but a captive, an old bag of bones without a motherland tossed on the waves of the ocean — instead he believed he was back as Kondo the Shark, ninth son of his father, watching his future dawn. Sitting cross-legged on his bunk he counted the imaginary gifts the French had brought in homage: a green-plumed dragoon helmet, a marine telescope, pieces of silk, pieces of velvet, a music box, cases of liqueurs, and a yataghan with a dark red sheath. He spoke of battles he had waged beside his father, especially the one at Abeokuta when four thousand prisoners had been expedited to the other world. He told how he had managed to escape the ruse of one of the Leopard mothers who hated him. He got angry when he recalled Juliano de Souza, henchman of the Portuguese, who had tried to take advantage of his father. The more the journey advanced, the further back in time he went, and when the ship docked in Marseilles he was nothing more but a little child, scarcely out of Mehutu's womb.

When he was a boy he would lose himself in the maze of the palace courtyards. He drank cold water from the earthenware jars placed at the corner of every wall to quench the thirst of the spirits. Sometimes he mounted the rainbow and dismounted not far from his father's residence, where day in and day out the *bokono* were studying the round divinatory plates. Once he interrupted a full session of the council and was led out by the ministers with a frown. From a very early age he had known it was forbidden to go beyond the rainbow where the *daadaa* slept for eternity in their huts of pearls. He was not frightened of the dried heads of the slaves that adorned the high walls that blocked out the sky. He knew they had chosen to take their lives and that they protected him from where they had gone. He dreamed of going outside to decipher the bas-reliefs that a throng of royal servants were painting with vegetable dyes. But the eunuchs were guarding every door of the palace, those squares of inaccessible light symbolizing freedom.

The journey from Marseilles to Algiers had been a difficult one. Settlers sailing to take possession of acres of land in the Hodna, the regions of South Oran and the Mzab, openly engaged in racist remarks, murmuring words such as "cannibals" and "filthy niggers." They frightened Princess Kpotasse to such an extent that everyone thought she was going to pass away at sea. Finally they arrived in sight of the shores of Algeria burned by the sun and the salt.

At Blida, the villa allocated to the old man and his family, in front of which three Arab guards in tarbooshes stood yawning, had belonged to a high Moslem dignitary whose property had been recently confiscated by the French authorities because he opposed the Native Code of Laws. It was a sumptuous dwelling set behind a garden of flowering mimosas and oleanders. The center was composed of a rectangular courtyard in the middle of which glistened water in an ornamental basin. The garden was encircled by a wide gallery enhanced by arches and colonnades onto which opened a dozen rooms. At each end of the rectangular courtyard stood the main buildings connected by a high wall. One of the rooms housed a library full of bound books from the twelfth century, a *minbar* (a carved pulpit from a mosque) from the ninth century, a gazelle-skin astrolabe from the eleventh century, and coffers of orange-wood encrusted with ivory. In the courtyard an olive press intrigued the Leopard wives, who could not understand what it was meant for.

Ouanilo, who hated Fort-de-France, had expected so much from this return to African soil. He wept when he was told the distance that separated him from Abomey and the kisses of his mother whom he had not seen for almost seven years. He was emerging painfully from his childhood, and the injustice suffered by his father outraged him. His despair was completed by what he saw around him in Algeria, and he dreamed of becoming a lawyer in order to right the wrongs the white man was constantly doing to people of black and swarthy skins.

During his exile in Algeria the old man's spirit had already departed. Sometimes he thought he was in Kutome, eating and drinking with the *daadaa*. At other times he was back in Martinique reliving moments of his existence there.

At the end of his stay in Martinique he had been cared for by a Dr. Arsonot, an old mulatto with very delicate hands who was extremely interested in the history of Africa and had read numerous accounts by explorers, in particular those by Sir Richard Burton and Doctor Répin, with descriptions of the powerful kingdom of Abomey lost in the heart of the dense forest. His imagination had especially been captured by the Amazons, that elite corps of three thousand women armed with bows and arrows, and he had cut out prints of them from the *Journal des voyages* and the illustrated supplement of the *Petit Parisien*. He did not let himself be influenced by those stories of human sacrifices, skulls, and blood, regarding them as mere morbid fantasies of journalists. Unlike those who had no scruples, calling the old man "savage" or "cannibal," he believed him to be an authentic sovereign, a king in his own right, as legitimate as the one who used to live in the palace at Versailles. He therefore set about writing a report addressed to the President of the Republic, drawing his attention to the tragic situation of the exiled king. He concluded by saying that the sovereign was suffering from a sickness called *lenbe*, homesickness, and that there was only one way to cure him.

He waited three months, then six, but his report remained unanswered. Since the ancestor continued to grow weaker Arsonot said to himself that if they wanted him to live he would need to be entertained with amusements and excursions. He resolved therefore to take him on an excursion to Saint-Pierre from where the Arsonot family originated.

The ancestor took a long time making up his mind. He could not overcome the fear of his taboos. What would the *daadaa* do if they saw him traveling by sea, this time by his own free will? Not bound and forced by the French!

Finally he let himself be persuaded by the queens, Prince Ouanilo, and Princess Kpotasse, who were bored to death in Fort-de-France.

At six o'clock one morning the group set off for the port, the ancestor, his silver pipe stuck in his mouth, bringing up the rear under his parasol held by Queen Fadjo. The children ran for joy in front despite the recommendations from Prince Adandejan. They did not stop until they arrived at the wharf. There, the dejected Ouanilo looked in despair at the ships of the Compagnie Générale Transatlantique from Nantes, Bordeaux, Le Havre, and Marseilles, none of which could take him back to Africa. The coal women, their skirts hitched over legs as straight as palm trunks, their baskets balanced on their heads, were already filling the bunkers of the steamships, while the washerwomen, elegantly turned out and bedecked with jewels, were bringing back in large trays the passengers' laundry they had washed as white as cotton. Everybody settled down as best they could in the steamer belonging to the Girard Company. The traveler Lafcadio Hearn said of Saint-Pierre that it is "the most strange, the most amusing and yet the most lovely of all the towns in the French Antilles." Others ascertain it was the busiest port in the Caribbean, and neither Willemstadt nor Havana, Port of Spain, nor even Caracas could rival it. Dr. Arsonot was overjoyed at the idea of showing the ancestor the harbor district and the landing stage on the Place Bertin with its flocks of white pigeons; the fort and the Perinelle Great House, built on the site of a former Jesuit convent from the eighteenth century; the church of Notre Dame du Bon Port; the iron market, the *calles*, and especially the rue Monte-au-Ciel marching its eighty-four steps up the sides of the hills; the fountains and their spray of silvery water; and the house fronts without window frames or glass, fitted with wooden and zinc canopies painted pale yellow. He also hoped they would spend a few hours in the botanical gardens travelers the world over came to admire for its plants imported from India, China, Brazil, and Guyana. People still remembered the lavish entertainment the governor held there to the great delight of Prince Alfred of England, one of the youngest sons of Queen Victoria.

At that time of year the roses of Caracas must have perfumed the whole town. But they had not counted on the curiosity of the inhabitants of Saint-Pierre. As early as the day before the rumor had spread, goodness knows how, that the ancestor was coming to Saint-Pierre. From early morning a crowd had swarmed into the port, preventing the dockers from unloading crates, barrels of codfish, and casks of wine. A good many pupils who had escaped from the neighboring lycée could be recognized by their uniform of black blazers and ties, waistcoats, and straw hats. Oblivious to all this commotion some ragged children were making the wings of their bird-shaped kites dance above everyone's heads. Lanky youths were taking advantage of the crowd to sell their newspapers in a frightening tone of voice: *Les Antilles, Les Colonies, L'Opinion.*

Latecomers continued to swarm in from the rue Victor Hugo, the rue d'Orleans, and the rue de l'Abbé Grégoire. Only at Mardi Gras could such a crowd be seen.

People's feelings were divided.

"An African king? Whatever next!" some scoffed.

Others were curious.

"What does he look like, this African king?"

And some were proud.

"A nigger and a king! And they chose our tiny Martinique as a prison for him! It's an honor for us!"

And others sincerely pitied him.

"Po guiab! (Poor devil!) So far from his own country! And what's more they say he can't even speak French!"

Around nine-thirty a shout went up from everyone's lips:

"Bato la ka rivé! (The boat's coming in!)

The crowd rushed forward, the stronger pushing and trampling on the weaker ones, some of whom fell into the water and thought they were going to drown. The noise of the crowd drew the attention of our group of travelers on the deck of the steamer. At first, nobody understood what was going on. Then the ancestor realized he was the one attracting all this attention. He sadly murmured a few words in Fon and went inside never to come out again. They had to return to Fort-de-France under full steam.

From that day on Dr. Arsenot never again attempted to entertain the ancestor.

Debbie had a younger sister, Farah, married to Charles Thomas Jr., a prosperous lawyer practicing in Piscataway, New Jersey. In the past, when they still confided in each other, Spero would get sick of hearing stories about the sisters' rivalries during childhood and their teens. Farah was their father's favorite, Farah was the prettier of the two, Farah had stolen the heart of a cousin, Farah judged people only by their money — and he knew that Debbie still had fits of jealousy even as an adult. He, however, quite liked Farah. Unlike Charles Thomas Jr., whose few words were heartily paternalistic, she treated him like a normal human being. She knew where Guadeloupe was on a map and did not mind its being so small or French-speaking. As a young girl she had been an activist and even read poems by Césaire. Spero understood full well that by taking refuge in Piscataway, Farah had wanted to escape the rigorous rules of life in Charleston, but he could not see what she had replaced it with and did not know what to think. Whenever he visited her at Thanksgiving or for a wedding anniversary he was always struck by the fragile nature of her life. As if once you removed the center beam this lovely edifice of Italian furniture, Porsche automobile, tennis matches, Dobermans, and public displays of interracial friendship would collapse from one moment to the next. At Farah's you never discussed anything that could be remembered more than an hour later. No politics, no social issues, and strictly nothing racial. The word race was held in contempt! In the end, her two sons, like Anita, had rejected Yale, Harvard, and Princeton, all those prestigious "white" universities, and David had gone to study at the University of Atlanta, and Ken at Columbia College, not far from Charleston. As if they were intent on discovering at all costs what *nigger* meant. Try to understand that!

Ken often came to spend weekends at Crocker Island. He was a strapping fellow, over six feet tall, drinking milk and orange juice of course, and somewhat livening up the house on the island. But Spero hated seeing him occupy Anita's room and never said a word to him. His visits were Debbie's triumph and revenge: on her sister, on Spero, on Anita, on her entire existence, in fact. She regained faith in herself. She stuffed the boy with the myths and clichés with which she had stuffed Anita and which people such as Farah and Charles Thomas Jr. had vainly tried to forget. As for Spero, who spent his life making fun of people, you can see how he ended up! *Let my people go. Up you mighty race. We return fighting. We shall overcome. I have a dream. Free at last.* Ken lapped it all up devotedly. Although he did not go as far as to accompany

Debbie to Sunday service, preferring to jog for two hours, he did leaf through the family albums sitting next to her, went and meditated on the grave of Uncle George, presumed martyr, and set up the tape recorder at Agnes Jackson's. With voices lowered and heads together they would both talk of the ancestor. They left out nothing. The confrontation with the French. The defeat. The first, then the second exile. Death. The triumphant return of the ashes. After these conversations Ken would steal frightened looks at Spero as if he were trying to establish a possible link between this hero who had just captured his imagination and the man sitting in front of him: grouchy, taciturn, overweight, graying, and good for very little. As if on trial, Spero would have liked to prepare his defense, but then he repented his weakness. Did he still need to be understood? Loved? In order to punish himself he left the aunt and the nephew alone, their heads lost in the clouds of their imagination and their daydreams, and went off to drink at the Montego Bay. When he returned home in the early hours of the morning, half drunk, stumbling on every step on the stairs, the very image of what they expected him to be, he was ashamed of himself.

Spero carefully washed his plate and cutlery in the sink and put them away. What would Justin have said if he could see his *ti-mal*, his adored little son, transformed into a domestic creature? Justin, who couldn't even boil a pot of water, waited on hand and foot by Marisia as if he were the Good Lord himself, the good-for-nothing that he was. Spero could never get out of his head the picture of his father, ensconced in a tub of hot water, surrounded by clouds of rising steam, black and hairy, like a hog ready for the Saturday slaughter, with Marisia fussing around him with a scouring brush.

As for the ancestor, his wives would wash him, shave him, cut his hair, and dress him. At his death they would bury themselves next to him in his grave. When his father had passed away, although they had not held the customary ceremonies, forty-one of his wives at their request were entombed with him while two hundred others took their lives using poison or other means. That's how black women used to behave with their men. Even in America! Debbie had told him somewhat scornfully of her mother's blind adoration for George, her father, the presumed martyr, at the same time a great womanizer and absentee husband. Never a word uttered in anger. Never a reproach. Never a complaint. Always lavishing him with attention.

Hey, for goodness sake, what had gotten into the heads of black women since those days? Here too they had wanted to imitate white women, at war with their men. Not only did they close their hearts and their bodies to their companions in the secret of their homes, they publicly wrote books to revile and ridicule them. Or else they prattled away on television. Last year Debbie had invited to Marcus Bookstore a female writer from Alabama who gave the impression she wanted to banish men from the face of the earth. In her latest book she had portrayed a whole generation of women who seemed to have appeared on this earth through the works of the Holy Spirit. And to think that people went into raptures over such books! Spero had not even wanted to know how that evening had gone and had preferred to get drunk at Linton's.

He refrained from looking at his watch and wondered once again what Debbie was doing. Generally at this hour of the afternoon she would turn off her tape recorder and let Agnes Jackson, exhausted from three hours of chatter, sink into a rocking chair and take a little nap. While Agnes slept, her mouth half open on teeth yellowed by age, she would play back her tapes and take notes. When he used to be a visitor to the house this was the time Spero chose to ask his questions. He didn't care two hoots for Langston Hughes and other luminaries of the black world. He tried to discover the other side of the coin: the hidden side that is just as significant.

In that wave of white folly that had struck the Jackson family, Judah, son or grandson of James Earl, tired of hewing beams and putting up barns like his father and grandfather before him. The enviable position of being a freed craftsman no longer satisfied him. He wanted to possess the land like a white master and make it bring forth its riches. So he bought a few acres of land down by the river Santee from a mulatto like himself and began to dig them over with two slaves from the leeward coast of Africa, Quaquah and Samuel, whom he had purchased for a small fortune. After a few years he owned one of the finest rice plantations in South Carolina and was getting ready to marry his children to authentic whites. That was the moment General Saxton chose to plant the Union flag in Charleston and hang Judah's burned remains from the branches of a sycamore tree on his estate, having tarred him and all the members of his family beforehand. Only one of his sons, Judah Jr., escaped the massacre. Unable to erase from his memory the picture of his father's tortured and humiliated corpse, he became a wandering preacher, setting off across the state to preach the Word of God. For five years he preached from Hampton to Newberry, from Conway to Cheraw. His beard grew down to his navel and he was called "the Second Christ." Between two visionary sermons he purged his humors at the local brothel. It was there he met a Southern belle who was ruined by the Civil War and forced to convert to whoring. He married her and had a bevy of children — including Agnes's paternal grandfather, whom a photo showed as a small boy with neatly combed hair sitting beside his solemn, dignified mother, who had forgotten her years in the bordello.

Debbie did not like hearing these somewhat unorthodox tales that Spero relished. They deeply shocked her while they offered Spero a welcome change from the official history she was determined to serve him up. The history in the history books.

It's true Debbie's ears only liked to hear what she wanted to hear. She and Spero had quarrelled loudly over Senior, who had left Barbados with his master Arthur Middleton, whose business had started to fail in Bridgetown and who wanted to treat himself to an entire continent. Spero had called him an Uncle Tom, and she had not tolerated this. Yet Senior was his master's henchman. He was the one Arthur sent to buy slaves at the market, and his own color did not bother him. He inspected the whites of their eyes and their teeth. He pinched their skin and weighed their genitals like any white planter.

Maryse Condé

Perhaps even a little rougher. Some claim Senior was a mulatto, Arthur's own son, which explains why he brought him with him from Barbados and subsequently gave him such preferential treatment, very quickly making him into a freed artisan. Debbie denied anything of the sort, swearing by all the gods there was not a drop of white blood in her family. How would we ever know? How could we speak with authority on events that went as far back as 1677 or 1678?

At that time Charles Town counted only a handful of houses, as black as the mud from the swamps, scattered between two constantly swollen rivers, the Ashley and the Cooper. Yaws, dengue fever, malaria, and a sickly cough carried off the newborn from the cradle to the grave in the space of a day. And the Kiawah Indians, who had no idea of the fate that was in store for them, presented the new arrivals with the skin and the meat from the animals they hunted. No, at the Middletons, they did not like talking about Senior. The only tangible souvenir they kept from that time in the family affairs was an anonymous drawing from the famous engraving by Samuel Copen depicting Bridgetown in the second half of the seventeenth century. A line of jagged hills whose tops were lost in the clouds. A row of houses weighed down by their Dutch gables. Geometrical forts. A forest of ships' masts. Up to this very day the drawing was still hanging on the faded striped wallpaper in the entrance hall, totally unnoticed.

Spero often told himself that Debbie had only married him in order to have a family tree she could boast about. For all those things she loved to talk about so much — slavery, exactions, and humiliations to blacks — her family had undergone very little in actual fact. Among the first freed artisans, barbers by profession in their shop with swivel chairs, the Middletons thought only of increasing their fortune at a time when their brothers in race were living in hell. Not a hero among them! On the contrary. In 1820 during the famous conspiracy by Denmark Vesey, who almost won freedom for his brothers, Moses Middleton was one of the honest citizens who signed a collective letter to the authorities to dissociate himself from the plot.

When they first arrived in Charleston, Debbie got it into her head to translate Djéré's notebooks. With her usual determination, every day, as soon as she was home from college, she would sit down at her desk and work until late into the night. Spero, in love, would come and snatch her away from her manuscript, and she would eventually deign to follow him. What pleasure-loving children men are! He did not know what to think of her well-meaning resolutions. He himself had read the notebooks over and over again with Justin to such a point that he knew certain passages by heart. When he was small they were to him like a wonderful tale with only the illustrations missing. At the time he was especially responsive to their fantastic and supernatural content. He adored the descriptions of the forest and its inhabitants. Bats. Butterflies. Monkeys. Agoutis and calaos. His favorite passages were the meeting of Posu Adewene with Agasu the Leopard and the very warlike and bellicose adventures of Tengisu, their monster-child, and those of his son, Hunugungun, master of the deadly lances. As he grew up he read them in a completely different way, as the tale of a defeat, a dispossession and an exile that had no end. It was not only the ancestor who had lost his possessions, but Djéré. Justin. And last of all himself. At times his eyes filled with water and the words the color of the South Seas blurred on the white page. On his return from Lille, however, despite his father's pleas, he had refused to reopen the notebooks, as if he wanted to finish with all those illusions that had done so much harm to his family.

So sometimes Debbie's infatuation annoyed him. What demon had got into him to let her read them? At other times he could not help feeling overjoyed at the idea that these notebooks that had delighted his youth would come out of the shadows and thereby avenge the sad destiny of their author.

Debbie had in mind a small black publishing house in New York that had a collection of tales and testimonials that included *Lemon Swamp* by Mamie Garvin Fields, one of her personal favorites. Which chapter should they send to get them interested? They quarrelled a lot on the subject, since they were of different opinions. Finally Spero went along with Debbie and accepted the choice of a short chapter from notebook number three entitled "Totem and Taboo." After sending off the manuscript they waited many long weeks, but Debbie refused to give up hope. In the end the publishers sent them a rather matter-of-fact letter of rejection that dashed her spirits completely.

The Notebooks of Djéré   *Number Three*

Totem and Taboo

My father taught me to fear and respect the animals. In their bodies, he told me, hide the spirits that possess all the powers of the Universe. Some are there to protect and defend us. Others, however, can cause sterility, suffering, and an evil death. One day — I don't know what came over me, for I was not a child to answer back and my father's stories always filled me with delight — I ventured a question of a doubting nature. Could the spirits also hide in the body of a miserable fly?

So my father told me this story.

Tadjo, one of his great uncles, was constantly challenging the spirits, believing himself to be their equal. His sole passion was hunting. But before setting off he never bothered to placate the spirits with prayers, magical practices, or sacrifices so as to ward off their revenge. He headed off into the bush, armed not with a bow and arrow, a spear or a javelin, but with a musket bought from slave traffickers along the coast, a weapon of war and massacre, hardly a fair match. He was not content to hunt for his own needs. Oh no! The smell of hot blood went to his head, and he killed and killed untiringly to his heart's delight. Oryx, gazelles, addax, antelopes, elephants, water buffalo, lions, panthers, hyenas, jackals, wild boars, anything went. But of course he never touched the leopard. One day Gnanhouman, master of the bush, approached him and said, "Tadjo, you are great. Your father before you was great. Your entire family is great. Beware, however, of the spirits' revenge. In order to hunt and draw blood from the beasts of the bush you must protect yourself with magical practices whose secrets I cannot reveal and would not know how to teach you. Listen at least to what I have to say and abide by these few precautions. If you spill the blood of a female animal, draw the blood of your own arm to show your repentance. If it's a male animal, collect a little of your blood in the horn of a gazelle or mouflon. Then pour it into a goblet. Pray for the resurrection of the animal you have killed and ask to be pardoned for having spilled the blood of a living creature. Do what I tell you, I beg you in the name of the ancestors, for if the eye of the animal in its dying moments meets your manhood you will be in grave danger. Remember too that you must never aim at the animal's head, for that is where the spirits live."

Tadjo merely scoffed at these words from the master of the bush and did not take them seriously. Resurrection of animals? Revenge of the blood? He took no notice and went on slaughtering even harder. By evening he would sleep exhausted beside bloody heaps of flesh.

For one whole day he tracked a Dorcas gazelle across the dry, bare, burning bush. While it was resting in the meager shade of an acacia, worn out by the heat and the hunt, he wounded it treacherously in the forehead and approached from behind to finish it off. The Dorcas gazelle turned to look at him before collapsing on its side. It was panting from the pain. Its big almond-shaped eyes stared at Tadjo and gradually veiled over with death. Taken by its beauty Tadjo was overcome with a violent desire. He quickly undid his loincloth and possessed it. The Dorcas gazelle died in a great stream of blood while he reached his sexual climax. Then he split the body down the middle.

As he was returning home, his game bag full, the spirits manifested their anger by making the rain fall and the thunder rumble in the middle of February, but Tadjo did not even feel the water pouring off him and arrived in his village singing. He did not notice that a fly was stubbornly following him, buzzing behind his left ear.

The day after his return from the hunt, as was the custom, Tadjo gave a great banquet with the game he had slaughtered. Over a fire of glowing embers, his slaves spread the meat mixed with all sorts of aromatic herbs on cross pieces covered with leaves set on vertical forked stakes. The musicians had already taken up their places in front of their instruments. Standing in the light of the wood fire a griot sang the exploits of Tadjo.

When Tadjo retired for the night the fly was still buzzing behind his ear, but he paid no attention to it. Who bothers about a fly, the smallest of God's creatures? He went to bed, fell asleep immediately, and had a dream. He had gone hunting; but out in the bush he no longer recognized anything. As far as the eye could see, to the very horizon, to the foothills of the mountains, the vast expanse had changed into an ocean of blood. The waves were flecked with foam and on their crests the bodies of every type of animal were being tossed. In his terror he ventured a few steps and found himself plunged up to his waist in the red, sticky liquid that soon rose as high as his mouth and nostrils and carried him off to where he did not want to go. The dream made such a strong impression on him that he woke up, haggard and soaked in sweat. His fourth wife, who was sleeping by his side, managed to comfort him. He went back to bed and fell asleep again as best he could. But another terrible dream woke him up again. The Dorcas gazelle he thought he had cut into pieces was alive and standing under an acacia bush calling him. Yet when he tried to lay hands on it, it decomposed and he found himself touching a sticky heap of entrails and coagulated blood. A second time he cried out; a second time the caresses of his wife managed to send him back to sleep. Only to be awakened by an even more terrifying dream. Then another and another and another. Soon he was unable to sleep any longer. Sitting on his bed he screamed and screamed, his eyes leaping out of their sockets and a trickle of blood flowing out of his left ear.

The *bokono* was quickly called in to make a diagnosis. A spirit in the shape of a fly had penetrated his left ear and was slowly eating away at his brain. After several days of suffering, delirium, and madness Tadjo died.

And that, concluded my father, was how the brave, the proud, the valiant Tadjo was killed by the smallest of God's creatures for neglecting to respect his fellow animals. My father had already told me about the Leopard and I knew we were his children.

2

The crabs emerged from every hole in the black volcanic sand that was papered with dead leaves and closed ranks. Jostling each other's purplish shells, waving their powerful, pincerlike claws, they careened and clawed their way to Spero's naked body. They plodded on unrelenting up his thighs, carefully encircling the massive hump of his manhood before tangling their claws in his pubic hair and scampering up the fleshy cal-abash of his belly. Their claws drew droplets of blood. Just as they were reaching the flat expanse of his chest, one of them sunk its claw into his flesh and delved as far as the heart that was thumping with fear. Spero cried out from the pain.

Awakened by the sound of his own screams Spero realized he had slept. Not a light, porous sleep, permeable to all types of sound. But a sleep as heavy as a boulder lying in the very middle of the river or a cartwheel long forgotten at the edge of a sugar-cane field that vines have overrun like nightmares. For two years, the same dream. Three or four times a week.

He stood up and went over to the window that had been left wide open.

The sky was empty. The sun had gone, setting behind the black wood of live oaks but still leaving a trail of light behind it. It had rained. A lot. A lot. The leaves on the trees had been washed clean and garlands of pearls hung along the branches as if they had been decorated for Christmas a good two weeks ahead of time. Gently the island was preparing to start its passage towards the night. The two would celebrate their reunion amid the darkness, the wind, and the rain.

This Christmas would be the second since their daughter had left them to go to Benin. What would she be doing in her village at the end of the world?

Remembering his postcard souvenirs, Spero tried to imag-ine her in a rust-colored decor set with round huts made of clay minus the cold, the rain, and the wind. A big satin moon hanging in the middle of an indigo sky spread its light. Wearing a head tie she would be going to midnight mass in the humble church made of logs built by the first missionaries and singing carols in the African language with the same devotion as the other worshippers. After mass she would share a frugal meal of cassava and boiled guinea fowl with her new friends. Not for one moment did her thoughts turn to her parents, alone, all alone, on Crocker Island like a decrepit old couple whose offspring has deserted them.

And they themselves, what would they do for Christmas? Christmas had always made him nostalgic, for if there is a season to be at home, a season that opens up all the wounds of solitude, it's truly this one. He would leave Debbie to do her thousand and one things. Already on a dresser in the dining room she had arranged some packages wrapped in shiny colored paper decorated with Christmas trees and sledges, each carefully labelled. Chaka. Paule. Jim. Agnes Jackson. Nobody was left out. Not even him. Last year she had given him a sumptuous album of paintings by the Rumanian painter Gheorghe Sturza, whom he adored.

As for him, he would probably idle about all day, then in the evening go to Linton's so as not to have to deal with the slowly darkening hours on his own. Every year Linton cooked a meal that he said was Cuban. Rice. Beans. Slices of avocado. Pork and a sort of sausage made of spicy hot tripe that he had cooked himself. He invited two or three girls of the sociable type. He would put some salsa records on his stereo player. They would dance. This year, Spero did not have the heart for such meager merrymaking. Besides, the girls no longer turned him on. However much they stuffed themselves in front of him with nachos and tuna sandwiches, he remained indifferent. What he wanted at the present time were endless chats about America, Guadeloupe, Africa, and life in general. Debbie was wrong to think his mind was a blank. He spent his time thinking.

What time was it? 5:45 P.M. At this moment Debbie was packing away in her bag two or three carefully numbered tapes filled with the useless chatter of Agnes Jackson. What had the old woman concocted that afternoon?

Spero also liked to get her to talk about her youth. In 1918, after the death of her mother, she no longer had the heart to live in Charleston and forced her father to let her go and live in New York. So she climbed aboard the *Comanchee*, a steamer of the Clyde Line that linked Charleston with the cities in the North. A little princess at home, she was now squeezed with five other passengers in a cabin for colored people with no air or light and a slop pail that you had to empty yourself into the sea. After three days and three nights of sheer agony she arrived at Ellis Island. That's where she had seen the immigrants. Whites. All whites. But a type of white she had never seen before. Gaunt. Haggard. Their features clawed by life. The women wore headscarves as drab as their faces to hide their hair. The men clenched fists as big as bludgeons at the end of their sleeves. Yet these poor wretches who had come to beg for hope guffawed and cracked a thousand jokes on seeing the blacks get off the boat and take their place in a separate waiting line reserved for them in front of the counter. For Spero, this story symbolized all the injustice of America.

On leaving Agnes's place, as the evening grew darker, Debbie would dash to the African Ballet Theatre, under the direction of Jim Marshall, sociologist by profession and dancer by preference, a good friend and confidant. Spero was in fact the only one to criticize the African Ballet Theatre, to deny it any genuine creativity and see it as a copy of those everlasting African ballets. The *Black Sentinel of Charleston* was of a different opinion and had no scruples comparing it to the Alvin Ailey company. Debbie too pointed out that the ballet had performed with great success in several cities of North and South Carolina, especially Durham and Columbia, as well as at the "Dance Festival of the Black World" organized in Sweden, where it had won third prize after Zaire and Burkina Faso. The highlight of the performance, which always brought loud applause, was the "Initiation Dance": twenty teenagers in red and black harlequin tights, silver bracelets on their arms and ankles, dancing energetically. The spectators also liked "Scenes from Village Life" a lot: men, women, and a few children serenely going about their activities during peacetime. KPFZ, Charleston's main black radio station, had broadcast a long interview with Jim Marshall, who explained where he drew his inspiration from. He had even had his picture in *Ebony* during the 1960s. Jim was a giant of a fellow. Six feet five. Easily able to dunk a basketball. A passionate baseball player too who kept all his student trophies. Slightly eccentric in his large embroidered African boubou. An excellent cook, too: a great specialist of vegetarian dishes, for he did not touch meat either. If life had the slightest sense of logic Debbie should have married Jim and not this Guadeloupean with the mud of the Morne Verdol still on his shoes. But it so happened — and Spero loved to snigger about it — that Jim did not like women! It was an open secret. Only Debbie refused to admit the truth that Spero wanted at all costs to get her to look in the face, drawing her attention to the thousand and one unmistakable signs indicating whether a man is a man.

Jim was always surrounded by usually very young and rather handsome men who handed round the trays during his receptions or served as decoration, like his potted rubber plants and his Ashanti masks, tapestries, and jewelry. But for two or three years now he had lived with Jeff, a waiter at the Good Old Days, one of the best restaurants in the heart of Old Charleston, as if love between men was above those class divisions that cause so much unhappiness to others. Anyway, Jeff was studying in night school to become a sociologist and had published some poems in the *Black Sentinel of Charleston* that showed a promising talent. In the meantime, however, before he became as pompous, perhaps, as his Pygmalion, Jeff was a charming young man who dressed like a model, had a liking for all sorts of liquor, and was not particularly bothered by the future of the race. From habitually sitting next to him at the end of the table during boring dinners where *grangreks*, scholars, untiringly analyzed the turn Martin Luther King's thoughts would have taken if death hadn't cut him down when it did, Spero ended up taking a liking to him. One evening, God only knows how, they landed at the Montego Bay, where

Linton was flabbergasted at Spero's friend's conversation. They drank and drank and in the great fraternity of inebriation Jeff confessed. He was suffocating among these bourgeois simmering in their eternal obsession with color and self-glorification. As soon as he had his degree they wouldn't see him again. He'd leave Charleston. America. Yes, he'd quit. And go to England. To London.

The secret love of his life was Dave, an Englishman he had met at a jazz festival when he lived in New Orleans. He had made him feel he was not a black, but a human being who deserved love the same as anyone else. In the letters he sent him every week, Dave urged him to come and join him on the King's Road. But he was only a musician, a songwriter and electric guitar player in an obscure group, and Jeff did not want to live off of him. So he was going to put up with Jim for a few more years.

This combination of cynicism and passionate love delighted Spero.

Jim and Debbie had met some thirty years earlier in Atlanta where they were both students. But at that time they were worlds apart. Debbie was the first to admit that during her student years she was just a parochial, middle-class girl from the South, knowing nothing about the outside world. Jim, however, was emerging from a childhood and adolescence along the lines of Bigger Thomas. Born in a Chicago ghetto to a mother who worked for whites and a janitor father lost to alcohol, his three delinquent brothers were rotting in state penitentiaries and his sister was a streetwalker on Central Street. He had only one idea in his head: escape, escape the hell of America. So in 1960 when John Kennedy appointed his brother-in-law head of the Peace Corps, Jim was one of the first to apply for a job. He was sent to a school in Kumasi, Ghana. There he met Malcolm X. Fascinated by the man who told him that the only real struggles are waged at home, he accompanied him to Tamale and Bolgantaga.

These three years had made him the man he now was, and on his return it was quite by chance he met up again with

Debbie at the college in Charleston. Their common political and cultural commitment threw them together.

Jim and Debbie had everything going for them. They listened to the same music; they read the same books. They shared the same ideology. For a long time they had lived with their eyes turned toward Africa, passionately comparing and discussing all the experiments of socialism. Jim, however, could not help being fascinated in an unorthodox way with the traditional power of the African chiefs. To his constant exasperation, Spero had heard him tell over a hundred times how as a new recruit in Ashanti country he had passed the procession of the Asantehene, Agyeman Prempeh II, on its way to the seat of traditional affairs.

First came four musicians blowing on horns and beating arm drums. Behind came the dignitaries and counsellors: Adontehene, Akwamuhene, Kontihene, and Gyasehege. The Asantahene himself walked bare-shouldered, superb in his kente-cloth toga, under a parasol a yard and a half in diameter decorated with a hanging fringe all the way round. The Kontihene noticed Jim, obviously a foreigner, standing open-mouthed with admiration and — here Spero imagined all kinds of irreverent things — invited Jim to come and visit him in his compound, a veritable city that housed his wives, his children, and his courtiers. Jim was soon to become a familiar visitor. Noon and evening palm soup and pounded yam, *foufou*, awaited him. At night he had a mat to sleep on, if he wanted to, in the men's quarters. They renamed him Yefrefo, which means "Come from Elsewhere." From that moment on, without ever actually forsaking sociology, he learned the arts of the royal dancers.

Jim would go on forever, a real chatterbox, like a *rara* rattle during Holy Week. He would describe the working of the Ashanti empire created by the legendary Oseï Tutu; its religion, philosophy, and customs; or else the role of the Asantehene in detail enough to try the patience of a nun. In their empire, he went on, the Kontihene was a prince of royal blood, the head of the army and the strategist of battles. He was one of the most illustrious members of the court and privy coun-

Maryse Condé

sel, and his friendship was a privilege few could boast. When Spero heard him bragging an exasperated voice inside him would ask: What would you have done if instead of taking you under his wing the Kontihene had really been your ancestor? Yes, what would you have done? It was people like Jim who had made him feel disgusted with his own origins and led him to treat them like a vulgar fantasy. They had made Africa into their carnival, their mardi gras procession whose rags they had looted. They did not attempt to understand either its sense or meaning and flashed it about without rhyme or reason. Jim also sanctimoniously described the funeral of W. E. B. Du Bois in Accra when the crowds thronging around the Osagyefo turned a page in the history of Pan-Africanism.

And above all, above all, the trip with Malcolm X to the North. The North is another land. There they pray differently. There they had met Islam in the shape of the wise man Abdou, who had presented Malcolm with an illuminated copy of the Koran dating from the fourteenth century. Jim himself had almost converted to Islam and changed his name.

Debbie drank in all these wonderful words like a child drinking a cup of *chodo* at a christening, her eyes shining, her body language signifying how she would have liked to exchange her days as a model student, the Caribbean cruise, the meeting with Spero, and even their love nest on the Morne Verdol for such enriching experiences. Spero hated Jim, yet always remained friendly with him. He would have preferred him to have an adulterous affair with Debbie, spending secret nights with her and waking up by her side, both exhausted in the predawn hours, drifting on an unmade bed. Anything rather than these bodiless attachments.

On this uncelebrated December Tenth, nostalgia grabbed Spero by the throat in an even more galling way. What wouldn't he give to go home? Turn up at Christmas amid the smell of pork casserole and simmering Congo peas! Attend mass at Saint-Jules, overflowing with a crowd singing "Christians Awake" but thinking of the feast afterwards!

Home?

Did these words still have a meaning? After years and years

of exile, is any soil still native? And do you still belong? You arrive home and no longer recognize the words or the music. You look but the tree with your placenta is gone. Chopped down by the property developers. When Maxo and Lionel wrote him Spero could see that the Guadeloupe he remembered was dead and buried. The factories had become graveyards. The cane fields, hiding places for vermin. Concrete had replaced wood. Already when he had returned home after his studies in Lille he had found La Pointe so changed. In the district called "L'Assainissement" a large hotel had sprung up, along with a church, a school, and other buildings in concrete. Gone were the stinking latrines and the standpipes with their never-ending lines. Now it was the magic of electricity and drainage! Only the Morne Verdol remained the Morne Verdol! Yet it too, it was whispered, was destined for the city planners. He no longer had any place to turn. He too, like the ancestor, was in exile.

The years the royal family spent in Blida were happier ones. Here at least there was no volcano with a cavernous voice to frighten them, no more terrifying storms or torrential rains. The weather was dry, sunny, and cool. Even so, Princess Kpotasse and Prince Ouanilo grumbled. The little Arabs called them dirty niggers and the women, drawing aside their veils, came out on their doorsteps to watch them amid shrieks of laughter. In his rage, the adolescent Ouanilo dreamed of killing them. Or else killing himself.

As for the ancestor, he did not realize what was going on since he had become an infant again. He left Ouanilo alone. He no longer dictated to him endless letters to the President of the Republic. Consequently, he was no longer prone to those fits of anger or melancholy that affected him when the answers never came. He no longer sobbed loudly at night. In Blida, all morning long, he would watch the shadow of the sun on the patio covered with *zellijs* tiles, in alternating blue and white. Around eleven, tired of watching the shadow play of the sun, he got up and, followed by Queen Fadjo, who did not like to see him go out alone in this foreign town, shuffled his old body under his parasol as far as the craftsmen's district in the very heart of the Medina.

On his way he would admire the houses, so different, so much lovelier than those in Fort-de-France, with their brick and stone facades decorated with mosaics. He would stop short in front of the wooden carvings on the doors. In a confused way they reminded him of the sculptures in his own palace. Then he raised his eyes to the roofs that rippled in terraces on which washing was drying and snapping like flags in the wind.

Above all he liked to linger at the market of the Jewish goldsmiths in their rattan sandals and black turbans in order to feel the weight of the gold rings and bracelets, lighter than those he once possessed, which had been chiseled by his own smiths. The Jews, who knew his sad story, would lament between their teeth, "Sh'ma Yisraël: Adonai Elohenu Adonai Ehad!"

He also liked to watch the potters, their cheeks tanned by the flames of their ovens, which they fed with big white thistles, wild carrot stalks, straw, and blocks of olive wood. But his favorite pastime was standing in front of the tailors as they embroidered and stitched, their needles threaded with long strands of plain-colored cotton. Cross stitch. Persian stitch. Stem stitch. Needlepoint. The sight delighted the ancestor, and if it had not been for Queen Fadjo he would have stayed there all day.

Spero imagined Debbie standing not far from Jim, watching the dancers exercise. From time to time she would make a small remark that he always took into account. What did she see in this chatterbox? This hot-air artist? This fake man? Women are always oblivious to those who deserve love.

You must admit, he hadn't had much luck with his women!

Neither his grandmother, nor his mother, nor his wife, nor his daughter had really loved him.

Marisia's color had undoubtedly made Debbie ill at ease. From the very first day Debbie had looked at her defiantly. The two women had lived under the same roof without exchanging a single word, Marisia barricading herself behind her Creole, Debbie behind her English, not a smile between them. In private Debbie had no qualms telling Spero she thought his mother crude, uneducated, and unworthy of her role. So he had always been ashamed to confide in her the feelings Marisia inspired in him, despite all that. She therefore had no idea of the blow his mother's death had dealt him. A little less than three years after his arrival in Charleston, two telegrams had arrived, one a few hours before the other.

"Mother very close to death."

"Mother passed away."

At that time you didn't take a plane like you do today. Too expensive! And the boat was too slow. So Spero had had to be content with a magnificent wreath via Interflora and imagine he was back on the Morne Verdol. Although Marisia, withdrawn and not very talkative in her unhappy marriage, did not have any friends, she did have clients: all those women she had dressed with her nimble fingers, tailoring straight skirts, flared skirts, pleated skirts, puff sleeves, leg-of-mutton sleeves, and bouffant sleeves. They invaded the house for the wake, rallying round Marisia for the last time as she lay stiff on her bed, the joyless face she had worn for a little under fifty-two years transfigured by an everlasting peace. Between two psalms they whispered you could see she was glad to be with Lacpatia again, her maman whom the Good Lord had called to Him last Lent. Her maman! The only person who had loved her! And the women stole reproachful looks at Justin, who as usual was swimming in rum and did not seem to realize what a wonderful person had spent thirty-five years beside him. Arthé was the only person Spero poured his heart out to about Marisia.

Arthé. For a time he had seriously thought of leaving Debbie for her. She was from New Orleans, and although labeled

Maryse Condé

black, in fact she had a mixture of three bloods in her veins. A husband had left her shipwrecked without money or children, with nothing to keep her in this life, and she drifted from one man to the next. She had given Spero the most precious thing that Debbie had denied him, the freedom to be himself. To be virtually no good. Except perhaps in bed. In her company he had for once forgotten the ancestor and talked of Jean Boyer d'Etterville, the *béké* in his mother's family, the descendant of the black sheep of a wealthy family who had come to sweat his sins out in Guadeloupe after spending years in the chaplain's cell in the tower of Saint-Pierre in Lille. While he was at death's door Jean Boyer had legitimized the seventeen-year-old Marisia with his sixty-one other illegitimate children. Owning neither factory nor plantation, but cultivating the land himself, he had lived like an animal. When Marisia, who lived in the Hauts-Fonds, passed by on the road with Florimond, her little brother, she could see the red roof of his house half hidden among the turpentine and Indian almond trees. She could not help thinking of a tale, the tale of a hideous beast who came out only in the darkness of night to pounce on its victims. At that time she did not know that the beast had attacked her mother twice and that Florimond and herself were the offspring of these skirmishes. Perhaps one's mother's family tree is as important as one's father's?

But Arthé had no desire to live in Guadeloupe. All those stories about the Morne Verdol bored her. In fact she was tired of black-on-black stories. Her one dream was to fly away with Spero to Paris. Wasn't he French? She herself laid claim to all the blood she had inherited from the planter ancestor from Saint-Domingue who had fled to Louisiana following the exemplary victories of Makandal, Boukman, Toussaint-Louverture, Dessalines, and the others. Isn't Paris the capital where color is no longer synonymous with pain? Josephine Baker, Richard Wright, Sydney Bechet, James Baldwin, and so many others were there to prove it. Spero took so long making up his mind, comparing his own gloomy memories of Paris with these myths made in the USA, that Arthé got tired. She left to sleep in another man's bed and Spero found consolation in alcohol, which is never consoling.

The window shutter banged. The night had slyly slipped in with the rain, and like a bird of prey was clutching the space around him with its claws. In the morning, after a serious scuffle, it would unclench them to leave room for the light of day. The rain would still be lingering, filling the hollow paths and varnishing the leaves on the trees. Wouldn't he do better to go back up to his room and numb himself to sleep? He started up the stairs, but stopped on the second-floor landing, turned the doorknob to Anita's room, and entered like a thief. Over the bed that Ken the intruder sometimes occupied he had hung one of his paintings inspired by *Le Douanier* Rousseau's little girl. Anita, five years old. Holding a doll in her right hand. A daisy in her left hand. A polka dot red dress. A red ribbon in her hair. Sitting in the middle of a garden planted with azaleas and zinnias. A scared staring look with a subtle beauty that would only be revealed years later. Spero, who did not give much credit to his own creations, liked this painting. He had spent a long time putting the finishing touches to it for an exhibition on the "New Black Painting" to be held in New York and had high hopes for it. But in the end the organizers wrote him a polite letter turning it down, as well as two other canvasses he had submitted. In disgust he had put it on show in Savannah. The critics had not even mentioned it.

If one of his women had spurned him it was surely Anita! And now, what was she looking for, carrying a lighted lamp out in the African daylight? Something he had been unable to give her — and Debbie too despite her grandiloquent speeches. What it means to be black?

Does it still mean anything?

One day when he was six, a day forever engraved in his memory, he was returning home with Justin. When Justin was in one of his good moods he used to take his *ti-mal* for a dip and a breaststroke in the waters of the sea that were as warm as a doe rabbit's belly. In actuality the child would bury himself in the sand and watch his father's head grow smaller and smaller above the waves, his heart pounding every time it disappeared. All that blue, all that spray frightened him. And then he was wearing a pair of cotton swimming trunks made by Marisia, while the other children had swimsuits made of jersey! After the swim, Justin joined the other thirsty throats at La Voilure, a fisherman's hangout in the Carenage district where he was a regular. While Spero sat bored in a corner with a glass of barley water, Justin would quickly play one or two winning games of dominoes or dice, down three or four neat rums, and finally make up his mind to set off back to the Morne. Spero, who was already exhausted from drinking in all that blue, used to find the journey home endless. One day they had crossed the bridge over the Voûte district, called the Pont Caca, walked all the way along the rue Dugommier and up the Canal Vatable. The sweat was streaming down Spero's back, sticking his short-sleeved shirt to his shoulder blades and mixing in with the dried salt on his face. While they walked, all makes of American cars, Oldsmobiles, Dodges, and Studebakers, passed them by with their fortunate occupants in crisp dry clothes and colonial helmets, kicking up clouds of dust that flew like wheat flour and forced them to make a hurried retreat to the sidewalk. Spero began to think things over. After a while, he picked up courage, caught up with Justin, who was swinging along in front with his long legs, and asked, "Papa, Papa! Why aren't we white?"

Justin did not know what severe meant. When Marisia merely thought about laying hands on one of her children he would grab hold of her arm and threaten her with the blows she intended to give. But that afternoon it was he who unbuckled his wide belt and tanned Spero's hide. The neighbors ran out, afraid he had made up his mind to finish the boy off. After that, pinching his son's earlobe with his nails of silex, he led him up to the photo in the dining room and gave him his first major lesson on the partition of the world.

Covered in bruises the child had not really concentrated and had gone to bed without dinner, a punishment graciously added by Marisia. He felt he had been the victim of a terrible injustice. What had he meant? Quite simply, why aren't we rich? Why haven't we got a car at our fingertips to take us wherever we want to go? Why do we live on the Morne Verdol among the poor while others are ensconced in white houses and water scarlet bougainvillea in their gardens? Why do we eat tubers moistened with a little fish stew day after day while others stuff themselves with French apples?

The next day, as if the offense had been a major crime, Justin sat Spero in front of him and described to him all the horrors of the past. The walls of the slave island of Gorée had neither eyes to see nor ears to hear the suffering and the wailing. The sharks danced around the slave ships, watching for corpses the crew threw overboard. They snatched them up in midair and snapped them in two with one joyful gnash of their scissorlike jaws. Not a Pater nor a Noster was said in their memory. The waves of the sea are but shrouds. The Negro women sank their rounded bellies into the soft womb of the earth, which also stifled the cries of their pain. Hot peppers sizzled in flesh wounds. Not an Ave nor a Maria. The maroon with his body lacquered in blood cavorted at the end of his rope among the red flowers and black pods of the flame tree. Not an Agnus nor a Dei. Who was to blame for all that? Eh? Who was to blame? Had Spero also forgotten why the ancestor had lost his kingdom? His big, beautiful kingdom. The kingdom of Alada. The kingdom of the descendants of Agasu. The descendants of the Leopard had emigrated to the east, taking with them the sacred objects, the royal throne hollowed out of an *iroko* tree, Tengisu's magic spears, and the statuette of the animal-ancestor. Then they founded the kingdom beyond the river, the kingdom where the sun never set, stretching from the mountains of Mahi to the ocean, from the Couffo to the Ouémé. Had Spero forgotten the desolation of the ancestor's last days?

Hosannah's body had not consoled him for very long. Neither had Djéré's funny little expressions. Of course he worshipped the boy. He took him in his arms and was entertained by his antics. But after a while, as if the child could understand him, he started to ramble on about times long past. He had appointed one of his brothers general of his armies and they had beaten hollow all those who had dared defy the Aladahonu. At the time there was no counting the number of men taken prisoner and reduced to slavery. Nor those delivered up to the traffickers who navigated the sea in exchange for pipes, steel knives, and brandy.

After Prince Adandejan had left for Kutome, the darkness of mourning totally enveloped the spirit of the ancestor and he sang over and over again the song they had composed together on friendship. When he came to the last word, his heart burst with grief. Now that his *honton* had left him, who would carry out his funeral rites? Who would sacrifice his ram? Who would hand out kola nuts, cowries, and drinks? Then he remembered he was in this land of exile where the ritual was unknown, and he wept even louder.

Queen Fadjo went into a fret, for she knew the situation could not go on like this. Since Hosannah had been of no use, she sought another remedy. For a time she thought she had found the answer in the Good Lord's prayer, and a Jesuit, Father Delaumes, became a frequent visitor to Bellevue. He had endless conversations with the ancestor. He spoke to him of Heaven and Hell. He made him confess imaginary sins and had him join hands on prayer books. He urged him to receive the holy sacrament of baptism and prepare himself for a Christian death through mortification. The ancestor emerged even more melancholic from these conversations and was haunted by the thought of his transgressions. One day, Queen Fadjo learned that the *gadé dzafé* Zephyr Marboeuf had found his master in the person of Troisfois Cheri, a Haitian. Troisfois Cheri had arrived in Fort-de-France clandestinely from Calvaire Miracle on All Souls' Day, an ominous sign if ever there was one. People said he used both hands to perform his works thanks to the loas of his native country. Queen Fadjo went and fetched him herself from his hovel in the Trenelle district, where he secretly tried to hide his powers, the only indication being a red flag to Ogun, the loa of war and fire.

During the ancestor's final year of exile on Martinique, Troisfois Cheri's remedies and endeavors ate up the meager pension the French government paid for the upkeep of the old man's family. He started by tying to the skin of the ancestor's left arm a magic handkerchief in the colors of Ogun — colors obtained from decoctions known only to him — and attaching tightly around his neck a necklace of porcelain pearls in the same red. He conversed at a distance with the loas back home, for the case was a difficult one. Morning after morning he demanded chickens dressed in white and goats with immaculate coats, marked only with a fiery spot between the eyes. He slaughtered them with a single stroke of his long knife then splashed their blood over the garden before daubing the base of the villa's doors and windows. Terrified, Princess Kpotasse locked herself up in her room and lowered the shades. Trois-fois Cheri also demanded demijohns of white rum, but these he took home and nobody knew what he did with them. At the end of months and months of work he rose up to his full height, threw his *bakoua* hat to the ground and swore, "Io two mové! Sé blan-la two mové!" (They're too wicked! The whites are too wicked!)

Then he left the house and never came back.

The old man nevertheless tried not to lose hope. He could not understand why the French would refuse him any longer a possession bequeathed him by his ancestors that belonged to nobody else. When he had finished dictating his endless letters to Ouanilo he would perch Djéré on his knee and describe the grandiose funeral rites he would hold for his father as soon as he returned home.

A bed would be dressed with everything precious the dead king possessed and a dummy laid on it wrapped in all kinds of rich fabrics. Then a huge grave would be dug in front of the palace of Abomey with an entrance big enough for one man to pass through. A hundred victims would be assembled whose heads would each be severed with a single blow of the sabre, wham! With their blood the earth would be kneaded into a coffin. In it they would place the remains of the king and lower it into the grave with loads of coral, brandy, pipe tobacco, pipes, three-cornered hats, gold and silver tobacco jars, and three canes with golden knobs and three others with silver knobs. Then eighty Leopard wives would be jostled down in tears eager to join in the sacrifice, as well as fifty healthy youths whose legs would first be broken.

After eighteen moons the coffin would be opened and the skeleton of the king shown to the people. Another three hundred victims would be sacrificed, and with their blood a structure similar to a great oven would be built in which the skull of the late king would be laid.

In actual fact, none of these marvels was performed. The ancestor died in the desolation of his Algerian exile, and Djéré had been unable to give his father the ceremonies his grandeur deserved.

And whose fault was that? Eh? Whose fault?

OK! OK! But all those stories took place ages ago. Things were no longer so cut and dried, and poor Justin had lost touch. In this day and age there were enough stories in which victims and tormentors were of the same color. All you had to do was glance through the papers, watch the news on television, and have eyes to see and ears to hear to have proof of it. It was that proof, blinding as it was, that Debbie considered a sacrilege. Their last quarrel occurred about eight months ago. Debbie had hurled at him so many unforgivable words that Spero had once more thought of returning home. To hell with his pride! After all, he would not be the first immigrant to return home with his pockets empty! The world is full of people who left to seek their fortune and ended up with misery. After a while, however, his lucidity returned. No use daydreaming; certain voyages have a point of no return. They come up against the grave that one day or another is dug for every one of us at the end of our lives.

Last winter the *Black Sentinel of Charleston* had remarked on the genius of Alan Rowell, a young black musician from Chicago who was touring the South. He had set to music the poems of Rita Coblens, the second black woman in the history of literature to win the Pulitzer Prize, having put to verse the story of her family and their migration from a Southern smallholding to the ghettoes of the North. Usually, Spero was highly distrustful of the enthusings of the *Black Sentinel*, which for thirty years, come what may, stubbornly repeated that black was beautiful. Yet the article came with an interview in which Alan ridiculed the same old pompous questions by journalists about the role of the artist and the meaning of his art, the links with tradition and mother Africa; intrigued, Spero had accompanied Debbie to the concert. It had been a long time since they had sat side by side in the hall on Poplar Street where they had been regular goers at the beginning of their marriage. The concert hall boasted of having hosted a performance of *Porgy and Bess* with Abbie Mitchell in person. It was overheated and solemn with its crystal chandeliers, its dark red high-backed seats, and its monumental staircase decorated all the way down with photos to the glory of black music: W. C. Handy, Scott Joplin, Bessie Smith, William Grant Still . . .

Nothing had changed with the times. Today was the same as yesterday: the same lights, the same chatter, the same crowd. The exact doubles of the neighbors on the Morne Verdol had arranged to meet, dressed up American style, the sisters having switched their tight little plaits and braids, their *choux* or *carreaux patates*, for scaffoldings of curls and waves carefully straightened and oiled, their loose dresses of printed calico for silk and lamé, and their sandals for high heels; as for the brothers, they had put on their best suits, strapped a bow tie around their necks, and encased their feet in boots of fine leather. The racist who said that all blacks look alike was not so racist after all. Spero's heart filled with nostalgia. He looked at Debbie, whose face had never really been very lovely but had once had such an effect on him, with her eyebrows drawn in parallel lines above the constant melancholy of her shiny black eyes, her full mouth, and the dimple on her chin. He remembered her amused surprise in the past at the thought of him recognizing childhood acquaintances in this new environment whom he wanted to greet with a *sa ou fè*— How are you? What had happened during these twenty-five years? Why did he now feel so alone, so foreign? It was because suddenly those he thought he recognized as a neighborly presence had revealed their true colors and unmasked the reality of their threatening, grimacing faces. It was because suddenly their looks and their fingers had shown him the door. Everybody loves a winner. Why bother with a down-and-out painter?

Deep in his thoughts, he hardly listened to Alan's music and had no idea whether he deserved the standing ovation he got. When they left the concert hall it was pouring rain. The streetlamps floated like buoys clinging to the sea, and the freeways heaved and rolled like the swell of the waves during a storm. While firmly in control of her four-wheel-drive, Debbie never stopped praising Alan, and Spero could guess the meaning hidden behind every one of her words. He who cannot see beauty in this world can only produce mean and mediocre works, rejected by the human heart. He who does not possess the fervor of faith in life cannot create. For to create is to believe. To believe is to live.

After a while Spero's patience tired of hearing these aphorisms. He laughed out loud. What a fuss for a wretched maker of sounds!

A woman's anger, goes the saying, is like a torrent that overflows. Although he knew by heart what Debbie verbally and silently reproached him for — being lazy, negligent, ambitionless, cynical, and nihilistic — he was unprepared for certain new accusations. What? She blamed him for Anita's departure and especially for her silence that was torturing both of them?

Spero stared the portrait of his daughter straight in the eyes as if he had in front of him not two blobs of paint, shining and blind, but the eyes of a living person capable of answering his questions and completely exonerating him. Was it true he had been a bad father?

On the Morne Verdol lived Amédée, a papa who raped his daughters. He had given a belly to his eldest daughter, Emma, then another to his second, Emmeline. The neighbors gossiped about it all day long; the men were quite prepared to find excuses for him. After all, he was the one who made them! He could use them any way he wanted! The women were more recalcitrant and offended. Méralda, his companion and mother of his children, went about her business as if she were oblivious to what was going on in her house. But when

Amédée approached the youngest daughter with the same intentions Méralda stuck a knife used for scraping hogs in his stomach. Public opinion and the magistrates from France acquitted her unanimously. A woman can do anything to protect her child.

If Debbie monopolized Anita to such an extent was she trying to protect her from him?

Yet there was a time when his heart had been as red as the sun and his dreams had grown thick as the hair on his head. He did not know exactly what he dreamed of. Simply not to end up like Justin and Djéré on the Morne Verdol; to breathe a bluer, crisper air than those two; to show all those who had taken him for an ordinary human being, son of Justin, one of the last of the African kings, what he really had in his blood and what type of man he really was. Looking back, things had subtly started to change after his visit to Monsieur Bodriol in Paris. When that man had shown him out like an impostor he had destroyed the very framework of his existence.

After this visit he had not gone back to Lille immediately, but stayed in Paris holed up in his hotel on the rue de Rivoli. While the rain pattered tirelelessly against the windowpanes, he had spent the time asking himself whether, after all, he had really believed in Justin's nonsense. Had he really had faith in Djéré's notebooks? Hadn't all that merely fostered his childish, then his adolescent, imagination? Perhaps. But imagination is sovereign. It nurtures dreams that in turn nurture the heart and guide one's life. If imagination perishes, life too perishes.

He could not stay locked up all the time.

At nightfall, hunger gripped him and he was obliged to go out. He walked bareheaded in the rain and dined in the first restaurant he came across. On seeing him enter the waiters muttered to themselves, "Here comes another filthy Arab! Why don't those people stay in their own country?"

He eventually returned to Lille. But his life was never the

same. Until then his shyness had always kept him from approaching the Africans and he had watched them from a distance. Suddenly, like a fruitfly, he started frequenting the spots where they met to speak their languages and dance their music. Nobody turned him out, and some even addressed him with friendly but mysterious words, "Are you Algerian, cousin? We're on your side!"

He who had never been interested in politics was intrigued to find out that a savage war was pitting Algeria against France and already a million Arabs had gone to their graves. One evening while he was drinking his third beer a woman with eyes of silk and mourning came and sat at his table. Her name was Youmma and she said she was a princess from a lost kingdom in the dunes somewhere between Nioro and Horodougou, driven from her country by the new democracy. For a while she had lived in the Horloge district in Brussels in the clutches of a Congolese pimp. Finally she had escaped and crossed the border in a cattle car squeezed between two cows. However much he had wanted to, Spero never made love to her. She simply came and sat down at his table every evening and talked to him.

"Cousin, you can't imagine what my country's like. As flat as the back of your hand. The cows are lovelier than the women and the men sing them songs of love. From October to June the harmattan blows its burning breath that sets thirsts ablaze and fans the bush fires. The dunes slide one on top of the other and the land is covered with ripples of sand. The sand is a seamless shroud. Only the acacia *raddiana* grows here, quenching burning throats and providing ropes for mooring, as well as mortars and pestles that grind the life-sustaining millet. My father was all skin and bones. He wore the edge of his rough wool burnoose turned down over his eyes. All day long he would read the *Jawahir-al-ma'ani* in the original and spit his saliva into a calabash. My mother would kneel in silence on both knees and set down kola nuts in front of him. He did, however, give her seven children. When? How? I don't know! I'm the last."

Taking his courage in both hands Spero ventured some questions.

"Cousin, cousin!" she shook her head. "You must be joking. Don't you realize what our countries have turned into?"

And she would roll off an already long list of deposed presidents, ministers fleeing for their lives, and triumphant upstarts. Yes, it had all begun from there, and it was a very different Spero who had returned home three years later.

He got up, closed the door behind him and went up to the next floor.

All around him the silence made the house vibrate with a dull rumor as if all those who for generations had loved and hated, lived in suffering or joy, were all giving voice to their experiences at once.

Debbie had relegated him to the very top of the house in a sunless room that children must have occupied when the house on Crocker Island was home to a tribe of Middletons and not to a solitary, dysfunctional couple.

It was the same as he had left it that morning. The bed looked as if it had been trampled by his nightmares. The sheets and blankets in disarray. The pillows dented. An aura of humidity hung everywhere. He went over to the window and the bird of night flying at eye level seized him in its powerful clutches. If only it would carry him off to his *krazur* of an island exiled in the Caribbean. December! The shafts of sugar cane would not yet have flowered and the soil manhandled by the great winds of the rainy season would be flooded. The fattening hogs would be stuffing themselves with tubers oblivious to their approaching death.

Where was the Debbie he had loved so much?

At this moment she would be taking leave of Jim while the dancers, soaked in sweat, took off their leotards. He would accompany her to her car and they would exchange a kiss as chaste as between brother and sister. She would roar off and stop over at George Street at the other end of the town to spend some time with Paule. Paule and Debbie teamed up to smother Chaka with attention. They gave him his dinner, watching his diet and forcing him to swallow large glasses of fruit juice with added vitamins. They checked the temperature of his bath water, rubbed him down, and slipped on his pyjamas. Then they would put him to bed, and while he was still sleepy and yawning from all these devotions they took turns reading him a story as if he were a little boy.

When he had gone to sleep they would sit facing each other in the living room and chatter. About what, for goodness sake? Knowing what they knew, what each was hiding from the other, how could they claim to be friends? What on earth could they talk about?

About men, of course! They were the common link. Their wickedness, their meanness, the dirty tricks inflicted on both of them. To start with, they talked about Paule's ex-husband, a bus driver who for years had humiliated her and beaten her, enamored of her almost-white skin and long thick hair, before leaving her for a Puerto Rican, next-door neighbor and mother of six. Then they came to Spero, who was hardly any better. Debbie recounted his infamous affair with Tamara Barnes, coming after so many others, and how she had not tolerated it. From that point on they were partners — mocking him, criticizing him, and cruelly comparing his feats. God! Women certainly had strength! What he had first taken for a victory over Debbie had backfired and become just another defeat. He had poked fun at Paule and Debbie in a portrait he had shown only to Linton called *The Difficulty of Making up One's Mind*.

Two choice morsels of black women, their hands joined at breast level, dressed identically in white albs, hair dishevelled, were receiving the visitation of the Holy Spirit standing in the very middle of a river. One of them was Paule, even lighter skinned, younger, and more appealing than ever with firm breasts, round shoulders, and at the end of her neck, ringed like a Fulani woman, her face with a sensuous mouth implanted with sparkling teeth. The other was Debbie, more buxom, more majestic, falsely serene, hiding under her inspired airs her raging desires. How did she manage now that she had driven him from her bed? Did she too take refuge in the Good Lord? He has a lot on his hands, our dear

Lord, comforting all these lonely black women, abandoned by their men!

For the first time he thought of breaking with Paule. Since he had not been able to drag her away from Debbie, he would have to leave them to each other as well as to the Good Lord she served so badly.

Spero sat down on his bed. Was it true he had been such a bad father?

A few hours before he died the ancestor woke up in the depths of the forest. The day had been like any other; he had taken his little stroll to the Medina and then gone to bed early. Ouanilo sat at his bedside and read him passages from *La Gloire du sabre*, which he liked when he was in Fort-de-France, but about which he now seemed to have lost all interest. Then Ouanilo retired without making a sound once the ancestor seemed asleep.

The forest! That's where it had all started. That's where it was all going to end! When Queen Fadjo heard the old man gurgle like a baby in a cradle she knew the fatal moment had arrived. She went over to the bed and he did not even recognize her. As happy as could be, his eyes gleaming, he was staring at a spot over her head. So she decided to hide the truth from the other queens, who were too fond of lamenting, like the over-emotional Princess Kpotasse, and went and fetched Ouanilo, the son the ancestor had always preferred over his other children.

Ouanilo sat at the head of his father's bed. He looked at this great body of iroko wood, once so heavy, now made frailer and frailer by the grief of exile and suffering, and his heart was in torment. When his father passed away how could he, still a child, alone with a handful of women, respect the custom and conduct his funeral with dignity in this land that did not share their beliefs? The long letter went through his mind he thought he should write immediately to President

Maryse Condé

Carnot to ask for the repatriation of his father's body, but his heart was in so much grief he had not the strength to put pen to paper. He went over and over again in his head every word of their last conversation together when the old man still had all his senses in Fort-de-France. His father had whispered to him in confidence that he had chosen him out of all his sons to be his heir. One day it would be his turn to mount the throne of Huegbaja and the world would bow down in front of him like the grasses of the bush under the breath of the wind. Elated, he had promised his father, sworn to him on the *daadaa*, that he would do everything to give the dynasty the lustre it once had when its very name was enough to make the greatest warrior tremble. Alas, he now saw that this would never happen. The sun would never again shine on the Kingdom of Alada.

Meanwhile Queen Fadjo took no respite. She called on all the gods she had learned to respect to ask that the ancestor die in peace and not lose himself along the secret path to Kutome with its difficult access. Not only the gods of the Aladahonu but also the gods of the Martinicans as well as those terrible, turbulent, insubordinate gods of the Haitians. Especially those! On the floor in the corner of the bedroom she had spread a white starched tablecloth and laid out a plate full of *manjé-loas*: corn on the cob, sweet potatoes, meat, and sugared almonds next to two bottles of barley water. She did not forget the white man's god, either, whom Father Delaumes had described over and over again during his catechism lessons. Since she couldn't read she had merely opened the Bible at random, and without knowing it had come upon the Book of Job:

> Why was not I still-born,
> Why did I not die when I came out of the womb?
> Why was I ever laid on my mother's knees
> Or put to suck at her breasts?

As for the ancestor he continued to coo like a wood pigeon in the forest. At 9:33 P.M. exactly the cooing stopped.

The death of the ancestor did not pass unnoticed. Noble

minds of all nationalities were moved. The French. The British. The Spanish. And even a few Americans, who sent a petition to President Roosevelt. The League of Human Rights voiced more protests. The world over, it seemed, weaker nations were being ridiculed by the stronger. Take the British, for example, who had exiled Nana Agyeman Prempeh I, king of the Ashanti, to the Seychelles. He too was strolling around Victoria with a parasol open above his head against the sun.

Eyes wide open in the dark Spero stared at the heavy beams supporting the ceiling and chanted as he counted. Bread. Wine. Poverty. Bread. Wine. Poverty.

Bread. Daubed in white, the beams of his room in the house on the Morne Verdol also stopped on the word *Bread*. In fact, for a moment, he lost track of time. Childhood? Middle age? Yet he felt his body overweight and flabby around him and remembered again where he was. At the same time the memory of his bad dream came back to him. In the past his nights had never been haunted by nightmares. On the contrary. Growing up poor he never left La Pointe, be it dry or rainy season, sweltering hot sun or torrential rain. The holidays boiled down to flying a kite in the sky over the sandbox and tamarind trees on the Morne. Or a game of soccer on the empty lot behind Saint-Jules. So he took his revenge in the dark, where his head roved and roamed as soon as it touched the pillow. Sometimes he floated down rivers as wide as an ocean sound, as clear as sparkling crystal, slipping his hand under the rocks as he went to waken the crayfish. Other times he crossed savannas filled with guava trees where green-breasted hummingbirds sipped the nectar of overripe fruit. There were times when he climbed to the summit of volcanoes and bathed in the sticky torrent of their magma. From up there he looked out at the ocean and swore he would cross it one day to the capitals of fame and fortune. Often he lay full-length on a raft tied together with five malimbé trunks and floated to an islet inhabited by crested

Maryse Condé

cranes that he captured with a lasso. Such were his childhood nights. Spero closed his eyes. Even so, he should have known he was no match for Debbie. He had been defeated time after time. The first time was when he had waged and lost his fight to keep Anita. He had lost count of the others. The last he had waged and lost two years ago. Anita was still at Liman College, but only surfaced with her occasional telephone calls to apologize for not coming home for Thanksgiving, Christmas, or Easter. The March before her graduation she had deigned to return to Charleston. Yet as soon as she stepped off the plane Debbie and Spero knew by the expression on her face that she was not coming to make peace with them but to escape a hell she had created herself. For the entire week she did not speak to them any more than she had done in the past. She spent most of her time wandering around the garden or locked up in her room talking over the phone to God knows whom and often in the very middle of the night. The only person who quite suddenly found grace in her eyes was Mamie Garvin, whom she interrogated for hours about her life.

On this topic she had not been the first one. There was a time when Debbie had had the idea of collecting the tales of Mamie Garvin as she had done with Agnes Jackson and publishing them as memoirs. She had even interviewed her and sent the first chapter to a publisher. Yet this text, like "The Notebooks of Djéré," had not found a buyer either, and the idea had been left at that. Mamie Garvin came from Kiawah Island, which you could see on a fine day lying across the sea. Unlike Crocker Island, in times long past, Kiawah Island had been green with the green of the most prosperous cotton plantations in South Carolina while her planters had been the most arrogant in the entire state. Around 1862, the Union army that occupied the islands before taking Charleston massacred them and freed their slaves. The latter had immediately taken refuge in the interior, going back to the old ways and languages they had brought from Africa, living off wild potatoes, mushrooms, and the hogs they bred and bled themselves. A few hours after she was born, Mamie Garvin was swung three times over the graves of her great-grandmother and grandmother in the tiny black cemetery at Sea Pines so that their healing powers could pass into her body. She had never been to school and until she was sixteen had spoken only Gullah, a language composed of African words and a little English, virtually incomprehensible to strangers. Gradually, however, the slaves' descendants left to look for work in Charleston. Mamie Garvin had held her ground. She remained hidden in the woods with the last of the rebels, the real Maroons, when the property developers from Charleston invaded Kiawah Island to transform it into a tourist paradise and build hotels with swimming pools and casinos and tennis courts and golf courses. They ruthlessly drove the island dwellers from the land they occupied. So Debbie, who on several occasions had consulted Mamie Garvin about Anita, had given her permission to build a small house behind the old stables in exchange for a few hours of daily housework. As a bonus, Mamie Garvin concocted mysterious herb teas the color of mud that Spero refused to touch but that Debbie obediently swallowed morning and night. At the four corners of the house she lit small burners fuelled with roots and aromatic herbs. Sometimes she talked out the top of her head and predicted the weather and disastrous events. From his window, Spero watched the silhouette of his child coming and going between Mamie Garvin's little house and theirs and wondered why Anita had come back to fuel their grief. Would this incomprehensible gap that had come between them be filled one day? Once Anita had left and taken her troubles back to Liman College, however, life on Crocker Island had seemed even more insipid and meaningless.

One evening, coming home from Charleston earlier than usual, tired of hanging out evening after evening at the Montego Bay, he had found Debbie in the kitchen with a very young girl, almost a child. Such visits were common, for despite her maternal setbacks Debbie could not get out of the habit of testing her theories of education whatever the odds. Moreover, parents consulted her with the trust they would put in a guru. Irritated, Spero was about to run up to his room when the girl's expression caught his attention. She reminded him of a portrait by Adolf Dietrich. High yellow. The secretive, desperate look of an adult in the chubby face of a child. Hair bristling with a thousand rasta locks, still yellowed by the sun and a lack of attention.

She said her name was Roshawn Johnson. Her mother had abandoned her shortly after she was born and she had been brought up by her grandmother, who, now old and tired of her getting into trouble, wanted nothing more to do with her. Her dealer boyfriend had just got ten years. They had not been able to charge her with collusion, but the judges had nevertheless placed her in Sunny Swamp, a juvenile detention center where most of the inmates were black and where three times a week Jim and Debbie preached their gospel as sociologist and historian. The magistrates of the juvenile court had also recommended she be taught a trade: mechanics.

When Spero came in Debbie was fussing around her like a broody hen, thinking perhaps that a large mug of hot coffee, a slice of apple pie, and speeches on the grandeur of the African past could heal the wounds America inflicted on her black minority. It was to teach Debbie a lesson and show how naive she was that Spero had first taken on Roshawn in his way, on his terms.

What did he hope to get out of it? In fact, absolutely nothing. He had always been frightened of youngsters. He was incapable of serving them up sweet lies, of persuading them that life is wonderful and that tomorrow the sun will shine again. But he had not reckoned he would gradually forget his plan of revenge against Debbie and become attached to Roshawn as you do to someone in great distress. To begin with, as a ruse, he offered to paint her portrait, a magical proposition which, according to him, would open up the doors of her imagination. So, early one afternoon, she turned up at his studio without so much as a glance at the canvasses on display. She took off her jacket, and wearing her red, grimy-necked T-shirt, she indifferently took up a pose for hours on end without saying a single word. Spero was dying to paint her naked body, as fragile as a fetus, but did not dare ask her to take off all her clothes. As silent as ever, she would go and have dinner with him after the sitting. She seemed fond of Chinese restaurants, and manipulating her chopsticks like a child would smear her mouth with curry sauce, much to Spero's delight. Sometimes she agreed to accompany him to Linton's place but was obviously bored by the wails of his saxophone. Once he even took her to the movies, but she stared at Eddie Murphy's clowning without a smile. In fact she never smiled and was no more talkative than a deaf-mute. It was Spero who filled the silences of their tête-á-têtes. Spero, who, like his mother Marisia, was by nature not very talkative, and now even less since he had to speak English with his terrible accent and erratic grammar, became effusive even without the help of alcohol and had enough to say for the two of them. About what? About everything. Himself. His daughter, so far away. Debbie. About the great shipwreck of their marriage. He would have loved to tell her other stories. The very ones that Debbie told her, for instance. Edifying, meaningful, optimistic, filled with hope and illusions that were never lost. But he did not know any. His own repertoire was limited, like an old singer who keeps on rehearsing the same old blues. Once while they were dining at the Jade Palace she suddenly laid down her chopsticks, looked up, and emerged from her muteness.

And Guadeloupe? What was the place like? Was it like America? Were there white folks down there as well?

Spero remained stunned, caught off guard. White folks? Yes, he stammered, there were some. And even two types: the *békés* and the French French! From the expression on her face he realized the effect this truth was having and hurried to make amends. However this did not prevent those of other colors living their lives as they wished, loving each other, bringing up children, and living the good life. And thereupon Spero started to describe as best he could a multicolored, babbling, spicy, sweet-smelling island paradise like an article in the magazine *Partance*. The guiab, masked devils, thronging the streets during the carnival season. Vaval is dead! Long live Vaval! The *gwo ka* drum thumping its heart out: rat-a-tat-tat, rat-a-tat-tat. And the fishermen in *bakoua* hats smoking their small pipes and mending their nets under the almond trees.

But he was wasting his time and his saliva; she had already stopped listening.

All night long he turned over and over in his head questions he had never asked himself. What can you really say about Guadeloupe? What can be said about it? OK! The island is no longer the hell it once was. The *békés* from the Great Houses no longer grow fat from the sweat of the niggers. Yet over there in his Elysée palace the great white president still lays down the law. In his predicament Spero resolved to get a book that would provide an answer to his sudden soul-searching and went to Marcus's. Alas! The section on the Caribbean had only a few rather yellowed translations of *Notebook of a Return to My Native Land* and *The Wretched of the Earth*, whose opening lines he found singularly discouraging.

Shortly after this dinner, Roshawn did not show up again at the studio. He waited for her feverishly from morning to night like a teenager who had been stood up. He went and stood at the corner of Meeting Street, where you can see up and down Market and Line Streets. He walked to the No. 5 bus stop where she used to get off, suddenly realizing the place she occupied in his life and how his days would fall back into their rut of boredom and solitude without her. After two or three weeks of agony he decided to raise the subject casually with Debbie. It was breakfast time with its watery coffee, which he had finally got used to after twenty-five years. She looked up and stared him right in the white of his eyes. Roshawn? She was getting along fine and had made up her mind to finish her degree in mechanics. Where was she? At her own request, the social workers and the juvenile magistrates had sent her to a center at the other end of the state. There, she was in peace. While she gave him this news in her everyday voice, not a tone higher, her eyes judged him, looked daggers at him, and aimed a charge of contempt that he knew he did not deserve. Did not deserve.

Yet what could he say in his defense? Nobody would believe him. The mixed black and white jury, required by law, of right-minded members would unanimously declare him "Guilty"! And it was true. He had everything against him.

A notorious womanizer. An old ogre's body lying in wait for fresh meat. Even Linton, who was troubled by it all, did not believe a word of his objections and cautioned him against playing with minors, which was not a game. He never saw Roshawn again. Her portrait, which he finished from memory and christened *Rasta in Red*, was the only painting he sold during the entire tourist season.

Roshawn! Anita! To this very day, at times, they were part of the same heartache, as if they had been two children of his own that he had been unable to look after.

Was it true he had been a bad father?

All his errors, big and small, filed in disorder past the tribunal of his memory. No, he had never accepted accompanying Debbie to those school performances where the children sang, acted, and played music in front of their proud parents, nor to the annual school picnic on Daufuskie Island. Yes, he detested Mickey Mouse and preferred westerns where the whites kill the Indians in scarlet hemoglobin to the films of Spike Lee. And yes, he refused to have anything to do with all those political rallies, even those in support of Nelson Mandela.

Outside, the rain was starting to fall again, and he decided to close the window he had left wide open. It would not be long before Debbie came home. The headlights of her four-wheel-drive would carve two shining circles in the darkness and scare the timorous animals of the night. In a ritual he was unable to break, however hard he tried, he would go down and welcome her in the hall; she would hold out her cheek, still firm and smooth, and they would exchange a few meaningless words. Then they would retire to the solitude of their beds. And what if suddenly he said, "Listen, let's start all over again!"

From when?

From the day they got married?

Everyone had given up hoping for a fine day, for September had been a washout. The rain had swollen all the ponds on Grande-Terre, and the rivers of Basse-Terre had overflowed their banks, oozing thick and yellow down to the sea like pus.

Hovels ended up at the bottom of the gullies, turned inside out among the giant dasheen leaves, wood climbers, and volcanic pebbles. The streets of La Pointe looked like creeks, and the inhabitants of the Morne Verdol were tired of slipping and sliding in the mud. Those who were born before the Great War racked their brains trying to remember a rainy season like this one. But on that Thursday, 28 September 1963, the sun was at its station at six in the morning in a cloudless sky. Stepping out the front door and looking up to inspect all that blue above him, Spero, superstitious by nature, took this to be a good omen. It had been over a week since he had been able to sleep or make love to Debbie, who, comprehending, put it down to nerves. He was so sure that failing her father, who was dead and buried, an uncle in America, a letter, or a telegram would come and bar his road to happiness. For the future bride was too lovely, too high-bred for him! Too clever! She had read too many books! She could speak too many languages: English, French, and even Spanish, which he had heard her speak with Roberto, the Puerto Rican tailor in the rue Frebault, while he was taking the measurements for his tuxedo.

Marisia was cutting a roll of Chinese silk in mother-of-pearl for the wedding dress Debbie wanted — no frills or flounces, and nothing white. The same way she turned down a complicated ceremony on a Saturday for a simple wedding service at ten in the morning midweek followed by a drink with friends. Spero would have much preferred to shout his happiness from the roofs of the Morne Verdol for the whole of La Pointe and Guadeloupe to hear and rent the magnificent Hotel Diligenti that had just been completed with its fifty-four hundred square feet of ballroom in which to dance beguines, waltzes, and tangos. But he hadn't a cent to his name. In order to give his son a worthy, though cheerless, wedding, Justin had already taken to Berlucci the Italian the two or three pieces of jewelry Romulus had given Hosannah that the family kept in the bottom of a drawer for a rainy day.

Animals, in fact, are more sensible than men! The mongoose would never think of setting up house with the rabbit!

Nor the green-breasted hummingbird with the shrike! The infatuation that had whisked Debbie off in a well-behaved young lady's first act of folly could not last forever. For the sediments of all those previous generations of Charleston Middletons had settled in her layer upon layer. In her fashion, she wanted to finish the cruise that had been interrupted. That's why she chose to spend their brief honeymoon in Dominica. With her Baedeker open in front of her she counted the island's three hundred and sixty-five rivers, one for each saint of the year; she got lost in the dense forest under the tall trees and the giant ferns; and she dragged the reluctant Spero, suspicious of all those English-speaking blacks, to the top of the Morne Diablotin.

They spent almost two days at sea. The hull of the *Captain Morgan* carved its way through the wild waves with such a creaking that the passengers thought their last moment had come and recited the prayer for the dying in tears. Sitting up front, as stiff as a drakkar's figurehead, Debbie pressed lemon rind to her colorless lips.

The Baedeker gives three stars to the Sweetbriar Lodge and its modest rates, some twelve miles from Roseau on the road to the Pointe Michel. So it was not surprising that Americans, black and white, constantly filled its twelve rooms, which had a view of the beach covered in gray pebbles and red ixoras. Debbie's and Spero's neighbors were Willard and Vivian. They came from Washington, where Willard was the first black to teach law at Georgetown University and Vivian, an architect, was working on the rehabilitation of one of the worst ghettos in the capital. Willard was a member of the Committee for the Prevention of Juvenile Delinquency, and both of them were very active in the government's War on Poverty program. The previous year they had traveled to Senegal to organize the huge "Festival of Black Arts" and been received by President Senghor, who had presented them with a leather-bound copy of his works.

Spero had naively imagined that Debbie had landed on earth at nine in the morning the previous June when she emerged from under the almond trees on the wharf. No papa,

Maryse Condé

no mama, no earlier life. Suddenly he realized she came from another country and that a thousand invisible ropes tied her to a family, a past, and a people. When they were together, Willard, Vivian, and Debbie paid no more attention to him than a teacher pays a dunce at the back of the class. It started with the glass of orange juice at breakfast and ended with the herb tea of a thousand flowers after dinner. It continued while on their excursions by country bus, in the course of which the grandiose landscape went to great lengths for nothing, while swimming, and while tasting the *titi-ri* cakes and sipping fruit punches. Debbie was already on her cruise when hatred and revolt had set Harlem alight, and she only learned of it in a letter from her mother that was waiting in general delivery at St. Kitts. With Willard and Vivian, she cried over the forty-three dead.

It was at the Sweetbriar Lodge that for the first time Spero's heart tightened in his chest. All those corpses between his Debbie and him! All those hoses dousing the fires he had not lit! And now she was taking their moments of lovemaking for a time of treason! Now she only thought of dashing home as fast as she could to her country of riots and violence! He hugged her tight, so tight, in his arms, but she wriggled free and kissed him like a grown-up irritated by an over-affectionate child. For the first time he had the premonition, quickly relegated to the back of his mind, that one of these days she might very well be ashamed of him. And in order to cast out this burgeoning shame hidden deep inside her she told Willard and Vivian what he had secretly confided to her: the story of the ancestor.

Yes, it was then he should have started making decisions. Having it out with her. A long serious talk. Instead of which, he did not say a word. He listened; he watched the sea, as gentle as a cat whose striped fur flecked as far as Guadeloupe, clearly visible on a fine day.

Willard had listened to Debbie's story as if it were part of the nonsense that men like Spero spun to make a place for themselves in a woman's bed. From that moment on every time he came face to face with Spero his eyes greeted him.

Honor and respect, brother! You're an honor to the black
male. Vivian, however, took it very seriously, interrogating
him about his memories. What had he felt, as a small boy,
when his father told him of the royal blood that flowed in his
veins? Did he discuss it with his two younger brothers? What
did they think about it? Which part of Djéré's notebooks affected him the most? Sometimes she casually broached quite
different topics. So he was going to settle in America? Did he
think he would get accustomed to living in Charleston, in the
South? The South is another land. People think and act differently. She herself, born and raised in Washington DC, could
never get used to it.

As a result of this stay on Dominica and the acquaintances
she made, the Debbie who returned to the Morne Verdol for a
few days began to be another Debbie, a Debbie who was turning back to what she had previously been: the daughter of
George, the presumed martyr, and Margaret, daughter of Andrew Putnam, preacher at the Baptist Church of Samaria,
known for his clean and honest living.

If Margaret had been a boy Andrew would certainly have
wanted his first child to walk in his footsteps and become a
preacher. But it so happened she was a girl like the other four
kids his wife Rosetta gave birth to four summers in a row. He
therefore ignored her, considering it a shame and a mockery
from God, who so loves to test the minds and hearts of those
who love Him, that his semen had not been able to father a
single son and all he had in his house were five weak-bladdered
women.

Yet, no matter how much of a girl she was, Margaret was no
ordinary girl, and there was no doubt the Holy Spirit dwelt in
her. Even before she could read she knew the Holy Scriptures
and could improvise sermons for her little sisters. She could
recite without a single mistake the book of the prophet Daniel,
a special favorite of hers. At the age of ten, right in the middle

Maryse Condé

of a service, she had fallen into a trance, and on gaining consciousness had described her vision down to the last detail. Exactly like the blessed prophet who inspired her. The four winds of heaven over the sea. The first was like a lion and had eagle's wings. A second like a bear. Another like a leopard with four wings of a fowl. And the fourth with horns that had eyes like the eyes of a man. At the age of fourteen she began to read the future, and Rosetta had her work cut out preventing people from bothering her child, whom they took to be chosen by God. Margaret could see the sex of fetuses as early as the third week, when they were hardly formed in their mama's womb. She could name the men and women who were about to have their lives cut short and meet with a violent death. She knew those who tried to hide the heart of a fornicator and adulterer in their breasts and those who harbored evil. (People say that is how she saw the death of her own husband in Stokane and warned him of it. But since he never paid her any attention he took her words in vain and died a bloody death).

How life never tires of surprising us! Margaret, that young girl whom everyone thought singled out from her cradle by the Holy Spirit and reserved for God's holy ways, at the age of sixteen met George Middleton at a funeral, fell head over heels in love with him, and gave herself to him under circumstances that were only cleared up later. When she realized she was pregnant she lost all interest in food and drink. At first Rosetta did not worry too much about it, putting it down to those blessed states her daughter was accustomed to falling into. Then she noticed that while the child was curled up on her bed with a tortured expression and quivering lips she was murmuring, "George, George!" There is no George in the Holy Scriptures. The unfortunate mama finally discovered the truth. George Middleton had no intention of putting a ring on his finger, hence a rope around his neck. However, when Andrew Putnam threatened him not with hellfire but with a 12-gauge shotgun, he felt obliged to make amends.

Ortus, the couple's first child, died at birth. Margaret then remained five years sterile. She saw this death and sterility as a sign of the Lord's anger against her and from that moment on dressed only in deep mourning. When Debbie came to inhabit her womb, three years before Farah, she threw herself on her knees at the foot of the cross, believing herself to be reconciled with God. Her daughters, especially the eldest, then became the apples of her eye.

Hardly had she sized Spero up at Charleston airport in that fall of 1963 than her thirty or so years of experience told her she did not need the gift of second sight to see the life her beloved daughter was about to lead with such a husband by her side. From that moment on she vowed a fierce hatred for Spero and did everything she could to bring Debbie back to her senses. What games does God play with the hearts of women? Why does He have the most deserving fall for the good-for-nothings? The most virtuous for the depraved? The most hard working for the bone idle? The most affectionate for the hard of heart? The most candid for those who lie through their teeth?

At every hour of the day and night Margaret turned these questions over and over in her head. Unable to sleep in the dark she listened for the creaking of Debbie and Spero's bed, knowing full well that such pleasures are short-lived and that her child would soon be left with her heartache and her two eyes to cry with. In the morning while she served a hearty breakfast of grits, smoked ham, scrambled eggs, toast, and an assortment of marmalades — at that time they still knew how to eat on Crocker Island! — her eyes cast daggers at Spero. At church when the preacher promised hell to the fornicators and the nonbelievers she looked round ostentatiously at her son-in-law. She had never believed in this story of an ancestor, finding in this ridiculous set of lies yet another reason to hate him. And then don't all niggers descend from Africans, king or no king? Whenever she had the opportunity she would ridicule his accent, his tastes, and his manners.

Spero did not give his mother-in-law a tooth for a tooth. He was too afraid of her, and he was prevented from going too far by her imposing height, her skin, the color of black-bird's plumage, her eyes shining like distress beacons at sea, and her voice used to speaking on equal terms with the Holy

Spirit. And then he knew full well the cards had been dealt wrongly. He did not deserve her daughter!

It must be said in Margaret's defense that Debbie, a loving and devoted daughter, never let herself be influenced by her mother. Margaret did not have the satisfaction of seeing the couple drift apart. Besides, while she was alive Spero did his best to act the perfectly faithful husband. After his exhibition flopped at Marcus's bookstore he divided his time between his studio and teaching art classes at Corpus Christi, a Catholic school that boasted of being integrated because apart from its three hundred black students it numbered thirty or so whites and a few children of Cuban immigrants. There, unlike the public school system where Debbie taught, the uniformed teenagers were disciplined and respectful. They greeted their teachers with an open smile and looked at them without seeming to have something to hide. The school's restrooms did not stink of alcohol or marijuana.

Even so, despite their docile looks, at the end of the spring semester the students submitted a thick book of major and minor complaints to the Father Superior. They could not understand a word of the new teacher's English. The African Americans, easily the majority, no longer wanted to learn to draw from the *Venus of Milo, David, Victory of Samothrace*, or other white paintings good for white folks. They did not want to copy the white models of Ingres, Degas, or Renoir either. Weren't there any painters of African origin who had magnified the race and the black woman, the life and beauty of this world? And not only that! During these times when America reverberated with the uproar of Malcolm X's violence and Martin Luther King, Jr.'s nonviolence, not once, not a single time, had they heard the new teacher mention their names. Didn't he consider them heroes? They swore that if this black-skinned white teacher returned to Corpus Christi, they would go on strike! The Father Superior, a Canadian from Ottawa who liked to think he could speak a few words in French, was obliged to accept the student demands and give Spero his notice.

Spero was very upset by this dismissal, and his students' complaints distressed him considerably.

He had unthinkingly used in his classes the methods taught at his school of fine arts in Lille. He had never thought of David being white, nor of Ingres' *Baigneuse* as a white woman. For him they were but masterpieces of art. Was he wrong? Was he in fact alienated, as the students claimed? Does art have a color as well? As for the other accusation, Debbie had already reproached him for his lack of interest in the major events of his time. While she had shed tears generally reserved for relatives over Kennedy and even Malcolm X, whose ideas and methods she did not approve of, Spero had not lost any sleep over the two deaths. Brought up by Justin in the belief that politicians are liars and illusionists, he believed that politics was merely a way of cheating the world and carried with it its own punishment. Why should it be any different in America, black or white? Why should politicians be gods or martyrs?

Yet what tormented him the most was having to leave a high school where he had experienced enormous personal happiness. Under the trees of the school's recreation yard he seemed to relive his brief time at the Lycée Carnot where he had idled and played hooky so often he would probably have been flunked out on reaching sixteen. If he had not left for Lille, he would have had to be content like Maxo or Lionel with some boring office job in La Pointe. Now he regretted this idleness and all those afternoons he had spent boxing or kicking around a football instead of listening to the teachers' lessons. If he had studied harder there is no doubt that today he would be more deserving of his Debbie's pride.

Verbally, Debbie was highly indignant at his dismissal. Yet under her angry expression Spero thought he detected signs that she had been expecting it, as if she had already understood that all his undertakings were doomed to failure.

As for Margaret, she did not hide her joy, a joy she was not to savor for long since she passed away at the end of that very same summer from a heart attack. Since the death of her husband her heart had become slow and irregular. It had also been worn out by all those years of violence. Switching on the televison you were bombarded with pictures of police dogs, fire hoses, police officers armed to the hilt, and corpses oozing blood. The slaughter had spared nobody. Neither president nor priest. Neither student nor soldier. Nor anonymous citizen. Margaret begged Debbie to be careful. She imagined the worst every time her daughter was late coming home. With her head wrapped in a scarf against the chill of the night she would walk to the little landing stage, and coming off the last ferry Debbie and Spero would see her loom up in the headlights like those apparitions from another world the people of Charleston frightened their children with.

It could be said that Margaret saw her death coming. For the entire week her soul was melancholic. Her eyes hung on every movement Debbie made, and at any moment, without rhyme or reason, they would fill with water that streamed down her cheeks. When she spoke her voice had sudden quavers. Once as greedy as a cat and always stuffing herself with candy, she no longer came and sat at the table, and at mealtimes read over and over again her beloved Book of Daniel, raising her voice from time to time:

"But go your way to the end and rest, and you shall arise to your destiny at the end of the age."

On the afternoon of the fatal day she began to talk of her husband in such a way that Debbie and Spero could not believe their ears. It happened at the Jackson brothers' funeral parlor, where Ebenezer Williams was stretched out in his massive deluxe oak coffin after living a life in the fear of the Lord. Owing to the heat from the hundreds of candles and high-voltage electric light bulbs, the wreaths were fast withering, while friends and relatives wiped away the sweat that streamed down their faces and made half-moons under the women's armpits. Cool and dry in his suit of tussah, contrasting with all those heavy serge and woolen mourning clothes, handsome George Middleton was pretending to pray; in actual fact he was eyeing the women and trying to imagine their bodies without all that heavy apparel. He spotted Margaret seated in the first row of praying women, managed to kneel down beside her, and whispered, "Tomorrow, 5 P.M., on the steps of the Museum of the Confederation."

She did her best to be on time for the rendezvous.

At that time blacks were not allowed into the hotels in Charleston, so the couple made love in the house of one of his equally lecherous friends. Her blood reddened the white lace scalloped sheets that covered the bed and he hugged her, murmuring, "You couldn't have given me greater pleasure than that!"

Leaving Debbie and Spero stunned, Margaret returned to her room and lay down to die.

It was the season when the days were long and the sun went on sinking never-endingly to the horizon. The perfume of the frangipani flowers drifted on the wind to the very middle of the dining room.

Deadened by his memories Spero heard the shutter on the living-room window bang several times against the front of the house. The late hour amplified the noise, and it was like one of those bursts of machine-gun fire that more often than not tore through the nights of Charleston. He decided to go down and close it.

The night the ancestor died some very strange things happened in Blida.

Two Arabs in deep discussion as they came out of a café where they had drunk endless cups of green mint tea saw, as if it were a shadow, a small column of black clouds whirling like a dervish as it advanced from the far end of the street, now deserted at this late hour. This shadow, this little pile of clouds, passed in front of them with such a roar and at such a speed that the air round about churned and sloshed like the waters of a pond when whipped by a fierce wind. The two Arabs were thrown against the wall of the house behind them. Terrified, they grabbed hold of the beads hidden in the folds of their

Maryse Condé

burnooses and recited the *sha'hada*. The shadow continued down the street spreading the same disorder.

When it arrived on the outskirts of Blida, at the place where the houses end, at the place where the town surrenders to the sea of sand and cacti sticking up like candles before an altar, the shadow hesitated like someone looking for his way. It advanced two or three steps haphazardly and looked up to see if there was a sign in the sky. But that night the sky was nothing but a huge empty Moroccan leather purse. All it held was a frail crescent moon and a few faded stars like fake jewels scattered right and left. Then the shadow uttered a great sigh to give itself strength and encouragement on the long and arduous journey to Kutome. It knew it would have to walk forty days and forty nights before reaching the steps of the city of the dead that towers upside down in relation to that of the living. Forty days and forty nights. All alone. Without slaves. Nor Leopard wives. Without anyone to help. Just a few pathetic prayers from the women and children to help it on its way. It set out.

Some caravaneers returning from the desert, perched on mounts swinging their long scrawny necks, saw this whirling black shadow skimming the dunes like a dervish. But they took it to be a mirage in their tired eyes and whipping their animals hurried to seek the haven of their beds.

In the meantime, in the very neighborhood where the ancestor lived, people could hear the wind moan outdoors like a woman about to give birth. They could also hear the mad roaring of the sea, the sea that was miles away as the crow flies, at the foot of the cliffs of the white city of Algiers. Small children sat up in their cradles and, frightened by the din, started to shed hot tears. The infants, wrapped in old clothes and cradled by the warmth of their maman's body, whimpered in fear, clutching in their tiny hands the white bladders of their mother's breasts. The more courageous of the men went out into the courtyards and shouted questions at the dark. What did all these signs mean? Was this another trick in the making by the uncircumcised? The French authorities had just confiscated the last of the property belonging to the religious dignitaries. Tens of colonists had again settled in the Mzab. Others were cutting down the pine trees and *thujas* to grow the vines for their vineyards. Yet Lallah Fatima, whose eyes had been blessed with the secret of second sight, predicted these uncircumcised curs would leave. They would leave in years to come and the country they had sold down the river would try to find the way of Allah again.

In the house that death had visited Queen Fadjo organized the wake as best she could. The French doctor who came to certify the death notified the authorities, who in turn notified Paris. Everyone was most preoccupied: what was to be done with this wretched corpse? Bury it double quick? But where? The ancestor was neither Muslim nor Catholic. What cemetery would think of accepting the remains of a pagan? Everything had to be done to prevent the partisans of Add el-Kadir, who were up in arms and always ready to hatch a plot, from taking this old king without a kingdom as a symbol and making a hero out of him.

Since nobody could count on the grief-stricken Ouanilo, Princess Kpotasse busied herself preparing a place of rest for the body. She cut all the flowers in the patio and arranged them in vases: frangipani, large white lilies, camellias, oleanders, mauve azaleas, mimosa, and spray orchids from Tahiti that need the heat of the sun to grow to the height of a child along the riverbanks and on the hills.

Down from the third floor Spero had been standing for a while on the piazza breathing in the salty wind from the sea. The great bird of night had spread its wings and plunged the sky into darkness. Not a star. Not even a tiny quarter of a moon.

The murky waters of the past surged forward and in doing so burst open the sluice gates of his memory.

It is a fact that the men in the Jules-Juliette family had always been bone idle and squandered the money of their mothers,

grandmothers, and wives. After his dismissal from Corpus
Christi, Spero found himself in the same position as Justin
and Djéré, obliged to beg from Debbie. She did not complain,
but proceeded in her own fashion. At the beginning of each
month she would line up on a table in the hall, beside a copper
vase always filled with fresh flowers, a series of envelopes bearing the names of their addressees in red ink: Mamie Garvin;
Flipper, the one-eyed gardener who four times a month
slipped on his rubber gloves to prune the azaleas in the garden
and burn the dead leaves; and Jeff, the handyman who un-
loaded the wood for the furnace, checked the pressure on the
radiators, and fed the toothless, cantankerous cats who, one
fine day, settled in as tenants from out of the blue. The enve-
lope with his name placed alongside those of the domestic
help humiliated Spero's heart. He would have liked to voice
his feelings to Debbie but did not dare. Linton, in whom he
confided, was sympathetic to his case and wanted to help.
That's how he introduced him to one of his acquaintances,
a certain Major Dennis.

Major Dennis occupied a suite at the Old Battery Hotel,
which had just been desegregated, and the good souls of
Charleston whispered that his mother had worked in the
kitchens there. He was an imposing jet-black man who spoke
with such a heavy southern accent that Spero's untrained ear
could make no sense of what he said. Fortunately, he spoke a
few words of French and even Creole that he had learned from
some Haitians while living in Belgium. He was one of those
unsavory characters who try to turn everything to their advantage. War profiteer and exploiter of the people, his color did
not bother him. Had he lived sunning himself under the slave
trade he would surely have made a fortune selling the flesh of
his own brothers. Once he had connections with the ghettos
of Kingston, Jamaica, and for a price procured the joys of
motherhood for the good folk of Charleston yearning for a
child. Once he had lived in Africa and was in charge of supply-
ing flesh for visiting presidents and heads of state. Wherever
he went he peddled soft and hard drugs. He had recently come
up with a very simple idea that he explained in great detail to

Spero. Since Charleston's smart set was wild about naive paintings from Haiti, why not give them their money's worth and roll off a series of Rigaud Benoits, Delnatuses, Wilson Bigauds, Sénèque Obins and even Préfète Dufaults? In order to dispose of them they would open an art center run by a Haitian from New York for the sake of local color . . . Spero was tempted. It was easy money. And then how would anyone discover the fraud? The Haitians outdid themselves copying everyone else. After some hard bargaining with Major Dennis, Spero managed to obtain a small advance, a few hundred dollars, but negotiated a fabulous contract.

From then on, coming to terms with a bad conscience without too much difficulty, he spent weeks finishing off copies of two Jasmin Josephs, *The Wedding of Adam and Eve* and *The Paradise of Animals*. This bestiary procured him such delight that he wondered whether these lions and elephants standing on their two hind legs, these giraffes clothed in pastel-tinted coats, and those monkeys playing with tigers in the depths of the forest had not come out of his own imagination. Was he really a forger?

Sometimes Major Dennis stopped discreetly by to see him and expressed his satisfaction on inspecting the canvasses. One morning while he was hard at work, instead of the Major it was Linton who rushed into the studio, stammering like a madman. Major Dennis had just been arrested in his suite at the Old Battery Hotel. Both men stared at each other in terror. The police were probably reserving the same fate for his accomplices. Without losing a second, they emptied the studio and hurried to the Montego Bay, where they set fire to the paintings. While watching his dreams of ill-gotten wealth go up in smoke, Spero likened himself to the killer Landru burning his victims.

For days on end he trembled. What would happen if they came to arrest him? What if his name appeared on the front page of the *Black Sentinel of Charleston*, but this time in a most shameful way? "Guadeloupean painter arrested for forgery and possession of stolen goods." What would Debbie say?

The mere sight of a police cap glimpsed by chance in the

street sent his body into a sweat and his legs into a tremble. He holed himself up on Crocker Island as if the island solitude afforded him protection. When Margaret passed away, he was in such a state he was unable to savor the death of his old enemy, as should have been the case. On the contrary, he thought of the shame he would bring on Debbie at a time when she was already sorely tried. As for Debbie, she took his expression to be one of grief and was surprised to see how much he mourned her mother.

However, his fears proved to be unfounded. The days went by and nobody came for Spero. Major Dennis's trial did not arouse much interest. Just a few lines in the *Black Sentinel* which, moreover, was not inclined to wash dirty linen in public and had enough on its hands with the murder of Malcolm X. Sure, the middle class in Charleston hated his ideas, but a nigger is a nigger. And death is death.

Soon the river of life started to flow again.

Farah, who had just married Charles Thomas Jr., arrived from Piscataway to bury her mother, and the two sisters who had not lived together for years found themselves under the same roof. It was inevitable that they — and all those who crowded in to offer their condolences to the remaining Middletons of Crocker Island — would compare husbands. But how could you compare the courteous, affable, polished Charles, with a smile on his lips and a promising future, to Spero? Debbie was perfectly aware of the low rating her choice would get her. She defended herself as best she could, casually recalling that Charles had merely profited from other people's struggles for racial equality to get into Harvard and study business law. It was these very same struggles that had allowed him to stash himself away in Piscataway and open one of the first integrated law offices with two white partners from his class. In a word, he had established his success on the backs of others. Debbie's mouth spoke like that, but deep inside her soul was telling her something else. As a result her attitude toward Spero changed. Since there was no longer any reason to be afraid of hurting the already sorely tried heart of her poor recently departed mama, she dropped all pretences and occasionally became impatient or angry with him. Yes, that was when their first real quarrels began: those that the caresses of the night cannot heal. Moreover, Debbie had started to turn her back on him in bed, and wounded in his pride he refused to lay hands on this hostile flesh. When he was far from Debbie he invented a thousand ways of making up to her. When he was near her he felt belittled, ugly, and pathetic.

At this point it was inevitable therefore that he thought of enhancing his image in the looking glass of another woman. Not very adventurous at the time, he did not venture very far, and looked at his reflection in the eyes of Jeanne, Debbie's first cousin.

Spero was intelligent enough to realize that he did not owe this surprisingly easy first conquest to the qualities of his own person. Jeanne and Debbie had been rivals since school. What one had, the other bent over backwards to obtain as well. However uninteresting he was, he represented a position to be taken in their strategy of combat. By spying on each other so much, Jeanne and Debbie had ended up becoming very similar. Making love with one or the other, Spero had to be careful not to cry out the wrong name. Jeanne was more kittenish than Debbie, less intellectual, taking pleasure for what it was. In private she knew all too well how to forget the thousands dead in Vietnam, the fires on the campuses, and other serious topics to indulge in her passion for spiritualism. She dressed in white veils, wrapped her head in a white turban, and called on all the dead in her family in turn — especially her younger sister, snuffed out in a car accident at the age of sixteen. She got it into her head to call on the ancestor and claimed he had obediently answered. And it was true, the evenings when with eyes tightly shut she called his name the round table cavorted about and kicked violently at the floor. According to Jeanne, the ancestor was happily at peace where he was, since he had found the way to Kutome without too much difficulty and sent for Ouanilo, his favorite son, very early on. His spirit was no longer tormented by events on earth. Yes, the French had deprived him of the company of his ancestors who were all laid to rest in Abomey. When they agreed to return his mortal remains to Dahomey, they had him buried far from his ancestors in his native village. But all that mattered very little any more.

Jeanne's other great passion was the meaning of dreams. She analyzed everything: light sleep dreams, deep sleep dreams, and especially dreams from the third type of sleep, those dreamed in the predawn hours when the spirit is preparing helter-skelter to leave the shadow of night to confront the glare of the sun. Spero did not believe a word of all this nonsense, which reminded him of the superstitions of the Morne Verdol, and refused to go along with her questionings. Until the day he described to Jeanne a dream of three fish lying on a large silver platter, their mouths biting woefully into a bunch of herbs, and she predicted he was going to hear of a pregnancy. The very next day Debbie announced she was pregnant.

Was it true he had been a bad father?

A bad husband, very bad, OK! But a bad father? So perhaps the birth of their child had been the chance to start all over again?

He happened to be with Jeanne when Debbie went into labor and had to call the nearest neighbors, a white family who lived six miles away on the cliffs on the eastern side of the island. In the past the Middletons had had words with these white folks, for they represented the invaders who gradually evicted the blacks from the Sea Island land they had occupied since the end of the Civil War in order to build villas with swimming pools and magnificent ocean views. But things had changed. Now blacks and whites had to learn to live together, and the white family had rushed to the rescue. While waiting for the ferry Debbie had almost given birth in their jeep, and everyone was all shaken up.

All this had angered Spero considerably. For weeks, as her time on the calendar grew closer, he had begged Debbie to go stay with one of the numerous Middleton relatives who lived in Charleston. She paid no attention. Her dream was to give birth at home like her ancestor Eulaliah, who had brought thirteen children into this world in the house on Crocker Island, all alone, with only the help of a servant. As soon as she was delivered she would tie a strip of linen cloth tight around her belly and go and bury the placenta under one of the trees in the garden, which she would name after the newly born.

All this nonsense was old wives' tales! Spero could not get it out of his head that Anita had emerged from Debbie's womb as she was today — doleful, whining, lacking strength and appetite — because of all those scares incurred at the dawn of her existence.

There was of course another explanation that secretly tormented his mind. Night after night the waters of love should bathe the fetus, lubrifying its little members and exercising its joints. The parents' kisses should dissolve into the blood so that it can soak them up. But despite all his grand resolutions he was unable to leave Jeanne, and throughout the pregnancy she came between Debbie and him. Despite his happiness with being a father and the father of a daughter, these thoughts made him feel awkward when embracing his child. He wondered deep down whether he was not the cause of her weakness, her failings, and her ungainliness. Finally, he was slightly ashamed of her as if his sin had come out into the open for all to see. Did Debbie in her adeptness see all that? Had he wanted to protect the child from all that with an irreproachable love?

Anita was about two years old when a retrospective of Jacob Lawrence's work was held at Marcus's Bookstore. The black painter had just been awarded national recognition, and coming after other signs it appeared to announce a wind of change. At long last America was casting off its tattered remnants of racism! At long last the dream of Reverend King was no longer a dream! In the euphoria of the moment Marcus had spared no effort. He had managed to convince the Whitney Museum to lend him *Toussaint-Louverture* and *Migrations*, which some considered to be the apogee of the painter's work, and sent out almost five hundred invitations to blacks as well as whites.

That day Spero and Debbie had quarrelled yet again. Debbie had her own ideas on education, maintaining that the earlier the senses are trained to behold beauty, the better they profit from it. Hadn't she herself, when she was hardly two, nestling in her mother's lap, seen Paul Robeson play Othello at the Schubert Theater? And didn't she religiously keep the magic in her memory?

So they took the child. Rigged out in silk and lace, puny and pitiful, she tottered around the gallery and suddenly stopped in front of *Tombstones*, Spero's own favorite. She went right up to the painting, close enough to touch it, then suddenly turned round to her mother and clapped her hands. Then after a triumphant look in the direction of Spero, Debbie picked her up and showered her with kisses.

How can we tell whether it was not this cloudburst of love, like torrents of rain, that lay the seeds for beauty to blossom within her, transforming her with a compelling force? How can we tell whether it was not this love he had been deprived of that made him what he was?

Who knows? Marisia showed a little tenderness only for Maxo, though he was the blackest of the three, stocky and thickset, with the crooked legs of a boxer. He was the one she showered with pet names and called *gason à manman*, a mommy's boy. It was for him she brought home from the market wrapped in a piece of paper a pistachio nougat or a *suk à koko*, a coconut candy with a pink topping! It seemed to Spero that Marisia had hugged and kissed him only once, as if she knew she was never going to set eyes on him again while she was alive: the day he had left for Charleston.

In those days planes were not a common sight. Those who could, dashed to Le Raizet airport to watch their wings skim the trees of the mangrove and make a dive for the runway. The others, oblivious to the cars hooting their horns, remained standing in the middle of the streets of La Pointe with their noses in the air to watch them fly over their heads. Since there were no direct steamer connections between La Pointe and

America, Debbie and Spero had to travel via Puerto Rico. The
family had accompanied them, therefore, with Justin grieving
in tow, to the end of the wharf, cluttered with crates, bundles,
packing straw, and canvas, where the *Tampico* was waiting
for them cramped between two colossuses bound for Saint-
Nazaire. The *Tampico*, which two days earlier had arrived
with a cargo of oxen for meat and drawing loads, was leaving
empty, except for crates of soap from Marseilles and jars of
olive oil ordered by a dealer from Fajardo.

Spero could not keep back his tears. He had a hunch he
would never see his family again in this world. He squeezed
Justin's hand hard enough to crush it. He hugged Marisia who
for once did not rebuff him. Yet, once they arrived in San Juan,
his eyes dried instantly.

Such opulence a few leagues from his Cinderella of Guadeloupe! He had always believed it a great misfortune to be born
a West Indian, that "West Indies" was synonymous with mediocrity. But here was Puerto Rico contradicting him. The
white facades of the five-star luxury hotels hugged the edge
of the ocean that was less blue than the blue of the swimming
pools. The eye got tired of measuring the expanse of the golf
courses and the height of the palms along the royal four-lane
avenues. In the windows of the shopping arcades all the luxury
goods were at dream's reach. Debbie wasted her breath repeating in every tone of voice that it was nothing but a tourist
trap. The Puerto Ricans themselves were huddled in the ghettos of El Fanguito and La Perla or fled to New York, where
they huddled in another ghetto, El Barrio, a new research
topic for sociologists. Spero wasn't even listening. He was
amazed. In the early afternoon they staggered up to the citadel of San Felipe del Morro overlooking the bay. While Debbie, armed with a guidebook, recounted the misadventures
of Francis Drake and his obscure death in Panama, Spero day-
dreamed astride a rusty cannon. During the voyage from San
Juan to New York a group of American businessmen on board
gave him a first taste of what Debbie, Willard, and Vivian
had tried to prepare him for. Never could he meet their eyes,
whose steely look pierced his body to reach a point somewhere

in space. It became his obsession. Though neither insolent nor quarrelsome, he got to the point of standing in their way on purpose in order to stare into the whites of their eyes. Nothing doing. Dressed identically in anthracite gray with blue ties and silvery hair, strolling along the deck, downing a beer after a scotch at the bar or taking their meals in the common dining room, the Americans ignored him totally, and in doing so signified he was not worthy to be called a man. That he was not even an ugly, repulsive animal. Or vegetable. Or mineral. Simply that he did not exist on the surface of the earth.

The few days he spent in New York only confirmed these impressions.

The Middleton named Daniel, who in 1917, against the advice of his brothers and sisters, left Charleston to settle in New York, had not gotten further than 135th Street in Harlem. With his inheritance he bought himself a three-story house with a basement, moved in his wife, ten children, and a widowed mother-in-law, then set about looking for work. But New York was not Charleston; he understood that very quickly. In New York, a Middleton was nothing but a very ordinary nigger, a nigger like all the rest, a black nigger, a nigger at his blackest. No employer would take his printer's certificate into account, and all he could find was a job as a doorman: six hours wearing his soles out on the sidewalk of the White Palace Hotel on Fifth Avenue, opening and closing cab doors and receiving tips from white folks. He never got used to it. At the end of his life, in 1940, for he died early, he wrote to his prosperous barber of a brother who had remained behind on Crocker Island, "Everybody's mistaken. The North is in the South and the South is in the North."

When Debbie and Spero arrived in the house on 135th Street its walls were weatherbeaten, its paint peeling, its facade uncleaned for ages. The building had the appearance of an old leper, ashamed of its pustules and stumps. Inside, the heating had been torn out and the radiators were purely decorative; the bathroom had no running water, the kitchen no gas, and in the bedrooms the springs had burst through the mattresses, piercing the cheap sheets. At the age of sixty-seven, Louise, Daniel's widow, still laced up her boots over her swollen ankles and come rain or shine valiantly marched down to 40th Street to empty trash in the offices. And yet these were seemingly false appearances, for the stairwell was papered with all sorts of diplomas awarded to all sorts of Middletons. Hairdresser's diploma. Nurse's aide diploma. Masseuse's aide diploma. Cook's diploma. Baker-pastrymaker's diploma. Dump truck driver's diploma. Auto mechanic's diploma. Boilermaker-galvanizer's diploma. Gardener's diploma. And last but not least, a theologian's diploma.

Standing in front of each diploma with its heavy copper frame, Louise obligingly recounted her children's success stories and, with eyes lifted heavenwards, gave thanks to God. She led Debbie and Spero to their bedroom for the night, cluttered with cups and trophies, and explained, down to the very last detail, how and where her athletic boys had won them. The next day, which was a Sunday, everyone who was a Middleton in New York, even small children and babes in arms, met to attend service at the Reverend Adlai Middleton's Baptist church on 118th Street. The Holy Spirit possessed Adlai at a moment when just like Ezekiel he spewed up the false prophets. Spero's stomach was still reeling from this religious bacchanalia when he had to ingurgitate chicken, spinach, rice, congo peas, bacon, pumpkin pie (which he took an immediate dislike to), and vanilla ice cream. It was on that day, with his hand clutching Debbie's under the table like a little boy clinging to his mother on the first day of school, deafened by a manner of speaking as incomprehensible as the gibberish of the Wayana tribe, that he had the feeling America would always remain out of his reach. A safe whose combination he would never possess. He had no key to its yesterday nor the days before yesterday. Even less the days before the days before yesterday. How could he understand today?

On leaving Adlai's they walked along streets as black as

hearses that the approaching night made even more sinister. All the despair of the earth had gathered on the faces of the men and women they passed. Upset, Spero swore he would never set foot in New York again. He kept his word, for he only came back twenty years later for Anita's graduation.

Back on 135th Street the family had a light meal of chicken paté. Someone sat down in front of the highly polished piano, the only luxurious object amid the sorry state of the house, and everyone sang "Amazing Grace" in unison. Then Debbie, who had managed somehow to tell Louise of the ancestor, read an extract from the notebooks of Djéré, "The Fire of Abomey," amid a religious silence.

In the train that took them back to Charleston, Spero could not refrain from asking Debbie for an explanation. Why were the Middletons of New York so content with their existence that they never stopped thanking God? She smiled with infinite compassion and whispered, "Because they are survivors!"

The Notebooks of Djéré   *Number Seven*

The Fire of Abomey

On 4 November 1892 the troops of General Dodds entered Kana, the town of the oil palm groves, and massacred
everything alive. The rumor of the slaughter spread as far as
Abomey, a day's march away, and my father recalled what his
bokono had been seeing and saying for several days: the fateful
day had come. So he removed the mortal remains of his father
from their refuge in the earth and conveyed them to a safe
place, which he kept secret. Then he spent the remainder of
the day in prayer, burning incense in jars. Finally, he made his
decision.

At nightfall, while his soldiers and Amazons set fire to the
four corners of Abomey as instructed, he applied the torch
with his own hands to the palace inherited from his ancestors.
The palace was protected by huge earthen walls pierced by
two entrances, one of which was exclusively reserved for the
king and those accompanying him. Inside these walls every
king had added his own palace to that of his predecessor for
the past ten reigns of our dynasty. Which meant that the palace covered a considerable amount of ground. (It could easily
house La Pointe and all its inhabitants.) The various buildings
of the palace — the quarters for the women, ministers, warriors
and priests — were roofed with straw laid on a ribbed framework of raffia palm. Holding a torch in his hand my father
heaved himself up onto the silk-cotton wood throne that
rested on the four skulls of enemy chiefs, stood up to his full
height, and tried to set fire to the straw. At first the flames
balked at the sacrilege they were being asked to commit, and
hiding behind a thick black smoke, uttered a series of sighs as
if they were trying to smother themselves. But greed got the
upper hand. The fire finally uncurled its coiled body and flick-
ered its flat, triangular head with huge catlike eyes. For a few
seconds it was content to lick the straw greedily until, unable

to resist, it devoured the roof, walls, and furniture in a single mouthful. My father and his family then hurried out of the palace and left the town.

Abomey is an island. The *daadaa* built it on a plateau some forty-eight miles from the low, swampy coast so they could defend it from all sides. Once he had descended to the surrounding plain my father stopped to look behind him. The entire plateau was in flames and the sky above like a calabash of blood. Clusters of stars whirled into the air and sparks were exploding just about everywhere. The din of the fire joined the noise of the wind from the ocean that fanned the flames like a jeweler's bellows.

Every time my father described this nightmare I started to cry. He would kiss my sticky, salty cheeks, and holding me tight he would say, "There is no need to cry. There is a need to avenge me. All my sons must avenge me." His words made me cry even harder. It was as if I could foresee the wretchedness of my existence and knew I would never be up to his expectations and that I could never avenge him.

After having watched his palace go up in flames, my father remained motionless with his head between his hands. Respecting his grief, the high priests went into prayer, and the *bokono* made divinations to know what the future now held in store for them. Finally he got up. Then with his faithful followers of Amazons, *bokono*, warriors, high priests, women, and children he set off for the forest. There in its womb he lived for almost two years, unbeknownst to the French who hounded him like a beast, protected by his gris-gris and the magic of his *bokono*.

With bitter heart, he mused. He had been stripped of everything. Palace. Army. Slaves. Prisoners. Silver. Gold. Palm oil. Not even a thatched roof over his head. No more wars to undertake. No more victories to win. All his flesh had shriveled, leaving nothing but bones that rattled when he moved. His hair was tangled and long like his subjects', who still wore mourning for his father and were already attired for him. His hair had changed color like the grasses of the bush in the dry season. So when he walked in the dark he was encircled by a moonlit glow. However, he still stood as tall and straight as the trunk of an ironwood tree.

The forest! That's where it all began! That's where it will all end!

Green on a green branch, a toad flicks on and off the glowing lights of its eyes. Down below in the hollow of the buttress roots run crabs with fierce pincers. The ancestor trudged on sure-footed, his head level with the giant tree ferns. He was struggling with his anguish. What crime had he committed on succeeding his father to the throne? Had he been too much in love with power and honor? Or women? Perhaps he had done something when he was a child? Or even before being conceived in the womb of Mehutu, his mother? Or else was it all her fault? Since she was a princess from Aja country who was unfit to give birth to a king. They said that only her magic had kept her son seated on the throne. They also said she had removed one by one all those who might challenge his glory. Oh, the vanity of it all! Now death, who goes sandalless and barefooted, was approaching.

In the black waters of the inundated forest float the fish and the dead corpses of the trees, as heavy as coffins. All that was left of his court assembled in a clearing. In the hollows of the earth the slaves managed to cook purple-flesh snails, monkeys scorched alive, and wild plantains. The children smoked out the bees with moss to collect the honey and snatched the soft fruit of the pupunha palm from its branches. Sometimes a quetzal firebird fell sparkling from the green canopy that soared out of eye's reach.

When the bats began to fly to the top of the trees with their large shroudlike wings, they knew night was approaching. So, together with his musicians, my father struck up some *cantilenas* he had composed himself while in Abomey. He sang of fame that is fleeting, glory that is tarnished, riches that melt away, and this life that nobody escapes alive. Listening to him, men, women, and even little children felt tears well up in their eyes, but hid them from him. For if my father noticed it he would have gone into a fit of rage. What were they crying for? Wasn't all this the hand of fate?

When my father recalled the treachery of the French who without reason had begun to wage war against him, he flashed his eyes and ground his teeth, and his sweet fatherly face became as frightening as a sorcerer's who thrives on evil. What did they want from him? Hadn't he honored their king with six large wrappers woven in gold thread, a parasol for a *cabeceira*— a warlord — and four children, two boys and two girls he himself had picked from the princes and princesses of royal blood?

During the two years he lived in the forest, the animals came to pay my father daily homage. The elephant, whose gray hide is cracked like the mud of a dried-up lake, the spotted bittern, the giraffe, whose head sways like a fruit on the end of a branch, the zebra, the Dama gazelle, the antelope, all the nocturnal and diurnal birds of prey, and even the lion with his coat the color of ripe papayas. All came out of their hiding to prostrate themselves before him. They recalled that he was the son of the animal king, he whose roar signifies death by stealth. Sometimes the high priests collected a little of their blood in buffalo horns and my father drank it as a beneficial potion, for blood and the milk of a woman are life-giving forces.

On awakening one morning there was no daylight. The blackness of the air resounded with the cries of bats. The water that seeped through the foliage was warm and black, like a rain of ashes, as if suddenly a volcano was angrily spewing its entrails. The *bokono* were gripped with anguish and lent over their divinatory plates. One of them seized a scaly anteater and cut it down the middle. Unperturbed by its nauseating smell he inspected in detail the insides of its belly. Then he spoke lengthily in muffled tones in the ear of my father, whose face turned the color of death. My father retired under the shelter the slaves had made for him with fronds and young branches of a palm tree. Throughout the day he could be heard calling on the *daadaa* and nobody dared utter a word. After many hours of meditation he emerged from his refuge, called five of his wives, took his son Ouanilo and the Princess Kpotasse by the hand, and walking straight ahead gave himself up to the

Maryse Condé

French officers who were waiting for him at Gobo where they were stationed.

As he spoke to me, however, my father forgot the bitterness of those days in order to remember their paradoxical sweetness. He wondered whether they had not been the happiest of his life. He had been stripped of everything. He had been as light as air. No more wars to undertake. No more victories to win. Only death to hope for.

When the cruel and arrogant French laid hands on my father and treated him like a prisoner of war, a great burning wind rushed down from the deserts of the north. It scorched everything in its passage. It scorched the trees. It scorched the plants. It scorched the water of the ponds. It scorched the animals. It scorched the children and even the fetuses in the folds of their mothers' wombs. It scorched the old folk. It spared only the men and women in the prime of life so that they could run and carry the terrible news to the four corners of our kingdom, to those who had not heard. *Zanku*! Night has fallen!

The women who remained alive then undid the hair on their heads. The men let the hair grow on their bodies. Some crushed their testicles with stones so that they could not beget, and there was desolation in the land.

An unkempt path led from the piazza to the garage, the former stable where in their days of splendor the Middletons had kept a thoroughbred. At the time, the other blacks, full of envy, said it was just as well all this opulence was hidden on Crocker Island where nobody ever set foot. For if the KKK got wind of it, they wouldn't hesitate to teach the Middletons a lesson and set a match to it.

It was the same envy that embittered their hearts when Thomas Middleton Jr. bought one of the first automobiles a black had ever driven in the streets of Charleston, except for a few powerful ministers of religion. That was in April 1929, and it was a salmon-pink Dodge. A photo lost in the family albums showed Thomas Jr. leaning against the hood of his new acquisition, his boys huddled up close to him; George, his favorite, sitting on the right fender, his elbow resting on a big round headlight, a cheeky kid in his double-breasted suit hiked up over a pair of knee-length striped socks.

On the other side of the gate, which opened with a grating sound under the trees, was the road that went all the way round the island: from the west side with its low swampy coastline and as many crab holes as a sieve to the east side bristling with bluffs and cliffs.

Without realizing it, like a sleepwalker in his sleep, Spero found himself walking in the rain close to the gate. The water clung to his strawlike hair then trickled down his neck and soaked his old sweatsuit. But he did not feel the damp. To the right were the pale flickering lights of the small landing stage. They would be switched off at half past midnight after the last ferry had arrived with its last few remaining passengers. It was now only 7:30 P.M. But because of the darkness and the silence it felt like the middle of the night. There was no record of any crime on Crocker Island. No theft. No rape. The only deaths

reported were those out hunting crabs or oysters who had
been carelessly caught unaware by the incoming tide. A few
days after they had been swallowed up by the sea their bodies
would be washed up like a heap of disjointed puppets on the
sand, already the color of mourning. And yet the darkness
fueled the imagination with fearful and disturbing pictures.

If Debbie had not stayed too long at Paule's she would be
home on the next ferry. What would he tell her when he
saw her?

"Listen, let's start all over again!"

But from when? What time? When had the record got
stuck in the groove? When had the tape started to grate and
the frames of the film overlap and accelerate before they finally
stopped? Dead. After the birth of Anita he turned over a new
leaf. Besides, Jeanne had got married to a brilliant economist,
one of the first blacks the government appointed to the diplomatic corps. People said the couple had been going out
together for ages, and anyone with eyes could see them in a
lover's tête-á-tête in the recently desegregated diners of Charleston. If that was true, Spero felt proud of having shared Jeanne
with such a man, a six-foot-six "piece of the Indies" who in any
fight would have surely punched him to a *chiktaye* of shredded
codfish. Jeanne had first gone to live in Guinea, then Senegal,
then Nigeria. Sometimes her photo appeared in *Essence* in
designer dresses, smiling beside her husband. At first she had
written Spero letters eight to ten pages long. It had somewhat
surprised him. Was she that fond of him? Then he realized
that those letters were in fact addressed to themselves. They allowed her to look her own doubts in the face. Instead of indiscreetly reading them he should have sent them back: return to
sender. For once over her initial enthusiasm, she became disillusioned. Africa was no longer in Africa. Temples to Mammon
were replacing the mosques and the churches. The charismatic
leaders had lost their charisma, and from the north to the
south, from the east to the west, the reign of the thugs had
started. During the last dry season she had accompanied her
husband on a mission to Benin. Her heart was beating with
joy at the idea of treading the native soil of the ancestor. Alas!

The palaces were in ruin. The people were only interested in their daily lot and singing the praises of their military masters of the universe. Only the priestesses with their flaccid breasts in the temple of Dan honored the memory of the past. Now Jeanne no longer wrote to him, and Spero had lost track of the African country where she lived. When he had any news it was through Debbie, whom the family kept informed of every echelon in her husband's diplomatic career down to the very last detail. Every time she heard them bragging, Debbie went into a fit. Was it for this that Malcolm X, Martin Luther King, and so many ordinary people had lost their lives? For blacks to go as far away as Africa to execute the orders of the white powers? While being careful not to argue with her, Spero put her words down to the old jealousy that after all this time had never healed. Black power, white power, it no longer meant anything. Just as money has no smell to it, power has no color to it. It's not white. It's not black.

Life's funny isn't it? Who would have thought Jeanne would have made the return trip to Africa?

Before Anita.

Spero had secretly written to the embassy to enquire about his daughter. Very quickly a reassuring answer came back from one of the secretaries. Anita was the pride of the Peace Development Team. Her village of Paogo had become a model village. Under her initiative the villagers had successfully tried growing rice and formed a food cooperative. Mademoiselle Jules-Juliette did not stop at field work. She had learnt the language of the region and was giving classes in development theory to the men and women.

His child, a development expert? Come on now! Spero saw the hand of the ancestor at work. Oh? So Spero had treated the memory of his name like a fairy tale? Oh? So he did not want to behave like the son of the Leopard? He had lived a spineless existence, without ambition, without ever turning his head toward the country he came from. His crimes could not be pardoned. Yes, it was the ancestor, and the ancestor alone, who was punishing Spero by snatching away what he cherished most on earth and leaving him nothing but an empty heart and mind.

When Anita had stopped being Anita, rebuffing Debbie or addressing her in cutting, grouchy monosyllables, Spero believed his revenge was at hand. At last, the bird's offspring was peeping out from her mother's wing, shaking her feathers and preparing for her flights of exploration. At last, his hour had come, for he was certain that in her desire for freedom Anita would venture into his camp and be persuaded to stay. He was already preparing in his head the words he would say to keep her:

"Listen, I'm not what they say I am. An old bag of bones, a dying man, a zombie who has not found his salt. I merely want to take life as it is: a potion that nothing can sweeten. I don't need lies or gilded illusions."

But once again he had calculated wrongly. Anita may have turned her back on Debbie, but she was not turning to him.

In early 1980, in February to be exact, a man came to occupy a house on Hearst Street where nobody had set foot for years, except for some shady niggers looking for some shady deals. Hearst Street was the main artery of one of those infamous black neighborhoods that mushroom on the outskirts of big cities to the utmost shame of the middle classes of the same color. The good people of Charleston, who like to trace back in time the great-great-great grandparents of all those who have the nerve to settle in their town, were acutely embarrassed. Nobody, but nobody, could say where this Brother Xangomusa came from. Because of his reddish dreadlocks that reached down to the belt on his jeans and a kind of angular face like Bob Marley's, some people thought he must come from Jamaica. But those who had heard the sound of his voice asserted that he could have been born and bred only in Brooklyn. The most peculiar stories were rumored about. Some said he had spent years among the Cholo Indians of Colombia selling wicker baskets to tourists to survive. Others, among the Pygmies of Gabon eating their diet of honey and smoked monkey meat. And others said he had lived with the leopard hunters of Kordofan on the borders of Abyssinia. Malicious tongues whispered he had been released from a penitentiary in Colorado where he had been incarcerated fifteen years earlier for the rape of a young girl. Even more wicked were those who asserted he was one of the few to have escaped from the Jonestown sect, which had the suicide of over nine hundred people on its conscience.

Brother Xangomusa had a following of a dozen rather shabby boys and girls, three of whom were white, all with identically shaven heads. The little band set about plastering over the holes and repainting the front of the house on Hearst Street, throwing out junk, scrubbing the floors, papering over the walls, and moving in benches, chairs, long tables, and various musical instruments. After all the commotion was over, one fine morning, Brother Xangomusa perched himself on the last step of a ladder and hung a banner on the recently whitewashed facade bearing the words

CENTER OF UNIVERSAL LOVE
beauty has not yet been born on our earth

The neighborhood jobless and drug addicts took no notice. Neither did the mothers with a family to support or the old folk left uncared for, worn out by the worry of surviving. Brother Xangomusa, so it seemed, belonged to a species all too familiar. For ever since the sun first cast its rays over our world, misery has made a bed for all sorts of gentle black visionaries and prophets to lie on.

From one day to the next, however, all these people started to prick up their ears when Brother Xangomusa began to preach on KZOR, a small religious radio station that only the bigots had taken the trouble to listen to up till then. Brother Xangomusa said that America was no longer America. It was begetting neither heroes nor gods. It was drifting like a vessel without a compass or a star to guide it on the bottomless ocean of materialism. Deprived of its guiding light, the rest of the world was walking on its head. Only ugliness abounded. Millions of men continued to exist without light in their eyes or hope in their hearts. This was why he, Brother Xangomusa, with the help of God, was launching an appeal. He appealed

to all the young people whose hearts had not yet been spoiled
and ruined by the middle-class values of their parents to join
him on Sundays for a day of love and prayer. Before the wrath
of God set America and with it the rest of the world ablaze,
they would attempt to find a way of hastening the advent of
beauty on our earth. The words of Brother Xangomusa did
not exactly sound new. It could even be said they had a jaded
ring to them. Yet, such as they were, their effect on the youth
of Charleston was amazing. The very next Sunday, Brother
Xangomusa's house was besieged by a crowd of young blacks
and a few whites who set about wildly shaving their heads and
praying and chanting with him. The number doubled the following Sunday and tripled two weeks later. Soon there were
no more weekdays or Sundays. Deserting their parents, the
young people set up house on Hearst Street where at any hour
of the day or night you could hear spirituals being sung to the
rhythms of rap and reggae.

His head burdened with his own problems, Spero had paid
scant attention to Brother Xangomusa. And then, was this
"Center of Universal Love" any different from the black Baptist Church of Samaria and all those places of prayer? So the
day Anita walked in with a head mown as close as a lawn he
made no connection and thought Debbie was making a lot of
fuss about nothing. Debbie was very proud of her daughter's
long, thick, curly (rather than frizzy) hair. For years she had
martyrized Anita to wash it, grease it, comb it, and braid it
on weekdays, and on Sundays curl it with great sweeps of the
Babyliss. She had dressed it up with ribbons, bows, and barrettes that carefully matched her clothes. During the ensuing
argument that flared up between mother and daughter and
raged for days to come, Spero was content to chalk up points,
supremely happy that Anita was carrying out his revenge
and screaming out loud what he thought deep down. About
Charleston and its black bourgeoisie. About the Middletons.
About the black Baptist Church of Samaria. About Jim. About
Debbie. Especially about Debbie. At certain moments he had
to restrain himself not to urge her on.

In June the police broke into the house on Hearst Street. A

young girl had got pregnant and confessed to her parents the true nature of Brother Xangomusa's love for his disciples. No charges could be brought against him. Absolutely nothing. The only suspect documents the prosecution could produce were numerous copies of letters addressed to heads of state asking them to make their country the "first universal love center" on the planet. One photo showed him shaking hands with the president of Zaire, one of the few who had listened to his message. But keep on slandering and something will stick. No matter how much some of the young people described in the press or over the radio the spiritual uplift he had given to their lives, Brother Xangomusa had to leave town and his center was declared a center of infamy. Leaving Debbie to make a clumsy job of interrogating Anita, Spero realized too late that in his war on Debbie he had perhaps played into the hands of a pervert. Stealing glances at Anita, he would have liked to have tortured himself a thousand times. He had kept in his mind's eye the picture of an adolescent, tall and gawky like a pole for poling down breadfruit, and now there she was like a datura that had secretly flowered in its sheath of green. Through his fault, a crazy nigger had perhaps laid hands on the treasure of his daughter's virginity.

He imagined Brother Xangomusa forcing the door of Anita's thighs, ransacking her hidden jewel, taking his pleasure, laying his semen at the very bottom of her lacerated flesh, and then and there he absolved all those papas on the Morne Verdol who wanted to kill all those who dared lay eyes on the children they had fathered.

After that, life, on the surface, resumed its normal course, no gloomier than before, even though Debbie's eyes bore traces of the wound. Anita's hair, frizzing around her head, gave her a halo like an Italian Madonna, and Spero infinitely regretted not having the hand of a painter from that period. Two years later she left them for Liman College and then abandoned them altogether.

He became aware that he was walking in the very middle of
the path under the hollow calabash of the sky, tacking left and
right like a man who is intoxicated with drink or has lost sight
in both his eyes. The rain had not let up and he was soaked.
Without realizing it he had arrived at the small landing stage.
The ferry was moored at the end of the jetty that extended
beyond the lights until it disappeared into the night, and you
could make out the name *Magdalena* painted in red letters on
its side. Two men with sou'westers and oilskins were directing
the manoeuvers of the few cars that emerged from the belly
of the ship and drove cautiously along the dock and sped off
along the road. Spero stood motionless, returning the wave
of the drivers masked by the darkness, but did not recognize
Debbie's four-wheel-drive.

Where was she now that he was waiting for her so impa-
tiently to start life all over again?

He walked into the waiting room, where the same old black
employee who had been selling tickets for the past twenty-
five years greeted him with a big smile. Like a wet dog he
shook himself before sitting down on one of the benches, then
looked out through the window at a point in space across the
sad face of the water on which the light from the lamps was
drawing circles. He felt like a kid whose mother wasn't waiting
for him at the school gate. Where was Debbie?

Couldn't she understand she should be home by now?
Chaka had been put to bed ages ago. By this time he must already be dreaming, dreaming of a time when his mother and
the friends of his mother would liberate him from their suffocating love. Opposite each other in the small living room the
two women would be talking as only women can talk. One
of those endless chats without beginning or end or middle,
where words beget words in order to lay bare life's setbacks,
from the childhood cuts and bruises to the trials and tribula-
tions caused by men. The way these two women ignored all
the pleasure he had given both of them made them appear un-
grateful in his eyes. Had they forgotten the salty water welling

up in their eyes, the moans and sighs? There they were, saying racy things about him, making up story upon story!

Did they have the right to accuse him behind his back? Debbie never gave him a chance to explain. She interpreted his behavior in her own way, and then lay the blame on him. The Spero she had once loved she now took for a man riddled with vice and without morals.

The summer Brother Xangomusa left Charleston, hounded out by shame and venomous newspaper articles, had been terrible for Spero. Now that the evil was done, and well done, he had tried to understand, but too late, too late. What had Anita been searching for at the Universal Love Center? First and foremost, he put all this business down to Debbie's theory of education, which he had never approved of. Too many lessons on the grandeur of the race and Africa, too many scales and violin lessons, too many African and modern dance sessions, too many concerts, educational films, and edifying readings, too many sermons at the Baptist Church of Samaria and Sunday school. Bound like a mummy with all these bandages, of course the child was suffocating and groping for air. Anywhere!

OK, but couldn't he have put a stop to Debbie's ways? In a great fit of anger couldn't he have pounded his fist on the table?

"For Christ's sake! This is not what I want for my child!"

But what did he want for Anita? He couldn't say. How do you raise a child?

He himself had grown up every which way on the Morne Verdol. Except for the ramblings of Justin, the catechism of Father Delumeau, and the lessons at school, he had not learned a thing. He learned about sex looking at his parents through the keyhole. About death by attending wakes. Much to his regret he ended up admitting that he too was responsible for Anita's failure. Through omission and irresponsibility. As a result, remorse and nightmares woke him up in the middle of the night. In his dreams he saw his Anita as a prostitute, naked and exposed like a datura on a bed of red velvet waiting for muscle men to penetrate her.

His bad conscience sent him prowling around Hearst Street. Way back, when they were still known as "Him and Her," he used to accompany Debbie on her monthly Saturday trips with half a dozen volunteers to one of Charleston's most deprived black neighborhoods. The longer he lived in America, however, the more convinced he was that all those efforts, however well-meaning they might be, were useless. A drop of water in the ocean of destitution where some sank straight to the bottom. At present he no longer ventured beyond the territory staked out by his studio, the Montego Bay, and Crocker Island.

Hearst Street looked like a lot of other streets in a lot of other ghettos in a lot of other big cities. No more sordid than the rest. The same jobless idling their time away on the front stoops. The same drunkards drinking liquor inside the bars. The same teenagers glued to their transistor radios. The same children playing the same childhood games. The Universal Love Center's banner, now faded and floating in the wind like a flag, was still draped across the front of the house that years earlier must have been the pride and joy of its owners. In a garden that was no bigger than the palm of your hand some azaleas were growing around one of those puny banana trees that always made Spero laugh. But he was in no mood for laughing the morning he walked inside. The ground floor consisted of a large room decorated with an odd assortment of reproductions of Hindu goddesses, Jesus Christ, and the Catholic saints and photos of Mother Teresa, Winnie Mandela, Notre Dame in Paris, and St. Peter's in Rome. A blue tarpaulin strung up between the trees in the yard hung over some tables and chairs. Upstairs were the dormitories. The police had placed seals on one of the doors. Probably Brother Xangomusa's bedroom. But it did not take much to push it open and reveal a filthy cell containing a futon, some sea chests, and an old wicker trunk. Perhaps it was here, in this hideous setting, that it had happened. Spero wished himself a thousand whiplashes, like the Christ on the wall.

On leaving the house he went into a bar and got drunk with a group of men as desperate as he was.

That's why he had been so happy when Anita had gone out with Roy, one of her high school classmates who drank milk and orange juice in the morning and imbibed beer and marijuana in the evening. Nothing unusual about that! He had felt reassured. Wasn't this proof that nothing had happened between her and Brother Xangomusa? That Anita was not fatally wounded as he feared? That nothing, in fact, a few months wouldn't heal? Roy Wilkerson Jr., son of the town's first black magistrate since Reconstruction, was one of those well-bred young men that Debbie liked to have around Anita at birthdays and other celebrations in anticipation of future alliances. The Wilkerson family had made a name for itself in the struggle for civil rights in Charleston, taking the lead in several sit-ins in front of the hospitals as well as on the playing fields and in the restaurants. That was how Roy Sr. came to spend three weeks without budging an inch from the front of the Old Battery Inn, a high-class hotel that refused to serve blacks. So as early as 1974 he had been rewarded for his trouble by this much-sought-after appointment. He was a short man with a sharp tongue who carried out his function with strict impartiality. So the blacks started grousing that he behaved like a white man. As for Roy Jr., he was a bit of an oaf, more interested in science fiction novels than this chattering about bygone struggles for civil rights. No better looking, no uglier than any other. Yet Spero was too much a connoisseur of bodies not to see that Anita and Roy were hungering for each other. In his joy, he decided to protect them. He signed Anita's notes of absence with a blind eye. He covered up her lies to her mother. If she missed the last ferry and came home in the early morning hours he secretly admired her for the stories she told Debbie and, with his heart glowing, took note of the rings under her eyes and the little wrinkles of fatigue around her mouth. Through constant spying he managed to find out where she met Roy: at the home of the boy's grandmother, an innocent old lady who was half blind and riddled with aches and pains and who thanked them from the bottom of her heart for coming so often to tidy up the house. He parked not far away for the mere pleasure of seeing her dash to the

Toyota that Debbie had given her for her sixteenth birthday, radiant, dishevelled, and half dressed.

How could he ever have imagined the way it would all end? Could he ever have suspected that Debbie would in turn discover the truth, but in a far more painful way than he? That one of those commonplace dramas was going to be enacted on Crocker Island — commonplace because they are played over and over again as long as there are young girls on this earth who secretly make love behind their parents' backs? It had been one of the most painful moments of their lives when they had to face Anita on their own after the killing of their first grandchild. She lay there, hostile and lifeless, refusing to look at them, refusing to speak to them, her every attitude indicating they were both to blame.

Yes, Anita was more precious to him than the apple of his eye, and yet all this love in his heart was as worthless as a devalued banknote. He had taught her nothing. He had given her nothing. He had guided her nowhere. Nor protected her with a high fence, tall enough to ward off life's reverses of fortune. In short, on this point like on all the rest, Debbie was right. He had been a bad father! A very bad father! He did not deserve forgiveness.

The old ferry employee, the one who had been selling tickets for the past twenty-five years, loomed up in front of Spero with his mouth stretched into a smile and handed him a plastic cup. The gesture touched Spero at a time when he was feeling so weak, so alone, and almost with tears in his eyes he gratefully drank the watery coffee. With the same smile that looked as though it was stuck on his face, the old man came and sat down beside him and started up an endless story about how proud he was of his sons joining the Marines and how his eyes were so bad one bill looked like another and he had trouble making change. This was why the whites of the steamer company, who all these years had not spared him his share of humiliations, wanted to pension him off. Debbie was perfect for listening to this type of story, finding the right words of encouragement to stand up to the whites, still a burning issue — you bet — while discreetly criticizing his sons for joining the

Marines. He must have heard of the dirty work the Marines did all over the world against the black nations? That's why some people adored Debbie. When she gave birth to Anita there was no counting the number of visitors in her hospital room, and the nurses did not know what to do with all the bouquets of gladiolus, Chinese hibiscus, and bird of paradise. Others, however, found her a little too Middleton for their liking, in other words, terribly arrogant.

As for Spero, he never knew what to say to people, and confronted with silence, the old employee launched into another story that was even more elaborate. When he was a child he had to ride in a rowboat to John's Island, the closest of the Sea Islands that operated a school. Like the others, John's Island was virgin territory, a thick tangle of pines, sycamores, and wide-spreading cypresses festooned with Spanish moss. The sharp-edged grass grew as tall as the schoolhouse roof and hid all sorts of snakes with venom in their mouths. It was the wives of the Methodist ministers who taught their classes; they were pale, so pale under their heavy hats of felt or straw, depending on the season. Since they did not know much themselves, all they taught the children was to sing and pray to God. The first time a real black teacher set foot on John's Island was in 1936, his last year at school. That's why he could neither read nor write. Would Spero like another cup of coffee?

Without thinking Spero nodded, and the old man wobbled over to the coffee machine. Bits of hair stuck out beneath his cap and brushed the collar of his jacket.

Where was Debbie? Was it true he could no longer count on her forgiveness? Didn't she know you have to forgive and forgive again?

When he was small, small enough to obey orders, and Good Friday lunch was over, with its single slice of pale fish cooked in a *blaf* and a baked potato, Marisia would dress him in a pair of shorts and a white drill shirt, white socks, and a pair of whitened tennis shoes. She herself was dressed in black, as if in deep mourning, buttoned up to the neck, her Roja-brilliantined hair brushed back into a chignon. Deep down he

thought she was very lovely, with her white complexion, almost as white as white folks, and those persistent rings grief
drew under her eyes. Without even taking the trouble to look
at herself in the mirror, she adjusted her hat, a black straw pill-
box with a feather of the same color draped from one side to
the other. Lacpatia, her maman, had worn a headtie, but in
consideration of her few years of schooling and her appren-
ticeship with a dressmaker, Marisia had always worn a hat.
Then she took Spero by the hand. Outside she opened a parasol made of mauve cotton strips above their heads and walked
down the hill to the church of Saint-Jules. Since the parasol
was held too high and offered him no protection from the dry
season's burning two-in-the-afternoon sun, hardly had they
stepped outside than the sweat began to trickle down his back
and soak his clothes. He endured it, for he knew that this day
was unlike any other: the Good Lord had died. Not for long
though. He would rise with the bells on Easter Sunday.

All along the Canal Vatable were women identically dressed
in black, their faces set in sadness, already in prayer, their children trailing a few steps behind with their arms hanging stiff,
made uncomfortable by the sweat trickling down their backs.
Like Spero, they all felt it was not a day to be rowdy or indulge in the usual fisticuffs, and they avoided each other's eyes
so as not to be tempted. On the square in front of the church,
Marisia made Spero kneel down on both knees on the burning
paving stones, like slabs left in the oven, and guided his hand
in the sign of the cross, from the forehead to the chest and
then the two shoulders.

When at last they got inside, the church was cool. Marisia lit
three candles in front of the alcove with Saint Theresa and the
Infant Jesus, whose statue, like all the rest that day, was draped
with a heavy purple cover. Since they had arrived a good hour
before mass was due to commence there were still some seats
left. Marisia chose a pew, fell to her knees on the prayer stool,
and with her head clasped between her hands, forgot all about
Spero. He could not help hear her sigh and mutter unintelligi-
bly. At times, tears trickled between the joints of her fingers.
Spero knew that her grief had something to do with Justin,

but did not know what exactly. It bothered him, for he had the impression of overhearing a confidence, a conversation that was not meant for him. So he turned his head and looked in every direction. Up toward the roof shaped like the keel of a boat. To the right, to the left, to the blues, yellows, and oranges, highlighted in thick black lines, of the big stained-glass windows depicting scenes from the Bible he could not fully understand. There were only certain points his eyes carefully avoided: the ceramic frescoes illustrating the stations of the cross of Our Lord Jesus Christ. Once the service had started the beadle would strike his cane hard on the floor as he led the little procession of priests and choirboys dressed in white surplices over their mauve robes, stopping in front of each station. Our Lord Jesus Christ frightened him with his crown of thorns laid askew on his head, his face dripping with blood, and this massive cross that threw him down under the feet of the passers-by. He dreamed about it at night. Marisia explained what it meant: the compassion of Our Lord forgives the sinner seventy times seven.

Had Debbie forgiven him seventy times seven?

He remembered the first time. The most memorable. Jeanne had left him in a state of dejection. At first he thought he had got over her without too much damage done. And then he found himself slapping on paint, depicting her with three enormous breasts, a mouth like the crater of Pinatubo, and four eyes at the four corners of a diabolical and lascivious face. As for Debbie, she seemed so taken up with her baby she appeared to be oblivious to everything beyond the cradle, an oak crib in which the Middleton children had been rocked for three generations.

Forsaken, he spent most of his time at the Montego Bay, wondering what use he was on this earth. One afternoon, tired of idling away his existence, he returned home to Crocker Island earlier than usual. By the 2:30 P.M. ferry. His key turned gently in the lock. The house seemed asleep, like the newborn despot who now reigned over it. He crossed the hall and entered the kitchen. Debbie was sitting slumped at the table, motionless, her head clutched between her hands, immediately bringing to mind the picture he had of Marisia, his maman, crying because of Justin. The difference being that when Debbie looked up her eyes were dry, black, and veiled by a bottomless despair, as if the facile consolation of tears had been refused her. He could not think of a single word to say. He slipped to her feet and put his arms around her waist, clutching her tighter and tighter as if he had lost control, while his head nestled in her lap. To start with, she had remained very stiff, rigid; then gradually he felt her soften as if she were melting under the heat of his remorse. After a while she laid her hand on his hair while through her dress he showered the center of her body with kisses, the very place where he had offended her in such an ugly way.

After this initial pardon, however, his fine resolution had not lasted very long; for adultery is a taste that grows on you. And then all these conquests gave him back his self-esteem at a time when he needed it the most. Even during the peak tourist season, when Americans from every state, Canadians, English, and Germans flocked to Charleston to admire the parks and gardens of the great colonial houses, his studio remained deserted. The few tourists who ventured in quickly swung round as if they had made a wrong turn. When Debbie's women friends and colleagues got together to discuss serious issues such as gang violence or the effects of the Vietnam War on the black family, or quite simply to chat as women do about women's things, he would spy on them from the kitchen, where he had been relegated like an offensive object, and perversely cast his desire on the woman who seemed to be the most decidedly adamant. He had a theory. Those serious attitudes always hid depths of despair and loneliness. Those lips, listing strings of statistics, were dying for rapturous kisses. And it was a fact that he could recall more successes than failures. It was true he quickly stuffed the failures in the back of his mind. Except for one, the pain of which even time could not erase the hurt. She called herself Amanda, even though her parents had christened her Louise. People whispered that she had taken refuge at her parents' place following a nervous breakdown and two suicide attempts. These were caused by her years in New York, where she had desperately tried to find jobs other than walk-on parts in low-budget films or sitcoms. And, Lord knows, Amanda was beautiful.

The first time Spero set eyes on her from his observation post in the kitchen her beauty lit up the somewhat joyless living room of the house on Crocker Island. It splashed over the blue-gray striped wallpaper, dotted here and there with big yellow roses, that he had said a hundred times he would change. It ricocheted off the Middleton family portraits and the photo of George, the presumed martyr, that Margaret had hung in evidence over the artificial fireplace. By the way she was nibbling on a cheese square Spero knew she was bored to death, and that the breakdown of the black church, topic of that day's discussion, left her stone cold. That very evening Debbie had her stay for dinner. There was nothing innocent in her invitation — he understood that too late — for Debbie knew what was bound to follow and did not want to miss the show.

Amanda was at war with her own image. Although she made such an impression on people, she had never been able to achieve the one thing in life she most wanted: to have her name in neon lights outside a theater on Broadway. This constant war with herself made her capricious, unpredictable, and impossible to fathom. She could switch on the charm as easily as she could switch it off. She did not rebuff Spero. On the contrary, she took to him as if she recognized a fellow soul mate. At the end of the afternoon, she would drop in unexpectedly at his studio. Peering nearsightedly at his canvasses with her sharp eyes, she would say in all honesty that they looked old hat. Wasn't that figurative style outdated? Leaving the studio, they would stroll arm in arm in the old slave market where he strutted like a turkey cock, the envy of all the men. During the Italian meals they took in her kitchen, speaking in low voices because her parents were dozing on the other side of the wall, she told him things she told nobody else. She did not approve of the ghetto black women locked themselves up in to lament the absence of their men. She herself had taken many white lovers, even a Japanese, and she had almost married an Englishman. She had broken it off because he hated children, whereas she, like all true black women, intended to have a house full of them. With languishing eyes she asked him about Paris. The City of Light. To keep her captivated he described everything she wanted to hear. The Place des Vosges. The café terraces of Saint-Germain-des-Prés. The footbridge of the Pont des Arts bridging a river of dreams. Montmartre. He did not tell her, however, about the Morne Verdol, for why pretend? The Caribbean did not interest her. She had gone to the Cayman Islands with her English lover and had been bored to death with all that sand and water. He did not tell her about the ancestor either. For according to her, Africa existed only as a myth in the sick minds of the Diaspora. She had gone to Abidjan with her Japanese lover and had seen nothing but high-rises, bridges, and pretentious hotels with swimming pools. The people there kissed her hands and feet when they learned she was an American. All through dinner they drank Hennessy cognac in champagne glasses, and she rambled on more than ever. They had to put an end to this business of black and white that was tearing at the soul of America. Black or white, men make love the same way, she could prove it, and the same red blood runs under their skin. Almost twenty years after the death of Martin Luther King, the sons of former slaves and the sons of former slaveowners could not sit down together at the table of brotherhood. In actual fact, he wasn't listening and did not bother to contradict her. His eyes were glued to the way her breasts moved unhindered under the silk of her blouse and to the shadow of her lashes on her dark brown eyelids. At 11:45 P.M. exactly she cut short her ramblings and turned him out, just in time for the last ferry.

On the evening that Spero, at his wit's end, declared his love, she laughed without malice, like laughing at a small child who wants the moon, and that laugh had rung in his ears for a very long time afterwards. After that, without realizing the agony she was causing him, she continued to drop in unexpectedly at his studio and invite him for fettucini in her kitchen.

One day out of the blue she flew off to New York and, amid

general disapproval, married a Jewish architect. Her name was never to appear in lights on Broadway. Debbie, who visited her while staying in New York, described her as apparently being happy, cradling her firstborn in her arms.

The waiting room, chilled by all these memories, suddenly seemed icy.

The old employee, turning his empty plastic cup over and over in his hands, was talking about the great march on Washington in which he claimed to have walked. Spero pretended to believe him. Yet he only had to look him in the eyes to know he had passed the month of August 1963 holed up in his house, frightened of being hit by a stray bullet. People told all sorts of stories to make believe they had been activists at that time. He got up and went and stuck his face against the window. Through the dense curtain of raindrops he could make out the lights of Charleston shining along the peninsula. Had Debbie forgiven him seventy times seven? And then was she so free of sin to cast the first stone?

Everyone believed she was worthy of mention in the Guinness Book of Records for marital fidelity. Was this the truth? He could firmly ascertain that in 1985 she had taken a lover. Of course, they would ask him for evidence. Does a husband need anything else but his heart and his flesh as evidence? People had always been mistaken about Debbie. People judged her by appearances. Instead of dancing the be-bop at her teenage parties, she stood around like a wallflower because the boys were scared to ask her to dance. At college, nobody could pick up enough strength and courage to speak to her of love, since all she could talk about was civil rights.

Yet Spero knew that behind those airs of assurance she was soft and fragile. Hadn't she melted under him the very evening they first met, releasing burning, torrential waters?

He had never taken women to the Morne Verdol, and had followed his few conquests to their wooden shacks on the Morne à Cailles. So he felt that for a first night of lovemaking his room was not suitable.

With the help of his friends, Romulus had enlarged the single-story house his papa had grudgingly left him. He had added a washroom fitted with three barrels to catch the water from the gutter, as well as a room for Djéré with a bed, a desk, and a wardrobe to pack all his stuff in. In case his father came to fetch him from Africa, he did not want any criticism. For thirty years the house had remained as it was until Marisia started producing children, one after the other. Three in six years. Since you couldn't count on Justin to do an honest day's work, she had asked her brother Florimond to lend a hand; Florimond, who — God works in wondrous ways — was a mason, had a concrete mixer towed to the top of the Morne Verdol, and abandoning his four construction sites in the Assainissement district, built two rooms onto his sister's house. Throughout the duration of the work he ignored Justin, who, with hands behind his back, gave orders on the height of the walls. When everything was completed, Justin chose the bigger of the two rooms for his Spero. The window looked out onto the hands of the clock tower of the church of Saint-Pierre and Saint-Paul. Behind the clock tower you could glimpse the transatlantic steamers lying at rest along the wharf and a great expanse of blue sea. On his return from Lille, Spero pinned to the walls he had painted over in white two reproductions he was particularly fond of — *L'Ile de la Jatte* by Seurat and *Madame Charpentier et ses enfants* by Renoir — giving the room a respectable air. But was this really the setting for a first night of lovemaking?

He had heard of the hotel-restaurant "Le Grand Large" at Bas-du-Fort. But in those days, I'm talking about 1963, only the *békés* and wealthy mulattos frequented the hotels of Guadeloupe. So it was a very flustered Spero who checked in at the reception desk. The receptionist eyed the couple from head to foot, then from foot to head, noting every detail in Spero's well-ironed twill Sunday suit and wondering in the back of his mind whether Debbie was not some English Negress from Dominica. Nevertheless he gave them a spacious room filled with the smell of salt from the sea. Anthuriums the color of pale flesh filled the vases and light shot out of a lamp in the shape of a goldfish.

Spero was shaking with fear at the thought of laying beneath his body this tall girl who was much too beautiful for him. While she undressed, he took refuge on the terrace, praying in his heart for a tidal wave to swallow him up in a single mouthful, as devastating as the hurricane of 1928, still engraved in the memories of the old folks of La Pointe. Yet the recollection of that night was still in his memory twenty-five years later, for together they had tamed the beast of pleasure without bridle, without saddle, and without halter.

Yes, his heart and his flesh could furnish evidence that in the year 1985, the very year he turned forty-five, Debbie had taken a lover.

And what a lover! A woman who takes a younger man is a case for disrespect. It has been the abomination of abominations ever since the sun has lit up the earth. She brings not only shame on her name, but ridicule as well. The year 1985 began where the previous year left off, in family disarray. Anita trailed through the house a face that grew more cutting and caustic by the hour. She had just announced her decision to study at Liman College. Pointing to her untouched trays, Mamie Garvin, the old servant, wasted her breath begging her at least to open the windows to let some fresh air in. Debbie and Spero continued to go their separate ways, without speaking to or looking at each other, while Spero was still bruised from having let Arthé get away. Yet it was that year Isaac Jamieson, a historian who had attracted attention with the publication of his book on the first blacks in California, chose to turn up in Charleston. For he now intended to tackle the extremely fascinating community of South Carolina's freed black artisans who in turn had been slave owners.

Isaac showed up one unusually cold January morning of this year without grace. For over a week Indian Swamp had been covered with a crust of ice, and day after day the frost hardened the hedges and the earth. On several occasions snow had fallen in big flakes, and dirty white heaps still hung around on the slopes, the roofs, and the bare branches. Her eyes black with dread under her headscarf, Mamie Garvin recalled that it had not snowed in the islands since just before the death of Martin Luther King. This was surely an omen of some other wicked deed white folks had in store for them. Her head swimming with her own problems, Debbie had little time to listen to Mamie Garvin. Likewise she had forgotten all about last summer's exchange of letters with Isaac Jamieson and looked at him like an evil spirit when Mamie Garvin showed him into the kitchen. Intimidated, he could but recall the forgotten letters while twisting a woollen cap in his hands. He only recovered his manners after the second cup of coffee, and it then became evident he was handsome, older than he first appeared — at least thirty — and very pedantic.

He immediately started talking about himself with great importance. He had graduated from Harvard. But since he was originally from San Francisco, the only son of elderly parents in poor health, he had rejected some extremely attractive offers in order to teach at Berkeley. He took no credit for his first book, *Longing for California*, despite the reputation it had gotten him. In certain respects, he was not the author. He had merely collected the words of his parents, grandparents, and their friends. Melchior, his grandfather, could neither read nor write. With his wife and two elder boys hidden at the height of June under thick blankets at the bottom of a horse-drawn cart, traveling under shelter of night, hiding from the glare of day for fear of whites, who at that time strung up any nigger who crossed their path, he left Alabama urged on by the desperate longing for a better life. In California he had worn his fingers to the bone working in the mines, in the hotels, and on the trains. Later on, his sons had found jobs in the shipyards at Oakland. The entire family had burst into tears when they actually held in their hands the book that recounted those years of suffering and odyssey. *Longing for California* was but the expression of his filial duty, and his real work as a historian was about to begin.

Spero loathed these collectors of degrees, these speechifiers, drivelling on with their same old stories. So at the third cup of coffee he had been in a hurry to leave Isaac and Debbie, nostalgic, thrilling to the same emotions, sitting on either side of the kitchen table, and set off for his studio in his old Volvo. In a country where everyone was judged by his car he had grown attached to this wheezing outmoded tank of an auto that often gave up on him in the middle of the freeway. After that, Isaac had often returned to Crocker Island with other chatterboxes of a similar category. Each time Spero invented an excuse to leave and let them feast on the past. He knew what they were all thinking, but not saying, so as not to hurt Debbie; but their contempt rolled off him like water off a duck's back. Besides, he returned their feelings. For him, these great minds were nothing but paper tigers and gigantic painted carnival dragons. Under their flowery language and speeches was hidden the shame and fear of their brothers in the ghettos hooked on drugs, whose growing numbers proved that their magnificent struggles had only bettered the lucky few. Brought up on the Bible, deep down they must have realized they were no better than those Pharisees vomited up by the Holy Scriptures.

Spero knew that Debbie and Isaac spent hours going through the papers of the Middleton family. Debbie attached great importance to Senior's act of emancipation, a document dating back to 1704, initialled by Arthur Middleton, Esq., and two witnesses, as well as the deed of ownership to the property on Crocker Island, dated 1865 and signed by General William Tecumseh Sherman himself. Even more precious was the bill of sale for Numah and Mamaduh, two Negroes from the coast of Guinea, sold by a certain Samuel Gullah, slave merchant, to Isaac Middleton in 1812. Spero would have liked to have listened through Debbie's study door to hear how they travestied a complex and ambiguous period in time into an edifying chapter of history.

Sometimes Isaac accompanied Debbie to the Baptist Church of Samaria where he sang all the psalms, even though he was not a Baptist, and escorted her to the Free Nelson Mandela Committee meetings as well as to Agnes Jackson's. He interviewed the old woman about her life in California. For around 1928 she had followed her actor husband to Los Angeles. He would have liked to hear her talk of the difficult conditions for black artists at that time. Instead, she told him stories of drinking, homosexuality, and vice, which he listened to somewhat disapprovingly. She showed him photos she had never shown Debbie, where in art deco bars she could be seen lovely and desperately sad, smiling beside her husband's lovers. One of them was called Willy. The two men left together arm in arm, never to return.

Spero knew that Debbie and Isaac were inseparable. But he did not see any harm in that, even if Debbie often spent nights in town and left him a note of excuse beside his plate on the kitchen table. The blinding revelation of what was actually going on behind his back hit him the evening of the farewell reception for Isaac at Marcus's. He had gone to the reception out of a remnant of politeness. As always, he had been bored to death. For once, the *grangrek* were not chewing over the memories of their struggles in Charleston. This time the object of their anger was Alice Walker's portrayal of black men in her latest novel. Amidst the ruckus, some were calling for calm and learnedly debating the discrepancy between the depictions in the novel, which Spero had not read — for he never read books by women, knowing in advance what he would find — and the representations in the film of the same name, which he had not seen either since he preferred a good old western. Other bores were carrying on endlessly about Jesse Jackson. They did not trust his Rainbow Coalition. Ever since the beginning of time, light-skinned individuals have detested dark-skinned individuals. So why try to make them get along together?

Spero was looking for the exit when he unexpectedly came upon Debbie and Isaac standing in a corner of the veranda, so wrapped up in each other that they did not realize he was there. Isaac was a head taller than Debbie, and strong enough for her to lean on his shoulder. Spero was struck by the pain on his wife's face that restored the infinite charm of her youth. He received such a shock that he almost grabbed Isaac by the throat like a rowdy nigger whose senses are inflamed by shots of rum in a local bar. Instead of which, like a coward, he turned tail and went back inside.

So that's where the interest in the free black artisans of South Carolina had been leading. Debbie and this young fellow! A good ten years her junior! Who was still in diapers when she, the pride of the Middletons, was already running off with all the first prizes at high school! The deceit of women! Outward appearances had not betrayed her. Only after his affair with Tamara Barnes did Debbie shut the door in his face. Up till then she had never rejected him, despite his cheating. Once he had mastered his bad conscience enough to approach her, she always received him back with the same somewhat pitying ease, as if she could not understand how inconsistent he could be. He himself was surprised at finding that, despite everything, he needed her body, which he knew as well as his own with its ever-visible imperfections that warned him from year to year of old age gently and insidiously creeping up on him. Nailed to the spot in this big noisy, bright room, typical of the houses in Charleston's black or white residential neighborhoods with their high ceilings and bow windows, he realized that four nights earlier he had still been making love to her. So she was sharing him with another man? Why? Didn't he satisfy her? Except for Jim Marshall he had never seen her cast her eyes on anyone else. What did she see in this Isaac? His youth? His good looks? His eyes without puffiness and his stomach without middle-aged spread? His dick that never lowered its guard and gave up the fight? For there could not be any other reasons! She of course would deny any such thing and would make believe in some intellectual, quite platonic friendship. This was nothing but a pack of lies, he was sure about that. Intellectuals are not made any differently from the rest of us. They experience the same passions. Like any woman in her forties, she was suddenly famished for fresh meat.

In the four-wheel-drive that drove them back to the ferry, Spero stole sidelong glances at this familiar face that managed so perfectly to hide from him any traces of deceit. Back on Crocker Island, when he asked to spend the night with her she pleaded as naturally as she could that she was too tired, it was too late; in other words she spun him one of those yarns women have been ridiculing men with since the Good Lord created them.

He spent the night in torture, picturing things that put his body on fire and asking himself the same question over and over again, which added to his anger. What would his father, Justin, have done if Marisia had shown him the same disrespect? He would have killed her, killed her with his own two hands.

The next day he confided in Linton. But Linton, although a constant critic of Debbie without really knowing her, just as he criticized all the black bourgeoisie of Charleston, had only soothing words to say. You can't go on appearances. What had Spero seen? Did he have proof of what he was saying?

Proof?

If he had needed more proof than that provided by his head and heart, the days following Isaac's return to California were proof enough. Usually so neat and trim from early morning, putting his slovenliness to shame, Debbie drifted around the house, letting herself go. A face without makeup. Hair combed in a hurry. A gloomy expression. Mechanical gestures. Watching her out of the corner of his eye he compared her to those masked characters dressed in jute sacks and perched on stilts that stride stiff and silent above the frenzy of the crowd at carnival. So Spero paid more visits to her bed than he had for a very long time. Because he wanted to watch her up close. To catch the groans of regret and remorse that lay behind the moans of an all too familiar pleasure.

One day he plucked up courage and dared broach the subject that was burning at his heart and ebbing his life away. At first she seemed not to understand. When finally the nature of his accusations dawned on her, she looked at him with a deep contempt — once again he was proving how mediocre he could be. And without even taking the trouble to defend herself she turned her back on him. He was left silly and sheepish with his pack of useless charges.

Yes, Debbie had sinned. She had no right to cast the first stone.

Maryse Condé

He knew her to be stubborn, difficult, pitching at someone at the slightest pretext, like a fishing boat on the high seas. If he went up to her and said, "Listen, how about starting life all over again," she would merely shake her head.

Then she would look him in the whites of the eyes and say in a don't-answer-me-back tone, "Listen, life doesn't start all over again!"

The air in the waiting room suddenly seemed stifling to Spero, as if he were standing next to a conflagration. Mumbling a few words of excuse he left the old employee, still talking for talking's sake, and went out onto the wet, dimly lit jetty, which was slippery in places. The rain was pounding feverishly into the sea, as black as the black expanse of sky, except for the rollers flecked white against the horizon. Spero liked to believe that if you set off in a small boat, by yawing and slewing, you would eventually end up in his archipelago of islands.

Where was Debbie when he suddenly needed her so desperately?

OK, the jury had made up its mind. There was nothing to say in his defense: he had been a bad husband and a bad father. Even so, she should not have rejected him and barred him from her life. She who was so conversant with the words of the Scriptures should have taken him over and over again into the forgiveness of her heart and her body.

For if the woman has lost patience with the man, what is there left for him to become?

As for the ancestor, however, he had managed to start life all over again. Emerging from the dunes of Blida he had not had too much trouble finding his way to Kutome after a journey of nine days and nine nights. There he had been bored to death again for a very long time. Of course he had joined the *daadaa* who, to his surprise, held nothing against him for what had happened on earth. Soon his beloved Ouanilo was reunited

with him as well as his other children and his 414 wives.
His slaves and concubines attended to him. Lying in a circle
around him his *bokono* predicted an uneventful future. Every
day the smell of animals sacrificed in his name wafted up to
him together with the drone of litanies of admiration. He
knew that on earth he was at the heart of a heated debate.
Some believed him to have been an example and a martyr.
For others he had been nothing but a bloodthirsty monster,
a prime example of a power that had no interest in common
mortals. Now he was past caring about all that. In Kutome he
was at peace.

Gradually, however, this peace started to bother him. He
missed the torments of his life as a mortal. Sometimes, quite
unexpectedly, the memory of the agony he had felt when the
gunboat *Topaze* bombarded the banks of the Ouémé, or when
he had seen with his own eyes the flames lick greedily at the
wood of his palace, gripped his heart and made it beat like a
funeral drum. He remembered his amazement at seeing for the
first time a boat cleave through the scales on the blue back of
the sea; his grief at arriving at Fort-de-France, tiny, so tiny under the crater of the volcano; his terror on hearing the secret
bowels of Mount Pelée rumble. He remembered too the happiness women gave him, and now as a spirit devoid of feeling,
he realized he had not gotten the most out of life.

He had been taught that if he felt like it he could slip into
the body of a newborn baby of his tribe who would then in-
herit his virtues and vices. Wasn't he himself the reincarnation
of a formidable ancestor who loved combat and waged war
against all his neighbors? The *bokono* had declared him such
the very day he was born. Yet, in the past, this lust for living
life over and over again had always seemed incomprehensible
to him. When he was on earth, his sole obsession was to leave
it. Give up the fight. Close his eyes. Lay his bones down in the
shade of a grave. But suddenly now the desire to return from
where he came burgeoned inside and gradually tormented
him. So at nightfall he began to draw close to the compounds
to eye the bellies of the women of the tribe under their wrappers. He caught them fast asleep and inspected them. Bellies

round as calabashes. Shell shaped. Taut and pointed. Sagging and flabby. Magnificent bellies. Pulpy bellies. He could hardly contain himself. Sometimes he slipped into the shadow of the midwife and approached the wide-open belly of a woman in labor. He prayed and chanted in unison with her. Then in the midst of the pestilential odor of streaming blood and pus he brought into this life the frightened, trembling newborn baby. While the *bokono* made their divinations, the ancestor inspected with a little shudder all these bulging faces no bigger than a fist with their wrinkled foreheads, their puffy eyes, and mouths contorted into a pout, and thought of all the distance he would have to cover again. He was about to give up the idea and resign himself to finishing his eternity in Kutome when, one soft moonlit evening, he met Abebi in a compound in Abomey. How times have changed! A princess of royal blood, Abebi had married a common scoundrel who, so proud of his military rank, got into bed and made love to her in his boots and uniform. He barely consented to remove his belt and lay it on a small bedside table so as not to lacerate his wife's thighs. Since the past had been eradicated and only praises of the lieutenant-colonel in power were acceptable, Abebi had lost all pride in her ancestors. Her only pride was the concrete compound her scoundrel of a husband had built her, the fans that blew air in every room, her gold jewelry, her indigo and kola wrappers dyed by the cooperative in Savalou, and the Mercedes-Benz sitting at the door like a faithful dog. Yet the people who had eyes to see and hoarded the past in the back of their memory could recognize the royal blood in the shape of her head that swayed like a flower of flesh at the end of her long ringed neck. Abebi was having a difficult pregnancy, for she was carrying twins who squabbled about which should have preeminence. She did not know this because she had refused to admit herself to the hospital, as stipulated by the lieutenant-colonel, and had entrusted herself to the midwife who sixteen years earlier had delivered her from her mother's womb. All day long, despite her fans, she drooped from the heat and gasped for air, too tired to push her belly in front of her, lying half naked on her bed while Adizua, one of her *boyesses*, fanned her with woven palm fronds. It was only in the evening when the breeze consented to ruffle the leaves on the trees that she could leave her room and lie down on a folding chair in one of the compound courtyards. She would then untie the cords of her wrapper and her masseuses would massage her young, temporarily misshapen body with shea butter mixed with a few drops of Yves Saint-Laurent that her scoundrel of a husband brought back from his missions abroad. And that's how the ancestor came across her. And that's how he became enamored with her. She reminded him of Hosannah when she had appeared in his bedroom at the villa in Bellevue carrying a heavy tray of fruit. Hosannah, the mother of Djéré! The ancestor often thought about this son begotten from his old age and exile, so dear to his heart, but that circumstances had forced him to leave behind. What had become of him? Had he had a good life? Had he fathered a fitting lineage? Peering into the immensity that lapped around Kutome, he turned his head in the direction where he supposed the islands to be. But he saw nothing. Only blackness on blackness. He heard nothing. Only silence on silence.

Every night the ancestor made a habit of sitting at the feet of Abebi. He watched her feed herself with the airs of a sick cat on a little mush or fruit salad carefully peeled and chilled by the *boyesses*. He watched her doze. He watched her cry and bite her lips in silence for her scoundrel was never at her side. Then one evening when the moon was in its first quarter, pale and fragile against the blackness of the sky, he saw her sit up, her face distraught and covered in sweat. Her labor had begun.

The *bokono* positioned themselves at their stations. The *boys* and *boyesses* ran in all directions. Since the scoundrel had still not arrived, Abebi's mother sent for the midwife. She hardly had time to recite a few entreaties and prepare the leaves of her compresses than she held a child in her hands. Stillborn. Fortunately, it was only a girl. Without losing courage the midwife laid the little corpse on the ground and continued her job, massaging and kneading the lacerated belly, giving orders and words of encouragement. Soon a second child made its appearance. A boy this time, but puny, so puny, and wheezy, so wheezy that those surrounding Abebi's bed wondered whether he would not go the same way as his sister, when opening wide his tiny mouth he screamed to claim his share of life. Alive, he was alive! The ancestor had just enough time to run for it and make room for himself inside the little body. All set for a new existence!

The scoundrel of a husband happened to be in bed with his mistress when they came to inform him he was now father of a son. He got up at top speed, buckled his belt and rushed home. On arriving at Abebi's bedside he embraced with gratitude her tired but radiant face and took his son in his hands. No doubt about it, he'd turn out to be a strapping fellow! They'd make him into a soldier, a real one.

Since all this happened on 6 January 1980, he named the baby Melchior.

Yes, he knew her well enough to know what she would say in an acid, commanding tone: "The same old nonsense! Life does not start over again!"

Stubborn and prickly! At least twice she had shown him how unyielding her character was. The first time was when Anita was quite small. His daughter made him want another child. Another child that would be rightfully his. Not just the property of its mother. A boy this time whom he would name Rupert — a first name he liked, strangely enough — who, clutching him hard around the neck, would plant big wet kisses in the hollow of his cheeks and all the niches of his face like he himself used to do with Justin. He would not fill his head with stories about a royal ancestor. He would not read him the notebooks of Djéré. No! He would teach him straightway to look the present in the eye. When he was old enough he would take him to La Pointe. They would ignore the neighbors, still as nosy as ever, coming out on their doorsteps to stare at them suspiciously, and walk up the Morne Verdol hand in hand under the sun. Stopping in front of the one-story house he would say to him: "Look! This is where your race grew up! This is the bed where your father was conceived by a poor beggar who thought he was one of the last of the African kings. If you want to be happy, don't follow his example. Forget all that nonsense!" It would be in La Pointe that his son would take his first mistress. He would choose her for him: a *bo kaye négresse*, the salt of the earth, who would know what giving pleasure means and would not ask for the moon. He would give his son a down-to-earth career. No dreaming of becoming an artist. Painter. Writer. Musician. He would teach him to keep both feet on the ground and not try and change the world, for all those who have tried have killed themselves on the job. In a word, he would teach him to take the good things from life without too much sentiment, ambition, or illusion that only gnaw at the head and the heart.

But Debbie had looked at him scornfully. Did he realize what he was asking? A second child requires careful planning! Was he sure he had progressed sufficiently, materially and morally, as a serious-minded, faithful, and mature individual? And then was America, so cruel to the underprivileged, the place to bring up more children? To give everyone an equal chance on equal terms? All these questions had not crossed Spero's mind. Back home they used to say: *Tété pa jin two lou pou lestonmak!* — The breasts are never too heavy for the stomach — and a child always brings joy with it. Realizing his recklessness, he had sheepishly had to retreat from his desire for fatherhood.

The second time was because of Tamara Barnes. When Debbie had informed him she was banishing him because of this affair, he had taken no notice, considering such threats part of the anger that fills the mouths of women. A few months later, when he had finally taken leave of Tamara, he could not believe it when he realized that her words of fury were by no means a rage of hot air, without weight or meaning, but words heavy with significance and loaded with determination and resolution.

Incensed, his punishment seemed out of proportion with his crime. Why had she forgiven him Jeanne, Arthé, Ruby, and so many others? White though she was, Tamara was but one woman among other women. One of those who had counted the least in his life, even though he had had such a good time with her. Banish him for that? Swallowing his pride he had begged and implored Debbie as he had never done, even when they were young and she fell into his arms so easily. He recalled all those nights with her, all those nights that, put end to end, would plunge the earth into darkness for years and years. What tormented him the most was not so much the pleasure and bliss of those nights, but the times when they had just chatted, lazed around, and slept curled up beside each other, as if she were condemning once and for all the most imtimate moments of their life together. She countered his words, his remorse, and his promises with an unbending argument. Never wavering. By taking a white mistress he had revealed his innermost self and humiliated her in a way she could not tolerate.

He ended up accepting the unacceptable.

At breakfast time in the kitchen, while Debbie bustled here and there, preparing for the thousand and one things of her day ahead and subtly convincing him of his uselessness, he eyed the traces of a sleep he had not shared and had as much difficulty accepting as an adulterous love affair. It was at that time he painted the biggest picture in his studio, a gigantic canvas that faced the door. It was a parody of those Haitian naïfs he had once copied and which now had their own Art Center without the help of Major Dennis. His own portrayal of Erzulie Dantor, supposedly the Goddess of Love, was in fact a formidable shrew that nobody and nothing could tame. She held in her many hands a knife to castrate men, a whip to lash them, and an open book to teach them to respect her commandments. It was a striking piece of art. The few people who were interested in his painting maintained it was his best composition. Tourists attracted by its strangeness would regularly offer him a good price — once even a collector made the journey from Canada. This singular painting marked the point when his life in America lost the little meaning it had, when nothing more tied him to Crocker Island. Thinking back,

Spero realized that this point in his life had marked the beginning of the end. Anita's departure for Benin had only precipitated it. His affair with Paule was but a pathetic effort at hiding it. Moreover, his body made no mistake about it as it often refused to go through the motions. Many times, instead of joining Paule in bed and making love to her, he started talking to her of Justin, Marisia, Anita, and himself. Only a sense of decency prevented him from talking about Debbie and everything that had stood in the way of their happiness. Paule listened to him fairly patiently, with a serious face, lying back on her pillows. When she realized another evening was going by without anything happening, she got dressed and quietly made her exit, after kissing him on the forehead as if he were a child whose mother is going out for the evening.

As for Linton, he wasted his time introducing Spero to lovely creatures with ravenous mouths, the way he used to like them. The previous week, driven by habit, he had courted Farida, a lovely specimen of youth come to drown in beer the hours she spent in front of a computer terminal. Then he had accompanied her to her tiny apartment on Sergeant Street, decorated with the same old reproductions and the same old potted plants. He had let her fill two glasses, smoke, and laugh. But when she came on to him and he caught the smell of a woman aroused, he was unable to do what is expected of a man in such cases. All he could do was make for the door and drive away in his Volvo, as heavy and sluggish as himself.

It was not just that at his age he had already become an old bag of bones whose virile member was as much use as an infant's. He realized he was living with one obsession, with the sole hope that Debbie would put an end to his exile and take him back. During the daylight hours spent at his studio, at the Montego Bay, or on the road that took him back to Crocker Island, he imagined he would find her the way she used to be, secretly disdainful, slightly aloof, but forgiving, yes, forgiving. Alas! Back home, once dinner was over and the horse-chestnut herb tea gulped down, she held out her cheek and withdrew to the forbidden territory of her bedroom. For two years she had not wavered. As for Spero, he regained his attic, his empty bed, his nightmares, and the voracious crabs that attacked his body. She was like that, Debbie. Inflexible. He was dying next to her and she did not care one bit.

Spero walked a few steps along the jetty, illuminated halfway along by the pale bulbs of the lamp posts, but seeming thereafter to disappear into the deep belly of the night. Under the lashing rain, the seawater slapped against the stone pylons and the big rubber tires that softened the impact of the boats. During the winter the ferry was the only service to Crocker Island. But during the summer season cruise ships came and went, chugging their load of tourists from one island to the next all along the South Carolina and Georgia coast. Some sailed as far down as Florida and joined the liners leaving for the Caribbean. Spero reached the middle of the jetty, at the end of the double row of lamp posts stuck in the ground like stakes. Neither did his daughter care one bit about him. What was she doing far away, so far away in that village of Paogo? Had she found what she was looking for? And if so, would good fortune be with her?

By this time, exhausted by its own virulence, the sun would have gone to set behind the rigging of baobabs. The black veil of the sky would be rippling under the long-awaited breeze. After her busy day's work Anita must be resting under the folds of her mosquito net encrusted with mosquito specks. What a mystery his child was! Was a man sleeping in her bed, giving her pleasure? And if so, had he found the key to her implacable heart, implacable and secret like her mother's? The Good Lord was a terrible director of humankind. On the stage of life he had cast women with strength, courage, and ambition. Men had to make do with the frantic need to be steeped in love like a fetus bathing in its mother's womb. Couples were really incompatible! It wasn't surprising if he didn't make the grade! Spero imagined the letter he would write to his daughter explaining what she meant to him. But would she even read it? Wouldn't she put it with all the others Debbie wrote to her week after week, never discouraged by receiving no answer?

He realized he had reached the end of the jetty and had the feeling of facing a locked door that opened onto another world. All that immensity that stretched as far as the eye could see oppressed him.

Sometimes, as a reward for getting good grades at school, Justin would take him to haul in the fishing nets with his friend Fredo, a regular drinking buddy of his at the Cerf-Volant. Fredo, son of a master fisherman from Anse Baille-Argent, had given up fishing himself, too enamored with rum and tired of working himself to the bone for a few fish, like his father and brothers, with very little to show for it. But you can't get the sea out of your system, just like that. At the slightest opportunity, Fredo set off to wage combat with the waves on his sailing vessel, the *Marie-Vertu*, and took Justin with him as his "mate." Justin and Fredo wedged Spero at the back of the boat on a pile of nets with the express recommendation not to move, and then they headed off for the open sea. The nets had been lying at the bottom of the ocean for several days, catching in their open mouths not only red snappers, wrasses, threadfins, and weevers, but all kinds of shellfish. One day, when they had gone to haul up the nets in the deeps of Carpot, they stopped to heat up the pot of rice and beans at the Ilet Cailloux, a large rock that rears its flat head, fringed with white sand, off the island of Antigua. The meal had been washed down with plenty of rum. While Justin slept in a deep drunken torpor, Fredo left him in charge of the boy and set off to haul in the nets by himself. Crouched in the shade of a sea-grape tree, Spero looked cautiously about him, for he was never at ease when at sea. The wind was sweeping the clouds to the other end of the sky. The sun was losing its strength, and, red as red can be, was sinking below the horizon. Fredo had still not come back. Silently, one after the other, the shadows slipped into their positions, and Spero began to hear every panicky thump of his heart. At last Fredo reappeared with a turtle he had dredged up, staining the mesh of the nets scarlet with blood. While the tiny boat, loaded fit to sink, was returning to home bay, darkness suddenly descended. It wiped out the limits of the sky and earth. It wiped out the color of the sea, now black as mourning, except for the breakers in the distance churning over the reefs. Terrified, Spero huddled

Maryse Condé

down in the back of the boat. He expected the turtle that lay agonizing at his feet to suddenly rear up with its viper head and crush him under its shell. He expected the squid to squeeze through the nets, waving their sticky fingers to tie him up. For the first time in his life he thought of death. What would happen if the boat capsized in this colorless, bottomless water? What's it like, this world from which nobody has ever returned to relieve the fears of the living? Desperately seeking an answer, he turned towards Justin. But he was too busy swigging a bottle of Feneteau-les-grappes-blanches, while Fredo, at the helm, was yelling bawdy songs. At the moment when his terror reached its height, the lights of Deshaies suddenly came into view.

All alone on this deserted jetty Spero was reliving the same fear and anguish of the twelve-year-old boy. The night, the color of Indian ink, was the picture of death. What lies beyond this darkness from where nobody ever returns? Is it a more ruthless, more implacable world than the one we know? Inhabited by beings even more unfeeling or cruel? That would be difficult to do! Perhaps, on the contrary, it's a place of peace, where the struggle is over. What is death? A veil of black crepe that gently, so gently is spread over our eyes and muffles all our suffering.

He sat down on the edge of the jetty, swinging his feet in the air a few feet above the water, the rain soaking his old sweatsuit and trickling cold behind his collar, which he automatically pulled up. Perhaps in the other world he would meet up with the few people who had loved him. Who, for example? Marisia? Perhaps she concealed her feelings from him. For it is impossible for a mother not to love her first son from the bottom of her heart. Or perhaps you don't meet anyone. Blank. Void. Nothingness.

He leaned forward as if he were trying to fathom what was under this big, soft, colorless, heaving blanket. Or else trying to make out the features of his devastated face, ravaged before its time. But the surface reflected back nothing.

Great was the temptation.

And what if he gently let himself down with his arms? If

with one stroke he went and joined the dreams lying on their side in the ocean depths among the debris of Spanish galleons sunk from times long past in forgotten combat? Forests of shellfish clung to their hulls; fish gazed at their reflection in the hollow eyes of the portholes and rough strands of kelp wrapped themselves around the broken masts.

No, this was not for him! You need courage to defy death and arrive ahead of time. His very cowardice kept him on earth, and what was left of his lust for life flared up relentlessly, like a bonfire you thought had been smothered under leaves and weeds. He would walk every step that remained to be walked on life's path. And perhaps one day, with the help of hope and patience, he would end up meeting Debbie again.

Wrapped in rain, Spero got up and returned to the passenger shelter. On the other side of the water, speckling the darkness with its lights, the ferry had begun its journey back to Crocker Island.